She was starting a new life in Texas—until old trouble turned up . . .

Scarlett Hall followed a job and a friend to Texas, but that cost her more than she'd bargained for. Now, wounded but determined to get past one of the worst days of her life, she decides she has to pull herself together. First step: cover up the physical scars left from her ordeal. That's easy. But the emotional scars are proving harder to handle . . .

Then she meets Ethan Calhoun. This bad boy seems ready to make his own changes and might be just what she needs to start a new chapter in her life. When he offers her a job as manager of his new bar, she decides to go for it. A change of pace and a hot guy who makes her forget her troubles while she's in his arms are a great cure. But it soon becomes clear that danger will be in Scarlett's life no matter how many changes she makes. As Scarlett comes face to face with her worst nightmare, it seems happiness was just an illusion. Maybe Texas is just too much trouble . .

Also by Gerry Bartlett

Texas Lightning

The Texas Heat Series
Texas Heat
Texas Fire
Texas Pride

Texas Trouble

A Lone Star Suspense Novel

Gerry Bartlett

LYRICAL LIAISON
Kensington Publishing Corp.
www.kensingtonbooks.com

Kensington Publishing Corp.
119 West 40th Street
New York, NY 10018

All Kensington titles, imprints, and distributed lines are available at special quantity discounts for bulk purchases for sales promotion, premiums, fundraising, educational, or institutional use.

Special book excerpts or customized printings can also be created to fit specific needs. For details, write or phone the office of the Kensington Sales Manager: Kensington Publishing Corp., 119 West 40th Street, New York, NY 10018. Attn. Sales Department. Phone: 1-800-221-2647.

Lyrical Liaison and Lyrical Liaison logo Reg. U.S. Pat. & TM Off.

First Electronic Edition: June 2019
eISBN-13: 978-1-5161-0716-2
eISBN-10: 1-5161-0716-0

First Print Edition: June 2019
ISBN-13: 978-1-5161-0719-3
ISBN-10: 1-5161-0719-5

Printed in the United States of America

Chapter One

Scarlett Hall was sick of feeling like a victim. She'd had plenty of time to heal both her mind and her body. There was nothing to be afraid of here. It was a beautiful spring day in Austin, Texas. No knife-wielding psycho was going to jump out of a doorway and drag her into a van like...

Stop it. Just go inside and get on with it.

Right. She'd done her research, a ton of it. This was the perfect place to wipe away the past. Scarlett took a deep breath and pushed inside. The place was clean. Good. And the woman was waiting for her. Because she'd made an appointment and she was late. Fifteen minutes of second-guessing and worrying had made that happen.

"Ms. Hall?" The woman held out her hand. "Casey Evans."

"Oh! Did you do that?" Scarlett stared at Casey's elegantly colorful arm. The scene looked like the Garden of Eden without the snake. Beautiful.

Casey laughed. "On my own right arm? I'm good, but I'm not that good." She waved at a man busy on a customer reclining in a chair who was getting a word written across his bicep. "This is Carl's work. My brother. We own Amuse Tattoos together. Isn't he amazing?"

"Yes. Can you do that art too? I want something floral like yours, only smaller. Where we discussed on the phone." Scarlett looked around the shop. There was a pair of special chairs in the open where the tattoo artists could work, and another man sat against the wall waiting his turn. He was young, probably one of the thousands of college students in town now that the huge University of Texas was in session. "You do have a private room, don't you? For situations like mine?"

"Of course. Come on back. I'm even better than Carl." That got her a grunt from her brother. Casey laughed. "He says otherwise. Anyway, let me take a look and then we'll talk." Casey had a friendly vibe. She was tall and toned, and she wore a muscle shirt to show off her body art. Her short white hair was buzzed on the sides and spiked on top. Her ears held multiple piercings, and she favored silver and turquoise jewelry Scarlett immediately coveted.

"I'm still not sure..." Where was this wishy-washy attitude coming from? Of course Scarlett was sure. She had to get rid of the evidence from that one hellacious day and move on. She stopped and stared at the pictures on the wall. So many options for tattoos—everything from simple butterflies to an elaborate battle of the Alamo, a Texas icon. But she had a folder under her arm. More research. She knew what she wanted. Remembering Texas wasn't high on her to-do list. Her life here had been a nightmare so far.

"We can call this a fact-finding mission if you wish, Ms. Hall. Ease into this." Casey opened a door to a private room where there was a table similar to a massage table. Just like the front, everything was sparkling clean.

"Call me Scarlett." She thrust her folder at Casey. "This is what I think I want. When you see what happened to me, you can figure out if it will work. Your résumé on your website said you have extensive experience hiding scars with your art. Camouflage, I guess you could call it."

"Yes." Casey opened the folder. "Very pretty. A little similar to the sleeves on my arms. We have our love of nature in common." She smiled. "You're going to have to show me where you need the work. You said on the phone..."

"That son of a bitch carved his initials on my butt." Every time she got out of the shower and passed a mirror, Scarlett was reminded of what had happened that horrible day. The monster was in jail now, for crimes even worse than what he'd done to her. She'd had to testify in depositions, but, thank God, she'd never had to face him after he'd been captured. She had told Casey some of this on the phone.

"Why don't you lie down on the table and pull down your jeans just enough to let me take a look? You did say you were completely healed. That's a requirement before I can do my thing." Casey waited for her to toe off her sneakers.

"I am. A plastic surgeon did what he could to repair it, but there is a permanent scar. He released me not long ago. You'll see." Scarlett unsnapped and unzipped her jeans. Her thong bared enough so her underwear wasn't in the way. Casey helped her climb onto the table. The curse of being short.

Nerves made Scarlett fumble as she pushed down her pants. Damn it, she didn't show her scars to anyone other than doctors and nurses. She hadn't even dated since the attack. Her best friend had seen her wound when it had first happened, but now Anna and her new boyfriend were off visiting her family back home in Boston. Anna was so in love, so happy, Scarlett hadn't wanted to tell her how freaked she still was or how many nights she woke up screaming.

So she held it in and pretended to be the same strong, together Scarlett she'd always been. Now she bared her ass and waited. If Casey said the wrong thing, she didn't know what she'd do. A meltdown wasn't off the table, but she might be.

But that's why she was here. She was sick of being alone and scared.

The silence was almost worse than if Casey had said something like "Holy shit!" Finally, Scarlett couldn't stand it anymore.

"What do you think?"

"Do you mind if I touch it? The texture could make a difference in what I do." Casey's voice was gentle but entirely professional.

"Uh, sure. I guess." Scarlett kept her cheek on her arm, her fists clenched, as Casey touched the slight ridges where Leroy Thomas Simms had carved his initials.

"I hope he's dead or in prison."

"Facing life without parole." Scarlett was surprised her voice hadn't trembled with her hatred.

"Good." Casey walked around so she could see Scarlett's face. "I can do a very pretty floral over it, and you won't be able to see a bit of what that bastard did to you. It might take a couple of sessions. And I want to offer you a discount. Covering scars is something I do to satisfy myself. I have one of my own." She pulled up her tank and showed Scarlett a tree climbing up from her navel. Bright red flowers bloomed from it. There was no sign of a scar. "Abusive first husband knifed me. There won't be a second husband unless I lose my mind."

"I'm sorry. You can't tell you were ever hurt." Scarlett lifted her head and clasped Casey's hand.

"Not on the outside." Casey smiled sadly.

"That's what I want. The outside to be pretty. I'm still working on the inside." Scarlett wasn't about to cry. Not in front of this strong woman. God, she admired her. "When can we start?"

"Right now. Let me get set up. I like what you chose—pretty colors, tasteful. I'll be back in a few minutes. Relax. It won't be painless, but I'll do what I can to make it easy for you." She nodded at a music system and headphones. "See if I have some tunes you like. Listening helps you zone out while I work." She helped Scarlett climb down.

Then she left the room.

Scarlett went through the tall stack of CDs and loaded the changer there with a variety of music she hoped would help her chill. By the time Casey came back with a toolbox and gear, she was lying on her stomach again, headphones on, and trying to relax to some slow tunes with a mellow vibe.

"Ready? I'm going to draw the design first. This is permanent marker so it won't wash off in the shower unless you scrub the hell out of it." She picked up a thin-tipped marker. "Once I'm satisfied with the design, I'll start with the ink. We can make another appointment to finish when we see how much I get done."

"Fine." Scarlett closed her eyes. Casey was still gentle, careful. No worries. She almost drifted off to sleep as the artist went to work outlining the pretty design of flowers. When the whirr penetrated through the music, at first it didn't bother her. Like she was at the dentist. A minor cavity, no big deal. Then the needle touched her, and she was back in that van. The man loomed over her. He gripped her breast, pushed against her and breathed in her ear all the things he wanted to do to her. He'd violate her. What a pretty little ass she had. He would like to come inside it and make her scream. He sliced into her, hurting her...

"No!" She threw off the earphones and fell off the table. Jerking up her jeans, she had to get out of there. Scarlett didn't see anyone or anything. All she knew was that she had to breathe fresh air. Run and get that hand off her butt. No one was going to hurt her, ever again.

"Scarlett!" Someone reached for her.

Blindly she slapped at them, pushing out one door, then another, until she almost fell on the sidewalk. Where could she go, where could she hide that he couldn't find her? She heard him coming. A woman stood in her way, staring at her. Hell, no. Can't trust anyone. Footsteps behind her. A door. Closed sign. He'd never look there. The knob turned, and she was in. She leaned against it.

Breathe. Turn the lock. She flipped the dead bolt and waited. Someone jiggled the knob, but it held. God. God. She sagged to the floor. Safe. Please let her be safe.

"Are you all right?" A man's voice came from across the dark room.

No, she was not all right. What had she done? Locked herself in with him. Scarlett searched for a weapon. Shit. She didn't even have her shoes.

"Calm down. I'm not going to hurt you." He was coming closer.

"That's what they all say." Scarlett jerked her cell out of her bra. She'd started keeping it there after the attack. "Don't come any closer. I'm calling 9-1-1."

"And say what? That you broke into my bar?" He was too close. He hunkered down in front of her. "Ethan Calhoun. How can I help you?"

"You own this bar?" Scarlett hit reality. Hard. He was right. What was she doing here? She tried to catch her breath, her heart stuttering as she looked around. She stared at the long wooden bar across the room as she tried to regulate her breathing. The room was empty except for the man who just sat there, still too close. She wanted to shove him away. Common sense finally returned as she gripped her phone and realized he wasn't making a move, just staring. Of course, she was acting crazy.

"Yeah, I do. Something scared you. Do I need to go outside and kick some butt?" He still hadn't moved.

Scarlett checked him out. Tall, good-looking, a little young, but not too young. He looked like he could enjoy some butt kicking but would prefer something more civilized in his vintage rock band tee and jeans. She waited, still breathing in and out, her heart finally settling down. If he tried anything that screamed danger, she had her fingers on her phone. But he just sat there, patient and, damn it, kind. She finally made a decision.

"You can buy me a drink."

"That I can do." He stood and held out his hand. "Usually, it's no shoes, no service, but I'll make an exception if you tell me your name."

"Scarlett Hall." Scarlett took his hand and let him pull her to her feet. "I have to warn you, I'm a head case right now."

"Honey, I'm way too used to those." He pulled her to the bar, then walked around and put two glasses in front of her. "Name your poison."

"Tequila. I've had a rough day. Rough month, rough year." She sighed. "Told you I was messed up."

"Then you've come to the right place." Ethan smiled and poured them each a splash of top-shelf tequila. "I think I've lost my mind too. Never owned a bar before. Now here I am probably about to lose my shirt. Moved to Austin because I loved going to college here. It's a common thing with Texas exes." He picked up his glass, waited for her to pick up hers, then clinked it. "Here's to crazy."

"Crazy." Scarlett threw back the shot. She wasn't about to turn to alcohol to solve her problems, but she liked Ethan's smile and that was a start. She needed her purse and her shoes. She had to go back and apologize to Casey. And she wanted that damn tattoo. She shook her head when Ethan offered her a refill.

"No, I've got to go back next door."

"To Casey's? You getting a tattoo?" Ethan walked her to the door.

"If I can find my nerve." Scarlett looked around. The only light came from the dusty windows and a laptop on the bar. No furniture yet, so obviously he wasn't ready to open.

"Want me to hold your hand?" He grinned.

Scarlett could imagine that. For the first time since the abduction, she didn't want to throw up a stop sign as soon as a man showed interest. And Ethan was definitely interested.

"No, thanks. This is something I have to do myself." She handed him her phone. "Can I call you if I need moral support?"

"Hell, yes." He tapped in his number. "Use that so I'll have *your* number, Miss Scarlett. And come back. I sure need moral support. I've spent years on the customer side of the bar business, but only six months learning about the behind-the-scenes part. I'm flying pretty blind here."

"I will." Scarlett realized this had the potential to be a nice place, but it needed something to stand out. She was no stranger to bars—in front or behind. "When are you opening?"

"Next month, I hope. Obviously, the place needs work. Furniture, staff. I hired somebody to help with that, but we weren't on the same page. She wanted to make it look just like every other bar on Sixth Street. I think it needs to be different. Fresh. I fired her yesterday." He turned the dead bolt and opened the door. "I'm getting desperate enough to call one of my sisters and see if they know somebody to come help."

"What do you have in mind?" Scarlett tried to picture the place cleaned out.

"I've got a name, at least. Fuel. Fuel for the soul with live entertainment. Then there's fuel for the body—I stole the best bartender in Austin from down the street. Luckily, she wanted to bring her brother, who is a chef. She's into those new craft cocktails, and he's known for his creative way with bar food. They've always wanted to work together but never got the chance before. This opportunity, a pretty free rein, and my offer to pay them more than the going rate sealed the deal." Ethan was excited, and it was a good look for him.

"I like it." Scarlett could appreciate the idea. "Austin has a great music scene."

"Yeah. I want a stage in here so we can feature up-and-coming artists on weekends." He pointed to what had been a raised area at one end of the large room. "I can see this working. I have some connections I can use to get some fairly big names in here." He paced the length of the room. "My family thinks I'm nuts, but then Calhouns take chances. Daddy was a wildcatter."

Scarlett let that pass. She had no idea what he meant. "You've never run a business like this before? You do need support, moral and otherwise. I worked my way through college as a cocktail waitress. I can't tell you how hard it is to get and hold good help. You need a strong manager to keep things organized and to supervise your people." Scarlett realized his enthusiasm was contagious.

She'd been stuck in office work since college, thanks to her sensible business degree. Her organizational abilities had brought her to Texas with the tech company she worked for. She enjoyed what she did, but it didn't excite her. Would she be insane if she took the leave of absence her employer had offered her after her traumatic abduction and decided to help Ethan? Hey, she could do the research and then organize the hell out of him. He needed someone like her. And she did have those years of cocktail experience. The bar business in Boston and Austin couldn't be that different. Her research would let her know about that. She was about to say something more when her phone rang.

"Hello."

"Scarlett, are you all right?" Casey had decided to try calling her.

"Actually, I think I am. For the first time in months." Scarlett stood in the doorway. "I'm sorry I ran out like that, but I'm coming back. Let's get this party started again." She turned to Ethan, who was on his own phone. He'd lost his smile. She decided to wait until he hung up to thank him for the drink. He finally laid his phone on the bar.

"Are you okay?" Scarlett walked back toward him. Casey could wait another minute. She didn't know Ethan, but she did know worry when she saw it.

"Not really." He reached for the bottle of tequila but stopped before he poured another shot. "Oh, hell no. Not going to try to drink this one away." His laugh was bitter. "Bar owners can't afford to do that, can they?"

"Nope. I've seen it happen, and it doesn't end well. You soon learn to leave the drinking to the customers." She touched his hand. "Bad news?"

"The worst." He looked her over. "I don't suppose you want a job. I could use a woman with experience." He shook his head. "That didn't come out right. A waitress with experience."

"I have a job. Office manager at Zenon Technology." Scarlett stepped back and looked around again. She really would like to get her hands on the place. It had potential, and Ethan seemed open to new ideas.

"Manager. Even better. Whatever you're making, I'll double it." He picked up his phone when it buzzed again. "Damn. I've got to take this. More shit hitting the fan. Think about it? The job? Quick. I'm in a time crunch."

"I will." Scarlett walked to the door. Behind her she heard Ethan curse. "How could you let this happen? She's dangerous. Who the hell is this person with her?"

Whomever he was talking to clearly didn't have good answers, because Ethan was cursing again when Scarlett stepped outside into the sunshine then shut the door behind her. She paused and looked around like she always did these days. Paranoid? Maybe, but then she had a reason to be cautious. No rough-looking men were hanging out between her and the tattoo parlor, but that woman... Wasn't she there earlier? Just standing and staring. She looked straight at Scarlett. Or was she watching the bar?

Was there a Help Wanted sign in the window? No, nothing. When the woman noticed Scarlett paying attention to her, she glared and started walking rapidly away. Weird. For a moment Scarlett had felt like she'd received visual hate mail. Damn. Now she really was being paranoid. She could swear she'd never seen the tall, thin woman before in her life. Forget her. She was gone, and Scarlett had a serious step to take.

She took a steadying breath. Time to start erasing her past and thinking about her future.

Chapter Two

Ethan hung up the phone after talking to his oldest sister. She was married to one of the sharpest lawyers in Houston. Thank God, Billy Pagan was already working on a way to keep Missy Calhoun out of prison when she was finally caught.

Damn it. His mother had tried to kill someone. And that wasn't the only law she'd broken. The only reason she hadn't been prosecuted for attempted murder was because the woman who'd dodged Missy's bullets was another Calhoun. Cassidy hadn't pressed charges, even though she certainly should have. She was a half-sister Ethan had never known existed until his father died and Daddy's will was read. Lucky for them all, she'd decided that her new sisters and brother didn't need the grief her testimony at a messy trial would bring. It had taken some fancy footwork on Billy's part to get a plea deal that sent Missy to Fairhaven for her "mental health issues." It wasn't exactly a popular notion to let the rich go to rehab instead of paying for a crime. If Mama pulled any of her wild stunts while she was loose? Well, it was just the excuse the prosecutor needed to forget the old deal and put Mama behind bars.

Cassidy was now running Calhoun Petroleum. Mama had hated the fact that Daddy had a daughter by another woman, and she'd wanted that girl out of the will and out of the way. Would she take another shot at her? Surely she realized it was futile. Besides, Cassidy had proven to be more like Daddy than any of them. She'd used her background in banking to help the company ride out near-bankruptcy when the price of oil had bottomed out. She'd brought Calhoun Petroleum through bad times and into the black again. Mama had ended up with Calhoun stock after her divorce from Daddy, so she had Cassy to thank for the great dividends landing in her bank account every quarter. But since when did rational thought and Mama dwell in the same hemisphere?

Ethan eyed that bottle of tequila again but left it sitting there. Nothing he could do about his mother, so he washed the two glasses and wondered if the pretty little blonde was getting her tattoo. She was obviously scared of something but had been determined not to show it once she realized she had an audience. He'd been crazy to offer her a job when he didn't know squat about her. So he did what he always did when he wanted to know something—he turned to his computer. What he found when he looked up her name almost made him reach for the tequila again.

Shit. She'd been the victim of a knife-wielding psychopath during an attempt at industrial espionage. No wonder Scarlett had run into the bar like she was being chased. What in the hell did Zenon Technology own that could be so valuable? The newspaper articles didn't give details, just stated that she'd been wounded when abducted at knifepoint. He dug a little more and found a story from Boston about the group selected to come to Texas when her tech company had been purchased by Zenon. Scarlett Hall was apparently sharp and valuable if she was one of only half a dozen employees invited to move across the country. She was the only one not in the software or hardware division.

Ethan shut down the computer. He needed someone to organize this new business, and she was an office manager. Perfect. Would it be stalkerish to hang out near the tattoo parlor next door and wait for her to come out? Yeah. She was obviously on edge and for good reason. But he could look up her phone number if she didn't call him soon. Thanks to the rising price of oil lately, even after buying the building that housed the bar and Amuse Tattoos, he could afford to hire an expensive manager like Scarlett Hall.

His phone buzzed and danced on the bar top. Blocked caller. He couldn't ignore anyone these days as he dealt with liquor distributors and contractors.

"Calhoun."

"Ethan, baby, it's your mama."

"Where the hell are you, Mama? Shannon called me all upset. You can't just take off from Fairhaven. It will mess up your plea deal. Promise me you'll go back." Ethan sat on the one rickety bar stool left from the previous owner. He loved his mother, and he sure didn't want her to go to prison.

"No, you can't make me go back, and I'm not telling you where I am until you promise to help me." She sounded like she was issuing orders.

"Help you? Break the law? Mama, that's not fair. What's wrong? Last time I visited, you seemed to be okay. Would you rather go to prison? That's what will happen if you don't go back right away. Fairhaven was the best we could do for you after what you did to Cassidy." Ethan knew Mama had endangered other people as well as his sister with her wild attempts to get rid of Cass. It had only been their lawyer's connections and fast talking that had sent his mother to a hospital room instead of a cell. Of course, she'd had mental-health problems for years. It was actually a relief for Mama to get the help she'd been avoiding since he'd been a kid.

"Baby, I had to get out of there." She sobbed. "They kept doping me up. I couldn't think straight."

"Mama, the girls and I could have talked to the doctor. Helped you get your meds adjusted." He knew she hated to be on medication, but her mood swings needed control. She sure hadn't responded to therapy. "Shannon talked to the people at Fairhaven. They say you left with someone else."

"Yes, Lisa Marie. She's wonderful. Took care of everything. You'll love her."

"I won't. She helped you sneak out of there and that's got you in a world of hurt." Ethan needed more information. "What's Lisa Marie's last name?"

"Lisa Marie Davenport. I went to school with her mama, Sylvia Conroy. We graduated high school together. Isn't it a small world? I swear Lisa's just your type. Pretty, tall and slim and born in Houston. You'll have so much in common." Mama sounded almost giddy, riding one of her highs.

Ethan stared at the phone. Was this for real? Was his mother matchmaking? Trying to set him up with a woman she'd met in a mental institution?

"Mama, I'm not listening to this. You have to turn yourself in. Shannon's husband can fix things if you do it right away. Forget this new friend of yours. She's trouble. In fact, that's something Billy can use to get you back in Fairhaven without adding time on to your sentence. Bet she used undue influence. You weren't thinking straight."

"Stop that, Ethan Calhoun! Lisa's the only one in that place who understood me." Mama went on a rant while he opened his computer. Unfortunately he was able to find Lisa Marie Davenport from Houston right away. There were plenty of newspaper articles describing Lisa's problem with anger management. The latest blowup had happened when a boyfriend had tried to end their relationship. Sweet Lisa Marie had run the man's Piaget watch worth half a million dollars down his garbage disposal. Too bad he'd had it on his wrist at the time. He'd almost lost a finger before he had been able to release the catch. Of course he'd wanted to press charges. A sharp lawyer and a quick trip to Fairhaven had been the only things that kept Lisa out of jail. Because losing her temper was a pattern. A wrecked Ferrari, paint dumped into a swimming pool, the list of meltdowns was long and troubling. All this had forced her parents to get drastic. Her mother was quoted as saying they were writing her out of their wills. Bad news for the daughter of a rich oilman. And this was the woman her mother had hooked up with at Fairhaven?

"Where are you, Mama? Why don't I come get you? I can take you back to Fairhaven and make sure you don't get more time added to your stay. Billy Pagan and I will work it out." Ethan hoped he wasn't lying to her.

"I don't want to go back. If you love me, you'll do me a favor. Go to my bank and grab my passport and credit cards out of my safety-deposit box. Withdraw some cash too. Please, baby. I need to leave the country. I'm never going back to that nuthouse again." She sobbed.

Fake or real? Ethan had no idea. His mother was a master manipulator. "I'm not in Houston, Mama. I'd come if it was to take you back to the hospital, but not to the bank."

"Where are you, Ethan?" All signs of tears were gone. Of course. Manipulation.

"Austin. I moved here months ago. I'm starting my own business. No one is going to get your passport for you, Mama, so don't ask. Step one foot inside that bank and you know the police will be called. You're a fugitive. If Billy hadn't known the right people, you wouldn't have been allowed to do the time in Fairhaven. You shot up a parking garage, almost ran over innocent bystanders. There's a list of crimes you could be put in prison for and you know it. Your psychiatrist—"

"That quack! Trying to put labels on me. Who could blame me for going a little haywire when your daddy's bastard showed up claiming part of the company I helped build." Her voice was getting louder. "I gave that man my best years, Ethan. You know I did. And he cheated on me. With his secretary! Fucking cliché! Then to put her daughter in his will?" Her voice rose. She was losing control.

Ethan recognized the symptoms. Soon she'd be ranting and lashing out. Was her pal Lisa Marie listening to this? Two women with anger issues. Some fun there. Of course he didn't say a thing about the fact that Mama was rewriting history. *She'd* been Daddy's secretary back in the day, cheating with him on Cassidy's mother, the first Mrs. Calhoun. He knew better than to try to set her straight. He was glad he only had to listen to this tirade on the phone. Growing up, he'd had to dodge Mama's slaps or high-heeled boot.

"Mama, there's no need to get worked up about it now. You should be glad Cassidy turned out to be smart. Look how she's turned the company around. When you get out of Fairhaven, you'll have a good chunk of change from those dividends you get from your divorce settlement. Right?"

"She's got your daddy's brains. Certainly not like that dull slut of a mother." Missy was coming back down. "I'm already out. Not going back. You talk to that lawyer, you tell him to figure out how to fix things." "Mama, that's not possible." Ethan had a bad feeling. "I've got to go. Austin, you said? I need money, pumpkin. You can at least spot me some cash. You know I'm good for it. I've got plenty in the bank, but thanks for the warning. I won't go in there if they're going to be watching, try to grab me and force me to go back to that horrible place. Lisa Marie can't get to her funds either, her parents cut her off. Lucky for us she left a car there, and I have a Calhoun gas card. It still works." She laughed, that wild laugh that made Ethan grip the phone.

"Mama, don't come here. I won't give you money. You have to go back to Fairhaven. You hear me?"

"Everyone is against us, baby. And for what? Because we won't let people do us dirty?" Mama was screeching again. "Don't you turn on me, boy. I'm warning you. You owe me. I'm your flesh and blood and don't you forget it."

"As if I could." Ethan realized his mother had hung up on him. She was headed his way. She didn't have his address yet, but she would track him down. Despite bad press and mood swings, his mother had friends. Those women had a network the CIA would envy. She could reach out and have every detail of his recent moves with just a few phone calls. Because, growing up, his pals had been the sons of the very ladies his mama spent hours with, drinking Bloody Marys and exchanging gossip at the country club.

When he'd bought the bar, he'd made it a point to get on social media and hit his own network in Houston. He'd sent everybody he'd ever known announcements about the proposed opening date. She'd have no trouble finding him once she found the bar. He lived in one of the apartments, right upstairs. Casey and her brother had the other two. It was a nice arrangement. Unfortunately, it would make finding him dead easy.

* * * *

Scarlett was a little sore, but it wasn't nearly as bad as the knife cut had been. Casey had given her some numbing cream. That had helped. She was dog-sitting her pal Anna's pup, YoYo, and had just finished walking him, her pepper spray in her pocket. She was trying to get comfortable on the couch with the TV remote when there was a knock on her door. The dog started barking, wild yips like maybe he was going to kill whoever was on the other side. As if a dog the size of her favorite handbag had a chance of that.

Scarlett had given up her old apartment because it had big front windows. Since the attack, she'd decided they weren't safe. Her door here also had a peephole. Which was too high to be useful without a step stool. She dragged it over and looked through the hole. The man looming out there had on a cap. Damn it, she couldn't see his face. How had he gotten past the locked gate, anyway?

"Who's there?" She made her voice as loud and threatening as possible. YoYo added growls. The message was clear. No one here was a victim. Go away.

"Scarlett, open up. It's Rhett." He pounded on the door again. "Hurry up. It was a long drive from the airport and I need to use the john."

"It can't be my brother. He's in Boston." Scarlett heard the man cough. The voice had been husky. Could it really be Rhett? Last she'd heard he was doing a book signing in their hometown. Anna had planned to go.

"I was in Boston until I heard you were keeping secrets from your family. Damn it, if I have to take a whiz out here on your porch, you'll be sorry." He pounded again. "I'm serious. You want me to hold my driver's license up to the peephole, Ladybug?"

"Oh, hell." That did it. Her childhood nickname won her over. No one called her that anymore. But the tiny red bugs had always fascinated her. She still had a few things in her bedroom decorated with them. She punched in her code on the security system, then began opening dead bolts. Yes, there were three of them, a chain and a slide lock. Finally she threw open the door. YoYo leaped at Rhett's feet.

"Out of the way, pup." Rhett looked wild-eyed as he tossed his cap on the coffee table. "Which way?"

Scarlett pointed, then bent over to pick up the dog while her brother brushed past her and ran to her bathroom. He slammed the door and made her glad she had the TV on and couldn't hear him take care of business. She shut the front door, carefully relocked the door, then reset the alarm. By the time he came out, she was back on the couch, pillows cradling her butt again.

"I assume you made it and that you put the seat down." She hid a smile when he turned back around, and she heard the thunk of the seat falling onto the toilet. "Thanks."

"You're welcome." Rhett sat on the other end of the couch, grabbed the remote, and cut off the TV. "Now, talk to me. What the fuck went down here? And why didn't you call any of us when you were attacked, kid?"

Scarlett shocked herself by tearing up. Not only that, but she fell sobbing onto her big brother's chest. Yep, just had an ugly crying jag. Okay, so it had probably been a long time coming. Holding herself together, being strong, that was her go-to position. But it was so hard sometimes. And lately, well, she was tired. And lonely. Rhett's arms around her took her back to Boston, a place where she'd always been loved and accepted. Here, she was an outsider, constantly having to prove herself. Even after the attack, she'd felt like she had to show a tough exterior. Why? Because she always had. With a shudder, she finally pulled back. YoYo was licking her foot and that made her laugh.

"Look at this. I'm a mess. Even the dog feels sorry for me." She grabbed a tissue from the box on the coffee table. The fact that it was close at hand said volumes about her state of mind lately. She'd been watching a lot of old movies, tearjerkers, and using them as an excuse to sob her heart out.

"Pity party over? Not that you haven't earned it." Rhett picked up the dog. "This is Anna's dog, isn't it?"

"Yes. YoYo."

"Silly name. Cute dog." Rhett set the dog in Scarlett's lap. "Now, I want to hear all about it. The attack, how you're dealing. Why you won't just come on back home. Mom is fit to be tied. Of course, I had to promise a full report, or she'd be here with me."

"Thanks for keeping her away. I couldn't deal with her right now." Scarlett ran her hands over the dog's back. It was soothing. She had a feeling Anna had left YoYo with her for just that reason. Maybe she wasn't as good at hiding her emotions as she thought.

"Mom's knee-deep in planning the garden club spring fund-raiser. Otherwise, she'd be here and no one could stop her. She's the chairwoman this year." Rhett stood and looked around. "She'd have a fit to see you living out of boxes. Why haven't you unpacked?"

"I just moved in."

"Mom said it was a new address." He glanced back at the locks and the security system, then patted her shoulder. "You have beer?"

"Sure. Check the fridge. It's nothing fancy. Not like your hero in the books drinks."

"That's fiction. I'll take whatever's on offer." He investigated her tiny kitchen. "Food?"

"Leftover chicken and bread. Make a sandwich."

"I will." He got busy and soon was back with a big sandwich and two beers. "So you moved after the attack."

"I needed a change." Scarlett took the beer, and they clinked glass bottles. She knew the comments were coming and braced herself.

"To a fortress." He nodded toward the locks on the door and the burglar bars on the narrow windows.

"The other place…" Scarlett took a swallow of beer. "Well, I didn't feel safe."

"I'll eat now, and you'll tell me all about what happened. Anna came to my book signing, dragging her new boyfriend. Nice guy. I liked him. He bought a couple of books. So I really liked him. Then we went out to dinner. He paid. Now I'm thinking he's my new best friend. Then Anna starts telling me how they met and what happened to her and to you." He put his sandwich on the table and set the beer next to it. When YoYo started sniffing the chicken, he said no and the dog sat at his feet, not moving. "You can imagine how that hit me. Finding out that my little sister had been cut up by a psychopath months ago and we never heard a word about it."

"What could you do? Telling would just get everyone there stirred up." Scarlett put down her beer because holding it made it obvious that her hand was shaking.

"I don't know. Come see you. Offer sympathy. Pay for a hit on that asshole who hurt you." Rhett's hands were fisted.

"Rhett, stop it!" She put her hand over one of those fists. "The man's in prison. There's nothing you need to do."

"Really. Nothing? That isn't what I want to hear." He watched her through narrowed eyes. "Why are you sitting funny? Aren't you healed yet? I'm not going to ask to see your ass, but seriously, it's been three months."

"I'm sore because I'm getting a tattoo, to cover my scar. I…I can't stand to look at it. He carved his fucking initials on me, Rhett. I can't bear to see it." More tears. No, no more of that. She wiped them away. "So I started today. The woman's a genius. I'm going back tomorrow for another session. You want to see my butt, I'll show you. I've become sort of numb to the whole thing."

"No, you haven't. You're locked in here like a prisoner in your own home. I've done enough research to know PTSD when I see it." He touched her cheek. "That bastard. Sick son of a bitch. Prison's too easy for him. Bet it wasn't his first trip there."

"Of course not. I'll show you his record if you want. I have it all on my computer." Scarlett reached for her beer. "You still want to hear what happened? A blow by blow?"

"Yes, I do. But let me eat first. You know they don't feed you on those planes." He picked up his sandwich. "Drink your beer. Have you seen a shrink? Talked this out with anyone?"

"I'll be fine." Scarlett drank and watched her brother eat. Fine? She wished she could believe that. Maybe it was time to see someone. Insurance would pay for it. But just telling her brother about the attack and the way the man had treated her made it all come back. By the time she'd shared it again, and they'd argued about where Rhett would stay—he wanted to sleep on her couch, she knew he was too tall for it—and he'd taken himself off to a hotel for the night, Scarlett knew she'd never sleep without that nightmare coming to call again. So she found one of the weepers she'd become addicted to and started a movie marathon.

She fell asleep on the couch with the TV on. And woke up screaming. It didn't help that her butt was on fire. The pain brought it all back. Sighing, she got up, rubbed on some of that numbing cream, then climbed into bed. The doctor had prescribed a sleeping pill. She didn't like taking it, but she was too tired to resist. So she swallowed one and fell into a black hole of oblivion.

Chapter Three

Waking up to the pounding on the door made Scarlett wish she'd bought a gun. Not that she was big on those, but she'd thought about arming herself after the attack. This was Texas. There was an indoor gun range not far from here that offered classes with a purchase. She staggered to the peephole, then deactivated the alarm and unlocked the door.

"You're killing me." Scarlett almost forgave Rhett when he thrust a cup of coffee at her. "What time is it?"

"Almost noon. Didn't you say your appointment is at two? We need to eat first." He looked upbeat and eager to go.

"We? Are you going with me?" Scarlett collapsed on the couch and sipped her coffee. Noon.

"I won't watch the procedure, but I want to see the place and meet the woman who's doing this thing." He sat beside her. "My agent called. I had to rearrange a few things, and now he's busy setting up signings in Texas. I'll be doing one here in Austin, going down to Houston, then over to Dallas. If they're on weekends, maybe you can go with me, see more of this big state."

Scarlett realized the caffeine was finally working. "Yeah, cool."

He picked up his cap from the coffee table. "I left this here last night."

"It's like the one your hero wears in your latest series. I loved *Seventh Avenue Sherlock*." Scarlett still couldn't believe her big brother had invented a hero who had become a national obsession. He'd hit bestseller lists with his detective series and had fans worldwide. Rhett had become a celebrity while she'd been stuck in an office. Didn't matter. She loved him anyway. And if being in an office wasn't making her happy, she should do something about it. She sat back, a little surprised at the thought. The urge for change fluttered in her belly. Was she queasy or excited at the idea? She realized Rhett was studying her, probably noticing the bags under her eyes. Time for a distraction. "Hey, Mom told me they might make a movie from *Sherlock*. Any news on that?"

"There's a lot of talk, but I'm not wasting time worrying about it." He frowned. "You look like hell. Did you sleep at all?"

"Thanks a heap. I finally took a sleeping pill, so yes." She finished her coffee. "Let me jump in the shower then slap on some makeup. Then maybe I'll look decent enough to take you to lunch. There are some great places with local cuisine near where I have to go for my tat."

"I'm sorry if I hurt your feelings, but I'm worried about you, kiddo." He helped her up from the couch. "Mom is waiting for a report. I'd like to say you are back to normal. But I'm afraid that would be a lie."

Scarlett gripped his hands. "Lie, please. I really don't need Mom to descend on me with baked goods and advice. I just lost ten pounds. She'd think it was her life's mission to help me put them back on. Not to mention hover."

"I get it. You never answered me. Have you seen someone since the attack? Therapy to talk about the trauma?" He stared at her until Scarlett squirmed away from him.

"You seem to forget who you're talking to, bro. I'm tough. The girl who makes grown men cry when she walks all over them with her five-inch heels." She patted his cheek. He was going for the stubble look and it suited him. Her handsome brother had probably left a broken heart or two in Boston. This trip to Texas had no doubt been an excuse to leave the scene of the crime after he'd let one more woman know he wasn't ready for a commitment. She and Rhett were both phobic about binding themselves to anyone for the long haul. Which was a puzzle to think about another day since their parents had been happily married for almost forty years now.

"You're changing the subject. I get that. So, lunch. Sounds good. I definitely want to get a feel for the Texas thing. I'm going to stay awhile, research my next novel. I have an idea that fans might like for me to take Darius Hunter to the Lone Star State. Texas is always popular in fiction." He got up and strolled around the apartment when Scarlett made a noise. "I get that it might not be your favorite place after what happened to you here."

"No kidding." She stood behind him when he stopped in the doorway to her second bedroom.

"What are you using this room for?"

"I planned to set it up as my office. When I moved, a two-bedroom apartment was all they had available with the amenities I needed." She flushed. Did he know those amenities included the gated entry with the code her mother had given him? Not to mention the security system next to her front door. And then there was the secret panic room hidden in the back of her walk-in closet in her master bedroom. The place didn't look like much on the outside, but it was a paranoiac's dream.

"What if I pay half your rent and bring in a bed, desk, and dresser? Fix up the space for myself? I'll need a few months to work on the book. When I leave you can have the stuff." Rhett walked in and opened the closet. It was empty, proof she really didn't need it. "It's a decent size. You'll be gone during the day anyway. I can do my thing and you can do yours. How much work do you actually do from home?" He was out again, next to her laptop on the breakfast bar. "I seem to remember you use this thing for social media and not much else."

"I pay bills on it now too. And I like it for my own research. As I get to know my new city." Scarlett thought about it. Rhett here. She couldn't deny she'd been lonely, especially since Anna had found King and fallen in love. She used to have Sunday outings with Anna to look forward to, but lately her best friend had been at her boyfriend's ranch or working nonstop. At least the important program Anna had created was in production now and she'd taken a break from that. But then she had headed home to Boston to introduce her new guy to her family.

"Hey, think about it. No pressure. Keep in mind that I'll be out doing my own research, then holed up writing. We should be able to stay out of each other's way."

"Don't you have a love life? Mom said—"

"Mom hoped I had something permanent going. I don't. My last relationship ended up a mess. I'll spare you the details. What about you?" He focused on her. "Boyfriend? I hope you have someone after that hell you went through, but where is he? He should be here, supporting you."

"No boyfriend. I'm taking a break from dating. I want my mind right and my butt pretty before I start anything new." She headed for the bathroom. Did she want Rhett moving in? Tempting. He was strong, brave, and could make her feel safe. She knew in the past he'd done more than just computer research for his books. They were thrillers, and so he'd learned to shoot, fight, even skydive. Not that she thought knowing how to jump out of a plane would come in handy if something bad happened to her again.

Oh, God, but she was a mess. The threat was over, wasn't it?

"Let's talk about this at lunch. I'll be out in a few." She slammed the bathroom door and jumped in the shower.

* * * *

Scarlett introduced her brother to Tex-Mex cuisine. He loved it. Not just the food either. He was into his second top-shelf margarita when her phone rang. She wasn't going to answer it until she saw who was calling. It couldn't be good news. No, silly to be pessimistic. The Texas Ranger might just be checking up on her. He'd been good about that since the attack.

"Mike. What's up?" She frowned when Rhett scooped up the last of her guacamole on a chip. She'd had plans for that.

"Hey, Scarlett. I'm in the neighborhood, thought I'd stop by." His deep voice was calm, just like it always was. Why did she think he sounded extra-serious?

"Which neighborhood? I moved on the first. Better security." She laughed. "I know, maybe I was being overly cautious, but I just needed to feel safer."

"No, it's a good idea. A woman living alone should have excellent security. Are you at home? Give me your new address. I have some news."

"News? What is it?" Scarlett felt the heavy lunch start to churn in her stomach.

"I'll tell you when I see you."

Scarlett glanced at Rhett. "We're just finishing lunch. Give me a half hour and I'll meet you there." She gave him her new address. "No, wait. I have an appointment on Sixth Street in about thirty minutes. Should I reschedule? Is it that important?"

He was silent. Obviously thinking about it. "Sixth Street. You by yourself?"

"No, my big brother's with me. He's visiting from Boston." Scarlett reached for her water and took a gulp. Mike knew her background. "You're freaking me out, Mike. What's going on?"

"Settle down now. I didn't mean to upset you. Your brother going with you to this appointment?"

"Yes, he is. Why? Do I have a reason to need an escort?" Scarlett heard her voice trembling. "This sounds like you have bad news for me, Mike."

"Yeah, well, it's not great. So go straight home when you're done, then call me." Mike cleared his throat. "I'm sorry if I'm being mysterious, but I want to see you to give you an update on Simms. Is that okay?"

"Simms? I'd hoped we were done with that asshole." She realized Rhett had put down his glass and was staring at her.

"Me too. Just call me."

"Will do. I should be home in an hour or two." She hung up without giving Mike the code to her gate. He'd have to wait for her to buzz him in.

"Simms? Isn't that who—" Rhett leaned forward.

"Yes. Let's get out of here. That was the Ranger who came to my rescue the day I was attacked. You'll get to meet him. Great guy. You might want to interview him for your next book." Scarlett waved at their waiter and held up her credit card.

"No shit. A real Texas Ranger. Of course I'd love to meet him. But what's this about Simms?" He grabbed her card and pulled out his own. "No way are you buying lunch. This whole visit is research."

"Mike has news. He wouldn't tell me over the phone. I hope like hell it's just something minor. If I'm lucky, Simms got killed in lockup." Scarlett wondered if another margarita was a bad idea. She decided it was. She needed to stay sharp for whatever Mike had to say. "You sure you won't let me pay?"

"Hell, no. This is tax-deductible. So, settle back, finish that enchilada, and let me play big brother." Rhett smiled but she could tell he was worried.

"You won't get an argument from me." Scarlett stared at the last bite of cheesy deliciousness but knew she wouldn't be able to get it down. Mike had been evasive. She didn't like it. She was suddenly very glad that tall, solid Rhett sat across from her. She touched his hand. "I'm proud of you, bro. We'll talk about this idea of you moving in later. There's the issue of privacy."

"Kiddo, I get it. If you don't want me in your way, I'll find a place for the short term." He signed the check and added the tip. "Now, let's go. Man, I can see already how a Ranger will play into the plot I'm thinking about. You can tell me how he helped you while we're on the way to the tattoo parlor. It's down the street?" He stood and threw his napkin on his plate. "I always start with a title. It helps me focus. How about *Sixth Street Standoff*?" He shook his head. "But that doesn't say Texas, does it? *Terror in Texas* has a nice ring. I may have to run it by marketing." He grinned. "This book is already cooking in my brain. I can't wait to get to my computer."

Scarlett wished she had just a fraction of her brother's enthusiasm for anything, much less meeting Mike. The Ranger usually touched base on the phone. Why did he insist on meeting in person today? Sure, he was kind, and he'd been a rock when she'd needed one the day she'd been hurt by that psychopath Leroy Thomas Simms. Mike had walked her through her statement when she'd had to tell every sordid detail over and over again for the Austin Police. The worst, of course, had been when they'd photographed her butt. The Ranger had let her hide her face against his broad chest during that part. Otherwise...

She'd spent the last three months trying to forget the day she'd been kidnapped by the men who were after Anna's valuable computer program. The tattoo was going to help her move on. By the time Scarlett was near Amuse Tattoos, she was shaking, certain that whatever news Mike brought had to be bad. Was she going to have to testify in a trial against Simms after all? She'd hoped he had taken the plea deal the DA had offered him and there'd be no trial. He'd been in prison before. Twice. So he would get life automatically, according to Mike.

They suspected he'd killed one of her coworkers at Zenon. Had they been able to prove it? Maybe not. But they had him cold on kidnapping and assault. She and her best friend, Anna, had both given depositions. If she had to see him again, at a trial . . . Horrible scenarios ran through her mind until she stopped frozen in front of the door to the tattoo parlor.

"Hey, what are you freaking out about?" Rhett stopped her at the door. "I thought you'd already started getting the tattoo. You want to put this off today?"

Scarlett shook her head. "No, the sooner I can erase what that asshole did to me, the better. Come on in. I want you to meet Casey and her brother, Carl. Maybe you can get a tattoo while you wait." She stepped inside, but it was clear Rhett would have to make an appointment if he wanted his own tat. Carl was working on an elaborate eagle on a man's back, and there was another artist busy placing a colorful butterfly on a woman's ankle in the special chair next to him. Two customers sat against the wall waiting their turns. A bell had announced their arrival, and Casey hurried from the back.

"I'm glad you're here, Scarlett. I was afraid you would back out." Casey smiled at Rhett. "You brought a friend."

"Casey, this is my brother, Rhett. He surprised me with a visit." She watched them shake hands.

"This is a nice place you have here." Rhett stared at Casey's face, seeming to not even notice her beautiful body art. "I'm glad my sister is getting some help."

"Happy to do it." Casey eased her hand from his. "Do you have any tats?"

"No, never saw the need." He finally looked at her arms. "Beautiful. I can see the appeal. I'd want something rugged. You know what I mean?"

She looked him up and down. "Oh, yeah. Definitely badass."

"Maybe the name of your first bestseller, Rhett. *Firestorm*. Surrounded by flames." Scarlett felt like she was watching a mating game. The instant chemistry between these two was obvious.

"Bestseller?" Casey tore her gaze from a journey over Rhett's biceps straining his knit shirt.

"I write thrillers, mysteries, whatever genre you want to stick them in, as R.B. Hall." Rhett smiled. "Yeah, Scarlett, I like that idea. With lots of color. Or maybe a snake wrapped around my bicep. A poisonous variety."

"Shit, man. R.B. Hall?" Carl had turned around. "I fucking loved *Beatdown in Boston*."

"Hey, thanks." Rhett grinned and held out his hand after Scarlett introduced Casey's brother. "I'm thinking about setting my next book here, in Austin. If you guys are willing, maybe you can help me learn about the scene here. Stuff my sister, who is new in town, might not know."

"We aren't into the hard-core things you put in your books. I know a few bikers. Do their tats. But I don't run with them, and I sure as hell don't do drugs." Carl frowned. "You really go there? For research?"

"I get a lot from interviews. I like to experience what I can, but not the drugs." Rhett glanced at Scarlett. "At least not that I'll admit to in front of my sister."

"Rhett!" Scarlett was horrified. She knew her brother had done some dangerous things in the name of research, but…

Casey pulled on her hand. "Let's get busy with what you came for. The men can talk while we get this tattoo done in the back room." Casey eyed Rhett. "Adventurous bestselling author. Interesting."

"He really is a nice guy. If you *are* interested." Scarlett had followed Casey into the same room they'd used before. This time she saw there was a stool she could use to climb onto the table after she took off her shoes. She was eager to get this tattoo finished. What had been done so far had looked amazing when she'd checked it out in the mirror at home. Yes, it hurt at first, but to cover up what Leroy Simms had done to her, she'd go through hell and back. Again.

"You ready?" Casey patted Scarlett on the shoulder as she lay down and pulled down her jeans. "I already loaded your tunes for you."

"Thanks. I'm more than ready. Your numbing cream helped." Scarlett took the headphones and slipped them on. She didn't want to hear the needle working or even see it. She closed her eyes when she felt Casey rub cream on the area then tried to relax. The sooner this was done, the better.

* * * *

An hour and a half later, she and Rhett were headed to Scarlett's apartment. She had called Mike and told him they were on their way, so he was waiting at the gate in his family car, the dull brown SUV that meant this was his day off. She waved at him, punched in the gate code, and drove through while he followed her. They parked next to her stairs and got out.

"Mike!" Scarlett gave him a hug. "This is my brother, Rhett Hall. Rhett, Mike Taylor, the Texas Ranger who was so amazing when I was attacked." The men shook hands.

"Thanks for taking such good care of my little sister, Mike." Rhett slung his arm around Scarlett. "She didn't let her family know what she'd been through. Her friend Anna Delaney finally told me when she came home to Boston recently."

"Scarlett was very brave through the whole ordeal." Mike looked around with a narrowed gaze. "Let's take this inside. Scarlett, I like the security here. Much better than your old place."

"Yes." She pointed as she walked up the stairs. "Look, burglar bars. And I have a security system."

"That's good." He frowned. "Why are you limping? Is that old wound bothering you?"

"I'm getting a tattoo to cover the scar. One more session and no one will be able to tell Simms ever cut me." Scarlett put the key in the lock, then hurried inside to disengage the alarm.

"This place is a fortress." Rhett walked in and headed for the kitchen. "Unless you're working undercover or the Ranger uniform is jeans and a Bat Festival T-shirt, looks like you're off duty, Mike. How about a beer?"

"Wouldn't turn it down." Mike sat when Scarlett smiled and gestured at one of her big armchairs. "Nice place." He took the beer Rhett handed him and twisted off the top. "So you saw Anna in Boston. Did you meet King Sanders?"

"Sure did." Rhett sat beside Scarlett on the couch. "They came to a book signing I was doing. I'm a writer." He took a drink. "Anyway, nice guy. I'm glad Anna found someone she can be happy with."

"A writer. That's cool. I've got some stories you wouldn't believe. Always thought I should write them down." Mike sipped his beer.

Rhett leaned forward. "If you don't, I'd like to hear them."

"Sure. Might as well share them. I'll never get around to putting them on paper." He nodded.

Scarlett wanted to scream. Why was Mike here? But she knew he'd get around to his reason for stopping by in his own time. Rhett had certainly made himself at home, offering Mike a beer. And where was *her* drink? She got up and limped over to the kitchen to get a diet soda. She picked up the tube of numbing cream but decided it could wait until after Mike left. She could bear the throbbing in her butt until after she heard the Ranger's news. She finally settled on the couch again next to her brother, who had just put Mike's number in his phone. Of course. For research.

"King and I go way back." Mike smiled. "We played ball together at UT here."

Rhett slapped his thigh. "I'll be damned. You're Mike the Missile Taylor! I remember watching you play football back in the day!" He bumped against Scarlett's hip as he leaned forward.

"Ouch! I'm sore. Remember?" She adjusted a pillow. "Mike the Missile?"

"One of the best quarterbacks the University of Texas ever had. I expected you to go pro. What happened?" Rhett was always looking for a story.

"Come on, Rhett. Maybe it's none of your business." Scarlett laid a hand on his knee.

"No, it's all right. I went down after a bad hit in the Cotton Bowl, senior year. Serious shoulder separation. And then my baby sister was murdered by a serial killer. Put those two things together, and I decided law enforcement was calling me." Mike set his beer on the coffee table. "Which is why I'm here on my day off."

"Man, I'm sorry. About both those tragedies. You were a star. Really talented. And, God, your sister. Did they catch the guy?" Rhett was very serious.

"The Rangers did. He was eventually put to death in Huntsville. Not that it brought Brenda back." Mike stared down at the brown bottle in front of him.

"I'm so sorry. No wonder you're so dedicated." Scarlett gripped Rhett's knee. To lose a family member like that would be horrific. She couldn't imagine it.

"So why are you here, Mike? Am I going to have to testify against Knife Guy in court after all? I hate the idea of seeing him again." Scarlett shuddered. She glanced at Rhett. "That's what I call the man who attacked me. He loved to use his knife on people, especially women."

"He did want his day in court and refused the plea deal, after all. Stupid, but what can I say? The asshole had you and Anna as witnesses against him and was a three-time loser, facing life. So, why go to court?" Mike picked up the beer again and took a deep swallow.

"To torture us, of course. He'd get off watching me on the witness stand, having to describe what he did to me. They'd show pictures of my wounds in the courtroom." Scarlett jumped up and ran to the kitchen. She grabbed a pile of paper napkins and handed one to Mike, then one to Rhett. "Jeez, Rhett, where are your manners? And use a coaster." She slapped one under each bottle of beer. Then she stomped over to the door and reset her alarm. Her heart was pounding. She leaned against the door, trying not to scream, cry, or fall apart. Then Rhett was behind her. He turned her around and pulled her to his chest.

"Ladybug, I'm sorry." He held her and rubbed her back.

"Dammit. I hate, hate, hate him. He hurt me. Put his fucking hands on me." She leaned against her brother but didn't cry. What was the point? Rhett settled her on the couch again.

"I'm sorry, but I've got more bad news." Mike set his empty beer can on the coaster with a clunk.

"What?" Scarlett shredded a napkin. She refused to imagine what else he could have to say.

"Friday afternoon Leroy Simms was being transported to the county jail from the courthouse when there was an altercation. He'd managed to make a shiv—you know, one of those handmade knives—and attacked a guard, got the handcuff keys and"—Mike took a breath—"escaped."

"What?" Scarlett froze. No. She didn't believe it. They'd worked so hard to catch the son of a bitch after a gun battle. Her heart stuttered. She was vaguely aware of Rhett gripping her hand and cursing. Why couldn't she move? Say anything? Finally she sucked in a breath and jumped to her feet, Rhett right beside her.

"Friday? He escaped Friday?" YoYo had been snoozing next to her feet. He was so alarmed by her screech that he started barking. She leaned down to pick him up and inhaled his doggy scent, tempted to throw him at Mike, who stared at her like he was braced for whatever she decided to do. No, she loved the dog. Mike? Well, he was on her shit list right now and he knew it.

It took everything in her to hand the dog to Rhett and say calmly, "Today is Sunday, Mike. Why are you just now telling me this?"

"I had hoped we would have him back in custody by now, Scarlett. The jail is in downtown Austin. We covered the area like a blanket after it happened. It amazes me that he hasn't been caught yet. Trust me, we're taking this very seriously." Mike was on his feet now too. He paced the small living room.

"What if he'd come after me? I was strolling down Sixth Street Saturday like I didn't have a care in the world." Scarlett sank back down on the couch, ignoring the pain sitting gave her. Not exactly true. She hadn't "strolled" since the attack. And then there'd been that flashback when she'd run into the bar and Ethan Calhoun.

"I should have called you right away. You're right about that." Mike stopped and stared down at her.

"God. You realize he could have caught me and cut my throat? Taken me totally by surprise." Scarlett felt like she could throw up or scream. But neither of those things would make her feel better. "He wants to finish me, Mike. He said as much after he was arrested." She buried her face in her hands.

Rhett cursed. "Scarlett's right. Someone from law enforcement should have warned her the minute he got away." He sat next to her and rubbed her back.

"Of course. I'm sorry. I've been distracted, involved in the massive manhunt going on. The guard he attacked is in critical condition. I guess I figured you'd see it on the news." Mike ran his hand over his short hair. "He's running, Scarlett. Why would he risk coming after you? Every cop who can has donated blood for the wounded officer, but it doesn't look good for him. If Ogilvy dies, then Simms will get the needle this time. Trust me, every cop in Texas is determined to bring in the son of a bitch."

"Scarlett doesn't watch the news." Her brother glanced at her. "You know why. Three days and you haven't caught him yet. How far could Simms go in a jail jumpsuit? Or did he take the cop's uniform?" Rhett was thinking like the detective in his books.

"He slashed the hell out of the officer. Six stab wounds. The uniform wasn't in any shape to be an option. A janitor in the courthouse was found unconscious in a closet and stripped. That's how Simms got away." Mike stood in front of Scarlett until she looked up at him. "Scarlett, honey, I mean it. He wouldn't hang around to come after you. I'm sure he's trying to get as far away from here as he can. He's mean, but he's not stupid. And he would have no idea where to find you anyway." He looked around the apartment. "Thank God you moved. Hell, *I* didn't know where you lived. This is good. Great security."

"It was my own paranoia and dumb luck that I did make a change." Scarlett wasn't in the mood to cut him a break. "Otherwise I might have been a sitting duck if he got my old address."

"Simms obviously wanted to blend in. That's why he got the janitor's clothes. I'm betting he hopped a bus and got the hell out of Austin." Mike frowned. "I came to warn you, just in case he's stupid enough to double back and try something. You're right, at first he did rant about wanting to get even with you and Anna. He also said"—Mike took a breath—"he'd rather go down in a hail of bullets than go back to prison."

"Damn it, Mike! Now you've really scared her." Rhett kept his arm around Scarlett.

He was right. She felt woozy, like she might faint. Oh, how stupid would that be? She remembered Simms way too well. Mike had said it. No one was meaner than Leroy Simms. But he knew what he was doing, every minute. He'd be running as fast as he could out of Austin. Sure, he'd threatened her, but talk was cheap. Why would he come after her now? Then she remembered the way he'd run his hands over her, how he'd squeezed her breasts and breathed promises so vile she'd thrown up on his shoes. That had infuriated him. He'd pulled out his knife and...

"She's going to be sick. Get her to the bathroom." Mike grabbed one arm, Rhett the other. Soon Scarlett was sitting on the toilet, her plastic garbage pail between her knees. No one had been paying attention to YoYo. The dog whimpered and licked her toes. Yes, he knew distress when he saw it.

She heard Mike and Rhett talking beside the open door.

"At least he'll have a hard time finding her here. Look at all the dead bolts. And the burglar bars. This is a safe place." Mike cleared his throat. "We've put a lot of men on this, working around the clock. You don't bring down one of our own and get away with it. There's some guilt here as well. Never should have been just one guard left to watch him, even if Simms was in shackles. The other had gone to take a leak. Simms saw his chance and took it." Mike must have banged his fist against the doorjamb from the sound of it. "We'll get the bastard and if he wants suicide by cop, hell, yeah, we'll oblige him."

"I hope you're right. That settles it. Scarlett, I'm moving in." Rhett stuck his head inside the bathroom. "You okay with that?"

"Yes. Thanks. Do it today." Scarlett slumped over the pail. She didn't think she could throw up, but she was sick to her stomach. Knife Guy out there somewhere vowing revenge. She swallowed, glad Anna was in Boston. Maybe...

"I have a gun, Mike, and will get a permit to carry concealed in Texas first chance I get." Rhett sounded unsteady, like he was as upset as she was. "But she can't just stay holed up in this place, you know. Waiting until Simms is caught. She has a job. A life."

"I know that. I'd like to get her protection, but we're stretched thin. Everybody is out there, looking for Simms. Now, about that gun." Mike threw some questions at Rhett. He must have answered them correctly because Mike finally agreed it was probably a good idea that her brother be armed.

"No one is getting past me here, but what about at her job? Surely you have someone who could go with her to and from work. Anna told me those criminals knew all about Zenon. That both she and Scarlett worked there."

"I just don't have the manpower. But Zenon has its own resources. Ron Zenonsky hired private security before. Maybe he will again. This all started because of industrial espionage at Zenon." Mike glanced in and saw Scarlett staring at him. "Scarlett, ask your boss to have a security guard walk you to and from the parking lot. I'd say it's the least he can provide."

She stood, her nausea suddenly gone, then picked up YoYo and rubbed his soft fur with her cheek. She was sick of cowering in her bathroom while her brother made plans to protect her.

"No, I don't think that'll be necessary. Ron offered to give me a leave of absence. To get over my trauma, he said. I had a job offer yesterday and I'm thinking I'll take it. As a change, and because Simms will never think to look for me there." She walked back to the sofa and sat. Ouch. She shifted pillows until she was comfortable.

"Wait. What kind of job offer? Where is it?" Rhett loomed over her.

"It's at the bar next to Amuse Tattoos. I'd be the manager." She waited for the judgment. Working in a bar? What about her expensive business degree? But Rhett was too focused on her safety to even go there.

"That's different from the tech field for sure." Her brother was obviously thinking about the tattoo parlor and what had been next door. "That bar isn't even open yet."

"I know. I'd be helping the owner get it set up. Organized." Scarlett realized Mike was frowning.

"You can't be serious. A bar? You'll be out where people will see you. Simms could walk in the front door to buy a drink and run right into you." Mike looked at her like she was crazy.

"Come on, Mike. On Sixth Street? Like I said, it's not even open yet. When it does open, it'll be trendy. I'm willing to bet Simms has never had a craft cocktail or designer beer in his life. I'm sure he favors beer joints and what I've heard they call icehouses here. They're the kind of places with garage doors and pool tables, Rhett. And why would a fugitive come into a bar with every cop in Austin and south Texas after him? Not likely." Scarlett could see she was making headway with her argument.

"You're right about that." Mike shook his head. "This is drastic, changing jobs. But time off isn't a bad idea. Stay here, inside. Lie low for a while. Binge-watch some TV shows and chill. You look tired. Maybe go home to

Boston for a few weeks. Surely we'll catch him soon, Scarlett." He glanced at Rhett. "What do you think?"

"This is my life, not my brother's, Mike." Scarlett was getting mad. "I'll decide what to do. And I'm thinking this is a good time to try something new and different."

"Mom and Dad would be glad to see you, Ladybug. Visit, recharge your batteries." Rhett sat close. "You sure you want to give up the job you came to Texas for?"

"I'm not a freakin' child, Rhett! Or a toy with batteries. Just listen to me." Scarlett had a temper, and she was on fire with it. Why not just pat her on the head and tell her to go away like a good little girl? No way in hell.

"I'm listening." Rhett glanced at Mike. "Tell us about this bar."

"Fuel, that's the name of the place. The owner offered me a job. He's eager for new ideas, and I've got one. I'm thinking the bar will be hidden behind a door that you have to know about or you'd never realize it's there. A secret bar."

"I guess I'm like Simms because I have no idea what you're talking about." Mike sat and stared at her.

"They're a hot new trend, Mike." Scarlett would have laughed at the look on Mike's face if she still wasn't scared out of her mind. "I'm going to talk the owner, Ethan Calhoun, into making Fuel a secret bar. And I dare Leroy Thomas Simms to find me there."

Chapter Four

Leroy was fucking brilliant. He had Austin's finest chasing their tails looking for him, but he had outsmarted them all. Everyone always underestimated him, going all the way back to high school. Just because he wasn't a thick-necked jock, he'd been a bench-sitter. Nothing could convince that asshole football coach to put him in a game. Until a timely "accident" had sidelined Coach's son. Then Leroy had his chance. He'd always been quick and was good with his hands, had even caught a pass for a touchdown. That had made everyone sit up and take notice, especially the girls. He'd showed 'em he had talents on and off the playing field.

Even college scouts were after him. But rules and studying were for losers. Why would he waste time in college? And forget marrying the first girl he'd knocked up. He'd helped himself to the Booster Club bankroll, then it was *adios* to that town where the Dairy Queen was the hot spot. Leroy Simms made his own rules, and no one better get in his way.

Friday's escape couldn't have gone better. Two guards to cover him. Seriously? He'd waited for his chance, then used the shiv he'd made out of a fountain pen his dumb-ass public defender had "lost" during one of their worthless sessions. Leroy hadn't been stupid enough to make a quick run for it, either. He hated cops and was happy to put one down, but he had nothing against a working stiff. He knocked out the janitor downstairs and then took his khaki pants and white T-shirt. There'd been a door propped open to the outside because the guy had been in the middle of hauling out garbage. Perfect. Leroy grabbed a can, snatched a battered straw hat from the trash, then stepped out to get the lay of the land.

His luck was in. He picked up a pair of clippers, rubbed a little dirt on his shirt, face, and arms, then joined the landscaping crew. Hell, yeah, he spoke Spanish. What boy growing up in South Texas didn't? So he clipped hedges and worked his way into the group of men gathering next to a white van. He climbed in right along with them. No one bothered with a head count. Sirens were screaming like crazy when the van pulled away from the curb. Leroy wanted to laugh his head off. Instead he just slumped like the rest of the guys, tired and obviously not through for the day, because, damn it, they stopped pretty quick in front of another government building in downtown. Everyone jumped out and began trimming more greenery.

You'd think he was screwed. They weren't that far from the jail, where he could see cops swarming like ants. They had traffic stopped and were searching buses. Like he'd do something as obvious as hop on one of those. There was a high-rise condo building on top of underground parking across the street, and Leroy had a plan. He asked one of his fellow workers where he could take a leak. He'd already been warned that whizzing in public on a bush could get them fired. The fella pointed to a restroom in the garage. Perfect. Leroy dropped his hedge trimmers and headed down the ramp. It was nice and cool inside, parking spaces marked with condo numbers. Some were vacant, like the owners were still at work.

When a couple came out of an elevator with suitcases, they chattered with each other about their spring break, a week in Cancun. They ignored Leroy like he was invisible. Of course, the hired help. He itched to cut them with the pocketknife he'd pulled off the janitor as they loaded their Mercedes, discussing the time of their flight and airport parking. After they were gone, he checked their condo number—1824. The elevator was right there. Leroy took his leak in the nearby restroom, washed the dirt off his face and arms, then turned his shirt inside out so it looked clean. Instant maintenance man. He had the gun from that cop he'd laid low, the knife, and a few tools he'd picked up in the janitor's closet where he'd stashed the guy he'd clocked. Good to go. He took a quick look around, then rode the elevator to the eighteenth floor.

The lock at door number 1824 was nothing. Once inside, Leroy spent the weekend working his way through their designer beer and wishing for some good old Lone Star. No way was he eating the kale in the fridge, but he had a steak thawing in the stainless-steel sink and wondered if he could fire up the grill on the balcony with a crazy good view of the University of Texas campus. Nope, he'd heard neighbors in the hall. But he did turn the TV on low to watch the news to see how the manhunt was going. Too bad the cop was still "clinging to life." Leroy relaxed when he heard they'd expanded the search for him statewide.

Because he had some unfinished business right here in town. First, he'd never been paid what he was owed. He knew there was someone here he could squeeze. Second? Well, there was that tasty little gal with the perfect ass. He hadn't got to finish what he'd started with her. And wasn't that a damn shame? He headed into the home office, where he'd discovered a laptop that connected automatically to Wi-Fi. Thanks, assholes.

Leroy got busy. He might not have a college education, but he wasn't stupid. He knew how to search for what he needed, thanks to hanging out with a techno-dweeb for way too long. Leroy Simms was just getting started in Austin Fucking Texas.

Chapter Five

Ethan grinned when he hung up the phone. He couldn't believe his luck. Scarlett Hall was really going to work for him, and she had some exciting ideas about the bar. God knew he needed her and her ideas. He looked around the deserted room. Fuel was still just a dream, the dusty reality far from what he'd imagined when he'd put down a massive chunk of change and bought the building. A knock on the back door startled him out of his mental vision of nights filled with capacity crowds and great music.

Probably another liquor delivery. The one thing he'd done right was apply for a liquor license early on. Texas was a land mine of complications when it came to getting permits for serving food and drink. His excellent choice of bartender had helped. Chelsea Dean and her brother were both old hands at the ins and outs of the hospitality business.

Ethan rushed to the back door when it shook with another hard hit. What the hell was someone using on the damn thing? A tire iron? He had security cameras mounted in the alley behind the place but had forgotten to activate them this morning after coming in. Hell, it was broad daylight and he figured the place looked deserted anyway. He threw the lock and opened the door, ready to tear a strip off of whoever was abusing his new steel door.

"Hurry, we don't want to be seen." His mother shoved him back, looking around furtively. "This is Lisa Marie. I told you about her." She dragged a tall woman in behind her. "Lock the door. Are you alone, baby?"

Ethan didn't like this. Locked in the bar with two women he didn't trust as far as he could throw them? Sure, one of them was his mother. But he had reason to believe she would as soon hit him as look at him. As for Lisa Marie? She carried a freaking baseball bat like she really wanted to use it. He'd read enough about her to know he didn't want to make her mad. He hesitated but finally gave in and took care of the dead bolt. No need to invite them inside. They were already scoping out the place like they were considering making it their hideout. No way in hell.

"Lucky for you two, I'm alone now, but not for long. Seriously, Mama, what are you thinking? I told you to turn yourself in. We've got a good lawyer in the family now. Hopefully Billy Pagan can help keep this mistake of yours from sending you right to prison once you're caught. You may have blown that top-of-the-line hospital stay we arranged for you, though." He deliberately avoided speaking to Lisa. This was a family matter, and he didn't give a damn what happened to the other woman. They'd escaped from a freaking mental hospital, which obviously had piss-poor security.

"Top-of-the-line?" his mother shrieked. "If that hospital was the top of a fucking line, I'd hate to see the bottom. The place was a living hell. I couldn't stay there another minute, baby." Missy Calhoun's eyes lit up when she spotted the whiskey behind the mahogany bar. "There you go. I see you're stocking your daddy's favorite brand. Mine, too, if you remember."

"I remember." Ethan thought about putting himself between his mother and the back of the bar, but the violence that simmered in her eyes and firmed her lips meant she'd be happy to trash the one part of the place he'd managed to put together if he got in her way. He mentally called himself a wimp as he stepped aside while she grabbed two glasses and poured a healthy measure for herself and her partner in crime. "Hold up, Mama. Is alcohol wise with your medications?"

"I'm not taking anything. I told you those pills they tried to force down me make me lose my focus." She clinked glasses with the silent Lisa. "Here's to freedom." She gestured. "Get yourself a glass, Ethan. Drink with us."

"I'd rather not. I need a clear head." Ethan leaned against the bar. He had a gun locked in a drawer in the office. Should he make up a reason to go get it? He didn't like the way Lisa kept staring at him and swinging that bat. She was a good-looking woman, different from the newspaper photos he'd seen. In those she'd looked hard-eyed and haggard. She'd filled out since then and it was an improvement. She had nice curves shown off in a tight T-shirt and jeans. Her hair had been lightened once but now showed a few inches of dark roots. His mother's hair looked good. He and his sisters had seen to it that her favorite beautician made the journey to her institution once a month for a color and cut. They'd do anything to keep Mama on an even keel. Or as even as she could be.

"I said, drink with us." Missy Calhoun glared at him until Ethan grabbed a glass and splashed whiskey into it. "Don't look at me like you're working on a plan to send me back there. I won't go and that's that. What you should be doing is figuring out when you'll get to the bank to get me a stake. And who you can tap to get me fake papers. Lisa here too. So we can leave the country."

"You can't seriously think I would buy you fake papers. How the hell would I even know how to do such a thing?" He sipped the whiskey and savored the taste, smoky and warm going down. Daddy's favorite. His old man would have already called the cops by now. Or at least refused to let these two in the door. Of course, Daddy and Mama had hated each other for years before the old man had died. Maybe Ethan *was* weak for not being able to turn away his mother. Daddy would sure think so.

"Figure it out, son. Look it up on the computer. You know how to find just about anything there. You know you do." His mother smiled at him proudly. "Lisa, Ethan is a genius with technology. He used to make robots in high school."

Ethan was surprised his mother remembered that. But he sure didn't have time for a trip down memory lane. He focused on Lisa. She was his age, not someone his mother would normally run with. "Lisa, you want to tell me why you've hooked up with my mother?"

"We're friends. Missy and I bonded over the shitty experience of being locked up for stuff we didn't do." She sipped her drink. "And the fact that our families abandoned us. Where's the loyalty?"

"Really? Is that how you're spinning this, Mama?" Ethan set the glass down hard. "Since when have we not been loyal? You did your best to fuck up our lives with your stunts. The last one, when you tried to kill Cassy, went too far. Yet we made sure you had a good lawyer who kept you out of prison. We got you help instead of a cell. How is that abandoning you?"

"That 'help' was in a mental hospital, Ethan. You think I should be *grateful* for that? Not even that son of a bitch who fathered you ever put me away like that." Missy refilled her glass with a shaking hand. "You owe me. All my children owe me. I sacrificed years of misery so you could have a home with your beloved daddy, a man who betrayed me time and again. That house where you grew up? That was his dream home, not mine. Everything we did was something he wanted—sending you to private schools, joining the country club, all so he could play the big man in the oil industry." She was spitting now as she got really wound up.

"Mama, calm down." Ethan knew she was rewriting history again. No one had loved the status of being Conrad Calhoun's wife more than his mother.

"Calm down? Why should I?" Her screech made Ethan's ears ring. "Conrad Calhoun picked out our friends, our cars, even our fucking dogs!

Then when he got tired of me, he bought me off. Like I was hired help he could just dump with a pension. Is it any wonder I have delicate nerves? And I sure as hell didn't want to see my children robbed of a single dime of their rightful inheritance. Your daddy naming that girl in his will... Of course it made me..." She looked at Lisa. "Temporarily insane."

Her new friend smiled. "It happens. I know."

"That's right. I lost my head for a little while. Who wouldn't? But do my children understand? Hell, no. They want to lock me up and forget about me. Just like their daddy did." Here came the tears.

Ethan let her cry, even handed her a bar towel to wipe her eyes. She had a point. His father had been dynamic, a steamroller pushing everyone in front of him. It was Conrad Calhoun's way or there would be hell to pay. If Daddy hadn't died when he did, Ethan himself would be chained to a desk or riding around in a company pickup, working for Calhoun Petroleum and answering to his father. This freedom to follow a dream would have cost him his inheritance. If he'd found the stones to face up to the old man.

"You're right, Mama. It's no wonder you had issues." Ethan put his arms around her.

"Thank you, baby. It's about time one of my children gave me a little sympathy." She picked up a pile of paper napkins and blew her nose. "You will help me, won't you? I just can't stand it in that place. They come at me all the time, calling it therapy, but they end up blaming me for everything. I'm out of control, that's the bottom line with those people. The only way to fix me is to dope me up until I can't see straight." She sniffled. "Ask Lisa Marie. They tried that with her too, but she's stronger than I am. She figured out a way to quit taking her meds. Hid 'em under her tongue, smart stuff like that." She reached out and squeezed Lisa's hand. "I'm so blessed she took me under her wing and showed me how to see clearly and take charge of my own treatment."

Ethan saw a look come over the other woman's face. Was it a genuine liking for his mother? Or could it be satisfaction that her plan had worked? Because, from what he had read, Lisa had nowhere to turn for the funds to leave the country. But his mother... Well, she had millions of her own if she could get to it. And rich kids, himself included, who might help her, if only to keep her from going to prison.

"Mama, where are you staying? How did you even get here? In Lisa's car? You know the cops will have an APB out for it. That hospital stay was court-ordered. Now you're both wanted by the police." He saw his mother sway. "Sit down." He dragged over his only bar stool and pushed her into it. "Sorry, but obviously I don't have furniture yet. Have you eaten?

I haven't stocked food, either." He didn't want to let her know that he lived upstairs and could let her lie down before he called for some takeout. "Do you have any money? How did you find me, anyway?"

"Slow down. First, we slept in the car, so my back is killing me." His mother glanced at Lisa. "Screw the cops. The first night we changed license tags with another car at one of those huge gas stations when no one was looking. Lisa saw that on a TV show. Wasn't that clever? We stole some snacks at the same place." Mama leaned on the bar. "I haven't done stuff like that since I was a teenager. What a rush. I hid a bag of nuts and some candy under my shirt. I wanted chips, but they'd have been too noisy." She giggled. "I'd never thought of that. Of course, the nuts made me thirsty, but Lisa had stuck two cans of soda in her tote. We're outlaws!" She grinned. "Can you believe it?"

Ethan shook his head. Outlaws. Like she was having some kind of adventure. He dug in his pocket. Lisa moved in on him with her bat. Did she think he was going for his phone? He *should* be calling the police right now. He pulled out some cash and she stepped back. Good thing. He didn't relish fighting a woman, but he'd swing his laptop at her if she came for him with that damn bat. Whose side would Mama be on? He didn't want to test it.

Was he aiding and abetting fugitives? Not if he could help it. He wanted them away from here, then he'd figure out this situation. An outright refusal would be stupid. Surely any court would understand and clear him of charges once they saw Lisa with her bat and read about her violent past. He wished he had a camera filming this now. But he hadn't set up any inside. Something to think about.

"You obviously need to find a cheap motel. And get something to eat. A decent meal, not snacks. You know you have to watch your blood sugar." He handed his mother a few hundred-dollar bills. Lisa watched his every move. If she thought he was going to give them a credit card, she could think again.

"That's my boy." Mama counted the money, then frowned. "This won't last long. I'm not staying where there might be bedbugs. I'd rather sleep in the car."

"Cops in this town will roust you out if they catch you doing that. I can get to the bank tomorrow for more cash. Then I'll start doing some research. Make some calls. A fake passport? I have to think about who I know who might have some ideas about that." Ethan said whatever he could to stall them both. He helped his mother stand, startled when she grabbed him around the neck.

"Thank you, baby! I knew I could count on you. Always my little man. My favorite child." Mama held on so tight he thought she was going to choke him. She finally let go and tucked the bills into her bra, something he wished he hadn't seen. She had on a velour tracksuit, the kind of thing she wouldn't have worn as a member of her country club. But the navy blue suited her.

She looked good for sixty. He actually wasn't surprised she'd run, now that he thought about it. He and his sisters had made the trip out to the hospital with a cake recently for her "significant" birthday. Spending it in that place had depressed Mama, and she'd thrown one of her screaming fits when she wasn't allowed to leave with them for a special dinner. All in all, the dinner in the hospital cafeteria had been a fiasco and proof that Mama was far from well.

"You'd better go, Mama. I'm expecting some people here any minute. Hired help for the bar. I know you don't want anyone else to see you." Ethan wrestled away a bottle of whiskey as he urged Lisa and her toward the back door.

"Thanks for the money. You know we'll need a lot more than this, baby." Missy looked around the deserted bar. "This place is going to cost you plenty. A good businessman doesn't sink all his own cash into a startup. Get a loan or an investor. Everyone would expect it." She patted his cheek. "I need three million at the very least. And get that sharp lawyer to work figuring out how to access my money. I don't trust Shannon's husband, that Billy Pagan. Your sister isn't sympathetic to my problem, never has been. She always was your daddy's girl. Took his side every time we had a fight." She sighed, then patted her chest where the money crackled. "Hire someone else. You know I can pay you back. No interest, of course. We're family. You understand that, don't you?"

Ethan had nothing to say to that. He was being used. No news there. Lucky him to be his mama's favorite. Ever since he'd been little and his mama had plunked him down on a bar stool at the club while she'd gone on a rant over cocktails to her friends about what a monster his daddy was, he'd been a handy prop. Now he was expected to be a money tree as well. Oh, no, he wasn't. Somehow he was going to get Mama back into the institution where she belonged, her pal Lisa along with her. Though it would obviously be better if Miss Lisa went somewhere else. Let her manipulate another person into being her accomplice.

"You never told me how you found me here." Ethan stopped them at the back door, disappointed that apparently they had parked down the block from his place so he couldn't get their new license plate number.

"One of my old friends forwarded me a copy of that email you sent out about this place. Her son Jason was one of your good buddies, you know who I mean."

Ethan nodded. Of course he did. The old biddy network was alive and well.

"Fuel. Clever name, baby. I guess you'll put up Calhoun Petroleum signs around the place. Might as well use your daddy's name for something good. The bastard made a mess of that company at the end." Missy's mouth turned down, and Ethan noticed new lines had formed since her last face-lift.

"Daddy made his share of mistakes, but he didn't ruin the company, Mama. The downturn in the price of oil did most of the damage." Ethan knew that truth wouldn't please her, but he had loved his father no matter what his mother thought of the old man. "The recovery has us all benefiting, and Cassy is doing great things now that she's in charge. Calhoun is turning around."

"I don't want to hear it. All I want is money enough to get the hell out of Texas for good." She kissed his cheek. "Though I'll miss you, son. You're such a fine boy. Maybe you can visit me when I get settled. While you're researching, find me a place that doesn't extradite. Someplace nice, though. Not one of those countries full of drug cartels." She handed him a slip of paper. "I got a burner phone. Call me when you get my money and we can meet. Make it quick." She patted her chest again. "This little bit of cash won't last long."

"You'll be hearing from me. I promise you that." Ethan walked back inside, locked the door, and finally remembered to activate his security cameras. When he checked the monitor, he was glad he got good views of the back alley and the area by the front door. He picked up his phone and hit a number in his contacts list. Would this call get him the help he needed? It was a slim hope, but better than none at all.

Chapter Six

"You're really going to take me up on that offer for a leave of absence?" Ron Zenonsky paced in front of his desk. "It's been months. I thought you were over the attack. You look fine."

"Don't you watch the news, Ron?" Scarlett hid her shaking hands behind her back. She was far from fine. It was Monday morning, and Leroy Simms was still at large. While Mike claimed the man was probably running as far from Austin as fast as he could, she couldn't shake the feeling that he might still be out there, thinking about grabbing her again.

The walk from the parking lot to this building where Zenon had its headquarters had been terrifying. The security guard at the door had been playing a game on his phone. She'd wanted to rip it from his hands and shove it... She had to get a grip. She was here inside now, and no one had bothered her.

"What does the news have to do with anything?" Ron stared at her like she was crazy. "I've been out of town. Took my daughter to Disney World for her spring break, and I just got back last night. Will you sit down and talk to me?"

Scarlett sat. Just a twinge from her new tattoo, not bad. "Leroy Simms, the man who cut me as part of the attempted robbery of your hot new program, escaped from custody Friday."

"No!" Ron fell into a chair. "They haven't caught him yet?"

"Afraid not. And I'm freaking out. What if he decides to come after me? I can testify against him when he's caught and goes to trial. Can you see why I might not want to come here every day? Where he knows he can find me?" Scarlett looked away from Ron's concern. No tears. Once she started, she might not be able to stop.

"He'd want Anna too." Ron jumped to his feet and grabbed his cell phone from his desk. "Does she know about this?"

"I talked to her last night. She's still in Boston, with King. They'll stay there until this situation is resolved. I doubt Simms could get that far, even if he knew where to look for her." Of course Anna was Ron's top priority. Her friend, the computer genius, had created the program Ron was counting on to make him even richer. It was all anyone at Zenon talked about these days. Simms had been part of the crew that had gone after that program thinking to resell the thing to some foreign entity. He'd used Scarlett to get to Anna. Thank God the plot had fallen apart when Isaac Crane, the nutcase behind it, had been killed.

"Anna's safe. That's good. Now we need to protect you." Ron leaned against his desk and studied her. "I'll get you a security team. No need to leave here, even temporarily. The office will fall apart without you."

"I doubt that. I know this isn't much notice, but I had a job offer recently, someplace Simms would never think to look for me. It's something I'd like to try. The truth is, I haven't felt the same here since the, um, incident." Scarlett stood and ran her sweaty palms down her black straight skirt. She'd dressed nicely for what she hoped would be her last day. The suit was her best one, a bargain at Neiman's Last Call outlet. She wouldn't need clothes like it at a bar. It was a good thought and made her smile. She realized Ron hadn't said anything and looked up to see his frown.

"Damn it, you were hurt because of my company and I didn't even offer compensation. Would a raise make you stay?" Ron reached out.

"This isn't a shakedown, Ron." Scarlett laid her hand in his. "Money won't fix this. It's honestly about two things— First, I'm scared to be here right now."

"And the other thing?" He squeezed her fingers but didn't let go.

"A challenge. I like it here, but office work just isn't satisfying me anymore. What happened when I was abducted made me take a hard look at my life." That was the truth. Something she'd wrestled with during the long nights when sleep had been impossible.

"But, Scarlett, you're very good at what you do. Everyone here admires your organizational skills." Ron was suddenly very close. "You think I haven't been paying attention? I have. You're intelligent, with great potential. If you want something new, let's consider how we can find it for you here at the company. Perhaps a promotion."

"Thanks, Ron. Your good opinion means the world to me." Scarlett backed up and eased her hand from his. The look in his eyes was a little too intense. Was he hitting on her? Her coworkers had whispered that

Ron had a reputation with the ladies, but she hadn't seen evidence of it at the office. She knew he dated, because she'd seen pictures of him with beautiful women on social media sites at charity fund-raisers. But he must have decided that the office staff was off-limits after a messy and expensive divorce last year from his former secretary. "I'm looking for a more radical change. I'll be helping a new business get off the ground. I like the idea."

"A startup." Ron smiled. "Those can be fun, but they can also fail. If you find yourself left without a job again, come see me." He looked back when his desk phone buzzed. "There's *my* boss. Mona's reminding me that I have an appointment with Distribution in five minutes. I dread telling her we'll have to interview for a new office manager."

"Give Damon Reed a shot. He's excellent and has seniority. I've been using him as my assistant since I got here." Scarlett headed for the door.

"And you're lucky to have Mona. We all live in fear of her." His secretary seemed to run Zenon while Ron spent most of his time courting investors and looking for the next big thing in tech.

"Yep, she knows more about Zenon than I do." Ron laughed and walked her to the door. "Stay in touch. Does Mona have your contact information?"

"Sure." Though Scarlett wasn't going to share her new address with anyone. "She can call me if you have questions about the office. I'm sorry, but today's my last day. I can't risk coming here again as long as Simms is out there. He made some serious threats after he was captured the first time."

Ron looked alarmed. "I get it. Stay safe. Let me know if you want that security detail. I can call someone right now."

"That's okay. I've got it covered." She knew whom he would call, and she didn't want the complication. Ron's new security company was run by Anna's brother, Scarlett's former lover. She wouldn't put it past Chance Delaney to swoop in and do his macho "I know what you need" bit. She really couldn't take the loss of control right now, no matter how well-meaning.

"Thanks, I appreciate the offer. I suggest you let Damon take over until you find a replacement. I guarantee you won't be sorry if you decide to move him up permanently." With that Scarlett hurried out of his office. Ron had looked like he wanted to give her a hug. He was attractive, a billionaire, and so not what she needed. She couldn't wait to be out of this building that still reminded her of the worst day of her life.

Her cell phone buzzed in her jacket pocket. She smiled when she pulled it out and saw who was calling. "Mike, please tell me you caught Simms."

"I wish I could, Scarlett. Where are you?" His deep voice was serious as always.

"I'm at work, at Zenon headquarters."

"What time do you get off? I'll meet you at the door and escort you home. I want to make sure you're not followed from there." Scarlett swallowed. "So, he's at large. Not even a sighting in Louisiana or Oklahoma?" "Afraid not. Did Zenonsky offer security?" "He did. But I turned it down. I just want to cut all ties. I live in a new place and will be starting a new job. Rhett can keep an eye on me too. I think being trailed by a bodyguard would just draw attention." Scarlett realized that Mona, her eyebrows raised, was listening to her side of the conversation. She waved at the secretary, not about to leave the office without telling Mona how sorry she was to go with such little notice. The woman was too powerful to piss off in case Scarlett did have to come crawling back. "Listen, I have to go. See you at five?"

"You got it."

Scarlett ended the call, then turned back to talk to Ron's secretary. Mona was staring at her computer screen like it held the secrets of the universe.

"Uh, Mona, I guess you heard some of that." Scarlett waited until the secretary looked up. Mona Delgado was a very attractive woman in her mid-thirties. She had dark hair pulled back into a bun at the nape of her neck. Her dark-rimmed glasses came off when she decided to give Scarlett her attention.

"Scarlett, I'm sorry. What did you say?" She'd obviously decided to pretend she hadn't been listening in on the phone call.

"Today is my last day. I'm leaving Zenon." Scarlett stepped back when Mona jumped up and ran around her desk.

"Today? Without any notice? Are you all right? What's the matter?" Mona grabbed her shoulders and looked her over. "Are you sick?"

Scarlett took a moment to process this uncharacteristic reaction. Calm and cool Mona was upset. Why? They'd never been buddies. She eased out of her grasp.

"Yes, I'm sick. With fear. That creep who attacked me is on the loose. I'm afraid he'll track me down here." Scarlett heard her voice shaking again. She had to get hold of herself. Mona stared at her. "I heard he used you to get to Anna Delaney. And hurt you. No wonder you're scared, Scarlett, but why would he bother with you now? Seems like he'd just run for his life. Surely you aren't the only witness against him."

"That's true." Scarlett wasn't about to satisfy the avid curiosity in the woman's gaze. She wanted details, everyone did, but Scarlett would be damned if she'd give them to her. "I just keep remembering things he said."

She shuddered. "I can't stand that he knows where I work. He could find me, and I'm not willing to take that chance."

"Aren't you overreacting?" Mona looked her over.

Scarlett itched to smack Mona's superior attitude right off her face. "I didn't say what I was feeling was logical." She fisted her hands at her sides. Control. She had to find it and keep it. "But I don't want to be near this place as long as Leroy Simms is free to come after me and that's that."

"So you're leaving us. Today?" Mona walked around her desk so she could look down at her computer. "Can you afford to just quit while you hide out?"

"Actually, Ron offered me a leave of absence right after the attack. With pay. I'm taking it. But I might not be back at all. I got a job offer. I've decided this is the right time to try a career change." Scarlett straightened her shoulders. Mona had always intimidated her a little, but she actually seemed concerned as she sat in her chair again.

Mona frowned and shook her head. "I'm sorry. It's just that you threw me there for a minute. I'm sure Mr. Zenonsky told you how valuable you've been in the office. How on earth will we replace you on such short notice?"

"I told Ron to give my assistant a shot at my job. Damon can handle it. I'm sure the transition will be seamless, and I won't stay even one more day."

"What is this new job?" Mona started typing. "You're not going to one of our competitors, are you? If you share trade secrets, that would be illegal. You did sign a noncompete clause when you moved from Boston."

"It's in a completely different field, Mona. Nothing for you to worry about." Scarlett sighed, more than ready to get out of there.

"Of course, I saw that Simms escaped on the news, Scarlett. I'm sure it does make you nervous." Mona stood. "Wherever you're going, whatever you're doing next, be sure to tell them to give me a call. I'll be glad to give you a reference. You've been a real asset here." She smiled, then sat again. "Now, I have to update your profile. New address? New job? Give me your contact information." Mona had her fingers poised over her keyboard.

"You have my cell phone number, and that's all I'm willing to share at this time. Knife Guy might be smarter than we think and hack into your files. So I'm not leaving him a trail, not even here. Thanks for the offer, Mona. I'll keep it in mind if I need that reference." With that, Scarlett turned on her high heels and left Mona staring after her. The all-powerful executive secretary had actually been rather nice for a moment. But she hadn't liked not getting that address. Too bad. Self-preservation came first.

The rest of the day was so busy Scarlett almost didn't have time to worry about the drive home. Almost. She got an inter-office email from Mona stating that Zenon was a computer company that had *never* been hacked and that it certainly maintained the highest cybersecurity firewalls, blah, blah, blah. She'd attached a form demanding Scarlett's new address and work information. Scarlett sent it straight to her trash can.

On a positive note, there was an impromptu celebration, a good-bye lunch in the break room at noon. Ron, which meant he'd made Mona do it, had ordered a catered meal and everyone dined on fajitas with all the trimmings. The big boss himself poured margaritas and made a toast to Scarlett, claiming she'd be a tough act to follow and announcing Damon's promotion. Mona smiled and said all the right things, then sat in a corner.

Scarlett was touched by how many people made it a point to tell her how much they'd miss her. Actually, she had been afraid she'd been something of a tyrant when she'd come in and found an office in serious need of reorganization. She'd tightened procedures until one woman had quit in tears. But those who had stuck with her claimed they loved the new methods she'd instigated and her fairness. Under the old ways, there had been lost papers, finger-pointing, and sudden firings when things went wrong.

Damon took her aside to thank her personally for her recommendation. He was thrilled at his promotion but had endured a grilling by Mona before he'd been given the job on a trial basis. Only the excellent performance reviews Scarlett had given him and Ron's reluctance to interview anyone outside the company had allowed him to move into her position.

By the time five o'clock rolled around, Scarlett had shed a few tears. She realized she had more friends in Austin than she'd thought, and she had to promise to set lunch dates in the future. She was careful, though, to keep her new job a secret. All she would say was that she was making a big change. She even let Ron hug her before he carried her box of personal items out to the parking lot. The car idling at the curb made them both stop in their tracks. The Texas Department of Public Safety emblem on the side was reassuring, as was Mike's bulk as he climbed out and took the box from Ron. The two men knew each other and shook hands.

"Wow. You really think Simms might come after Scarlett?" Ron looked around the lot that was emptying fast now that it was quitting time.

"It's possible. Not smart, but possible." Mike walked toward Scarlett's car. "You still have security, Mr. Zenonsky?"

"Here at the office? Of course." He pointed to the man in uniform standing at the entrance to the building. The guard was all attention in the presence of his boss and a Texas Ranger. "Do I need it personally for after hours? Do you think he might come after me or that program again?" Ron shook his head. "Wouldn't do him any good to come after the program. It's already in production. There's no value to him anymore. Besides, as far as I know, Simms isn't computer savvy enough to do anything with the software. It was Isaac Crane who had the skills and contacts to make money from the program."

"I can't predict what Simms will do. He talked big when he was arrested, but a lot of cons do. It usually doesn't mean anything. What I do know is that he's violent and a repeat offender." Mike set the box in Scarlett's trunk. He looked grim. "That policeman he knifed during his escape died today. We're searching for a cop killer now. So I'd say Simms has nothing to lose. In my opinion, that makes him even more dangerous. Get a personal guard, Mr. Zenonsky, if it'll make you feel safer. Simms needs money to start a new life. He might be desperate enough to try kidnapping. You do have a child."

"Dear God." Ron's face went white. "You've convinced me. I'm calling Security now."

"I'm sorry, Mike. About the cop." Scarlett laid her hand on his arm. He wore his uniform today and looked very official and stern. "Did you know him personally?"

"No, but we're all brothers." He kept looking around the parking lot, watching for anything suspicious. "In another hour I'll be driving in a motorcade escorting the body to the funeral home. So let's get going." He helped her into her car. "I'm going to follow you. If I run my siren, stop. That means I think we're being followed and I want you to let me handle something. Otherwise? Go straight home. Got it?"

"Got it. Thanks, Ron, for today. Lunch was great. A real send-off." Scarlett doubted he heard her since he was already on his phone. Of course he was concerned for himself and his family. And who could blame him? A cop killer on the loose. A desperate man who liked to use a knife. She shuddered and started her car, then locked her doors. Once Ron was safely inside the building, she backed out, then waited for Mike to follow her. They drove the speed limit home when they could, but Austin's five o'clock traffic was its usual tangle and crawl. There was a giant knot of tension between her shoulder blades by the time she finally punched in the code at the gates of her apartment complex. Mike parked next to her and trailed her up the stairs, carrying her box of stuff.

"I'm checking your place before I go." Mike stood behind her as she used her key.

"I can't imagine he could find me here." But then the alarm didn't beep when she opened the door. She glanced at Mike. He dropped her box, then pushed her aside, his gun out as he stepped in front of her.

"Whoa, whoa." Her brother jumped up from the couch. "Unarmed and friendly. Don't shoot."

"Why didn't you have the alarm set?" Scarlett heard her voice rise. Great, now she was screeching at her brother. "You scared the hell out of me."

"Sorry. You did give me a key so I let myself in. I was just sitting here watching TV. I knew you'd be home soon. Why would I set the alarm?" He walked over and put his arms around her. "Mike, you can put the gun away."

"You understand why she's upset, don't you?" Mike slid his gun back into his holster, then brought in her box, setting it on the bar. "Help her out. Set the alarm, even if you're just chillin' here. It makes her feel safer. That's important. You see the news?"

"That's what I was doing, checking the latest." Rhett shook his head. "Sorry about the cop."

"Yeah, me too. I've got to go." Mike sighed. "You okay now, Scarlett?"

"Sure. Fine. Thanks for bringing me home." She pushed her brother away and kissed Mike on the cheek. "Be careful. I know you want this Simms guy bad, but don't put yourself in harm's way to get him."

"That's the job, honey. I hope I have the chance to get him. I surely do." He took off down the stairs.

"What's his hurry?" Rhett shut the door, then engaged the locks and the alarm.

"The police are escorting the dead officer's body from the hospital morgue to the funeral home. He wants to drive in the procession." Scarlett walked to the kitchen and pulled out a bottle of water. She felt drained, and all she'd done was drive home. Ridiculous. How was she going to function normally while the killer was still out there?

She didn't have a choice. She'd called Ethan today and told him she wanted to work for him. Of course, that was after Rhett had done a thorough background check on Mr. Ethan Calhoun and the entire Calhoun family. Yes, the man came from money, oil money. After his father died, the company had suffered, but a long-lost sister had pulled Calhoun Petroleum up from the brink of disaster and Ethan had inherited a nice chunk of change as well as royalties from oil wells. Those would keep him flush even if this investment in the bar didn't work out.

Rhett had found out that Ethan had been a wild child as a teen, but he'd done nothing so bad that he had needed jail time. Just his bad luck that his prominent family made those youthful indiscretions land in the Houston newspapers. His mother had issues, but Scarlett knew better than to blame the man for what his parents might have done.

When Scarlett had shared her idea about the secret bar, Ethan was all-in, excited about it. She'd promised to meet with him at Fuel tomorrow morning. So, between now and then, she had to find the courage to leave her fortress and do it. How? That was the burning question.

* * * *

Ethan had spent the past twenty-four hours figuring out how to juggle resources. At least he had help coming. A private investigator was on his way from Houston. Hopefully he'd be able to track down Mama and her partner in crime and they could get the duo back into the hospital. At the very least, he'd have some ideas about how to keep Mama out of the bar. Unfortunately, both women weren't above hurting people to get what they wanted. Mama was probably already trying to figure out how to get a gun. She liked having a weapon and knew how to use it. Ethan also kept picturing Lisa with that bat.

The knock on the front door meant he had company. A glance at the monitor and he grinned. Scarlett was here, right on time. He hurried to throw the dead bolt and let her in.

"You've started locking your door." She glanced behind her.

"Yeah. I had some unwelcome visitors recently. You never know who's going to show up." Ethan noticed a man behind her. "You brought someone with you?"

"Let me introduce you. He's not staying, but my brother drove me here." She dragged the man in and threw the lock. "Sorry, but I agree with you. Never can tell who might come in."

"Ethan Calhoun." Ethan held out his hand. Scarlett was fidgeting and looking around. "Relax, Scarlett. The visit was from a family member, nothing for you to worry about. I handled it." He managed to say that with a straight face.

"I'm just jumpy. This is my brother, Rhett Hall." She flushed. "I'm sorry if you thought I didn't trust you."

"Scar, calm down. We're here. Everything's cool." Her brother shook hands firmly. "So this is Fuel. Interesting place. Obviously you have some work to do."

"A lot of it. I'm glad Scarlett agreed to come on board to help." Ethan walked over to the bar and turned his laptop to face them. "I've made some preliminary plans. What I think the place should look like. The bartender has told me what she wants as far as her space goes, and the kitchen has a good layout. I've already ordered the equipment and everything else the chef says he needs. It all should be here in the next day or two."

Rhett glanced at the screen, then patted his sister's back. "I'll leave you to work. What time do you think you'll be finished? I can pick you up whenever you say or you can text me."

Scarlett was totally absorbed in the layout on the screen. "Oh! Yes, text me." She glanced at Ethan. "I expect to stay most of the day. Unless you have somewhere else to be?"

"No, I'm meeting a guy later, but I can always talk to him in my office. Family business." Ethan wondered why Rhett hovered over his sister. And seemed reluctant to leave her. "Everything all right? Rhett? You're welcome to stay if you want to."

"No, I've got things to do. See you later." He headed for the door. "Would one of you lock up after me?" He waited until Ethan was beside him. Scarlett stayed at the computer, still examining the plans. "She's jumpy for a reason. Get her to tell you why." He nodded toward his sister. "See you later." With that he stepped outside, looking around before he headed down the sidewalk, only to slip into the tattoo parlor next door.

"Guess your brother is getting a tattoo today." Ethan locked the door.

"What?" Scarlett finally dragged her gaze from the screen.

"He just went into Amuse Tattoos."

"Oh. I didn't know..." She shook her head. "He met Carl and Casey yesterday. I doubt he's getting a tattoo today. Monday is Casey's day off. I heard them talking yesterday. I believe she's giving him a tour of Austin. Guess he's picking her up now. He also wants to interview them, especially Casey." She explained about the interview. "He's always looking for a story."

"And Casey is hot." Ethan grinned. "An author. Yeah, I've heard of him. I'm not much for reading fiction, but I'll have to pick up one of his books."

"I can bring you one. They're good. Men like them because they're full of action and things like what car his hero drives, with details about the engine. Stuff that I skim." Scarlett smiled, and the beauty of it made Ethan move closer.

"That stuff, lady, is important. Why is your brother driving you around? Is he borrowing your car? Does it have a decent engine?" He reminded himself that he was her employer now and backed up.

"No idea. He's rented something loud and cool, a Camaro or Corvette, something like that. He would rather walk than drive my ancient Corolla." Scarlett laughed, then pointed to the laptop. "I like your plans. What do you think about the secret bar idea, now that you've had time to mull it over?"

"I like it. I've been to one in Houston that's been in business for years. It's always packed." He would like to imagine Fuel like that. "The Houston secret bar is known as a make-out place. It's very dark, sexy. You have to find your way up some stairs to even get there. Then inside it's hard to see, with booths lining the walls, sofas too. The place has lots of nooks and crannies, and the music usually adds to the seductive vibe." Shit, she'd turned to look at him with her blue, blue eyes, and he could imagine how it would be, the two of them sinking into one of those deep velvet love seats... Uh-huh. Love seat was the right word for it. He'd sworn there was actual sex going on in some of the out-of-the-way places in the bar.

"Ethan, you're painting a pretty vivid picture. You've got to sell drinks to make money. Too dark, too much of the"—she licked her lips, and he almost moaned—"hanky-panky, and you're running a brothel, not a bar. Not that it doesn't sound cool."

"Cover charge." Hell, his voice had cracked. He cleared his throat. "I mean, that's how they make sure the place stays profitable. And it must be making money. I swear my parents went there when they were young and hot for each other." That thought was enough to throw cold water on his imagination. "I see your point, though."

"Let's put a pin in that vibe for a moment and think about how to get the word out." She fanned her face with her hand. So Scarlett wasn't unaffected. "We need to get on one of those lists, the kind that people search on the Internet. 'The Most Popular Secret Bars in Austin'." She put up air quotes, then stopped next to what would be the stage. "I did some research and there are several sites like that. We want to be on those as soon as we open. Austin already has several interesting places." She turned to Ethan. "We need to check them out."

"You're right." Ethan almost blurted out a cliché, like it was a dirty job but someone had to do it. Ha! He was already imagining bar-hopping with Scarlett. She'd be in some short little dress while they did "research" sampling cocktails. Damn, he did not like being her boss.

"You said you'd sent out emails to friends. We need to expand that list too. I'm sure your bartender has a following, since you said you hired her away from a popular spot. She and her chef brother can help you." She detailed plans for a media campaign, proving he'd been right to hire her. But she was talking fast, her fingers tapping on the side of her jeans in a nervous rhythm. She wore a blue sweater that matched her eyes and dipped low enough that Ethan had to be careful not to gawk. Tempting. She had the kind of curvy figure he'd liked ever since he'd hit puberty.

"Are you going to tell me why you're so jumpy? Why your brother has to drive you to and from the bar?" Ethan put a hand on her shoulder. "That's personal. We were talking about the business." She moved away from him, back to the computer.

"Your brother told me to ask you. If there's something I should know, then you'd better let me in on it now." Ethan remembered how he'd met her. She'd been scared then. And talking about being crazy. She looked entirely sane to him, but then he was no judge of what was rational behavior. His mother had been able to fool a lot of people for a lot of years before she'd finally done something so out-of-bounds no one could ignore it. The last thing he needed when starting this new business was to hook up with someone with "issues."

"I'm not crazy, if that's what you're worried about. I can see the way you're looking at me. Sure, we joked about it when we first met, but I had something bad happen to me a couple of months ago. It left me nervous." Scarlett sat on the lone bar stool.

Damn it, Ethan was going to order more furniture right away.

"Prove you're not crazy. Tell me what's bugging you. Because, I'll be honest with you, Scarlett. I cannot deal with someone working for me who is nervous or who might flake out when I need them most." Ethan paced in front of her. "Quite frankly, I've got a lot on my plate right now with my family. Yeah, it's personal too. I could say I'll tell you mine if you'll tell me yours, except if you knew mine it might get you into trouble." He stopped and looked into her eyes. She had long lashes, obvious now that she was blinking back tears. He couldn't quit pressing, though. This was important. He meant every word he said.

"Now, are you going to be straight with me? Or do you walk out of here right now and we forget we ever met?"

Chapter Seven

Scarlett couldn't believe he was giving her an ultimatum. What the hell? She barely knew the man and he was already dictating terms. But then she could hardly blame him. He'd hired her after meeting her in a pretty bizarre fashion. Apparently he had some serious stuff going on in his own life and he didn't need more drama. She'd probably be doing him a favor if she did walk out.

But she didn't want to. This was an exciting opportunity. If she let Leroy Simms ruin it for her, she'd never forgive herself. And it would probably be for nothing. Everyone kept telling her Simms was long gone from Austin. She should believe them.

She took a steadying breath and eased off the bar stool. "Ethan, you're right. I owe you an explanation. I've been dealing with something that happened recently. Anyway, my brother was helping by driving me here." She rested her hand on Ethan's sleeve. Another vintage rock band tee. She loved the feel of the soft cotton. And the obvious strength of his arm under it. He even smelled good, clean and masculine. No, she shouldn't be distracted by things like that.

"So tell me what's going on." Ethan leaned against the bar, giving her his full attention. He had an intent gaze that made her *want* to tell him everything. He was tall, fit, and had a nice tan, like he spent some time outdoors. Good to know. If all he did was hang out in bars after dark, that would be a red flag. Make her wonder. . . *Focus.*

Scarlett realized he was giving her time to decide. She owed him an explanation. So she started talking. "You know I was getting a tattoo this weekend."

"Sure." He raised an eyebrow. "I admit I've been looking for it. It's not on your arms, at least from the elbow down. Your jeans are hiding your legs, so my imagination is working overtime." He ran his hand through his short hair, dark brown, like his eyes. "Damn it, I'm having a hell of a time remembering that I'm your boss. Call me out if I get too personal and make you uncomfortable."

"I will." Scarlett realized she didn't mind his flirting. It felt good to have his complete attention. There was nothing sleazy about Ethan Calhoun. She'd had bosses before who had made moves on her, creepy moves. The bar business could be tough, and cocktail waitresses were frequently considered fair game. She'd learned long ago how to hold her own against handsy customers and unwelcome advances no matter where they came from.

"I mean it. I'll be up front here. I find you attractive." He smiled ruefully. "There, I said it. Feel free to shoot me down, any time. It won't cost you your job, Scout's honor." He held up fingers in a salute she recognized.

"Were you really a Boy Scout?"

"For a while. Until my mother got crossways with the troop leader. Mama is volatile, and that's putting it kindly." He stared at the back door for a moment, then looked at her. "Anyway, I keep my word. It's important that you know that. I don't promise if I can't deliver."

Scarlett really liked that. The chemistry she felt between them also appealed. He'd laid it all out there. He was her boss, but he wasn't going to use his power against her. Cool. "I'll hold you to that. I'm pretty hung up on keeping my word too. Let's see how things go. If I ask *you* out, feel free to shoot *me* down." She grinned, on solid ground now. She'd missed this, the sparks flying when getting to know a new guy. She'd let Leroy Simms steal this part of her life when the trauma of what he'd done to her had made her hibernate while she nursed her wounds. She'd been looking at men since then like they might pull out a knife and start carving on her. No more.

"Let me tell you my story before I lose my nerve." Scarlett could imagine dates—or more—with Ethan. It was way too easy. She blurted out the whole thing—why she'd gotten her tat and where Casey had to put it.

"Holy shit! No wonder you ran in here the other day like you'd seen a ghost. I'm sure the minute Casey hit you with that needle you had a flashback." Ethan shook his head. "That bastard. I hope he's dead."

"Unfortunately, he's not. In fact, the reason I'm so nervous is that he recently escaped from the Travis County Jail, right here in Austin. You may have seen it on the news. He stabbed a cop."

"Of course I've seen that. It wasn't that far from here. Scarlett!" He moved closer. "Naturally you're freaking out."

Scarlett shuddered. "I was there when he was captured the first time, Ethan. I managed to confront him, going on and on about how much I hated him, what I'd like to do to *him*. You get the picture. I said I couldn't wait to testify against him. Me and my big mouth." She looked down at her hands, clenching and unclenching against her thighs. "He marked me, Ethan. And wanted to, uh, do a lot more. Told me so in graphic terms. God knows where he'd put his knife if he ever got hold of me again."

"Son of a bitch." Ethan pulled Scarlett into his arms. "I'm so sorry. Of course you're scared. You just have your brother? You need bodyguards." He held her, his hands warm on her back. She could feel his heart thumping against hers. "Maybe you should leave town until Simms is caught. I've got a place in Houston, my family's home with plenty of guest rooms. I can call my sister. I'm sure she'd be happy to have you. He'd never find you there."

Scarlett leaned back to look into his eyes. "You hardly know me, Ethan. How can you offer such a thing?"

"I'd do the same for any woman who'd been hurt like you have." He let her go. "Well, that didn't come out right. I mean, I want you to be safe. I could tell the minute I met you that you have no harm in you."

"Don't be so sure." Scarlett knew Ethan had meant that as a compliment, but "no harm in her"? Did that translate as wimpy? Poor pitiful Scarlett? She'd felt homicidal lately when she thought about Leroy Simms. Put her in a room with him tied up and give her a knife… "Hey, my brother's no slouch as a bodyguard. When you read Rhett's book, you'll realize he's not just some soft author who sits behind a computer all day. He does extensive research for his action scenes and tries a lot of that stuff himself. So he's more than capable of protecting me. He even carries a gun."

"Good to know. I grew up learning to shoot and have a licensed handgun of my own. Maybe I should strap it on." He put some space between them. "If you're determined to stay in Austin, I'll start carrying it. It's not a bad idea anyway, because of some other things going on around me. My gun's in my office. I'll get it before we go to lunch." He looked her over, probably for signs of tears. "You will let me take you to lunch, won't you? We do have to eat."

"Only if it's someplace close by and popular. I hope a fugitive wouldn't have the nerve to come after me in a busy café." Scarlett realized this might be considered their first date.

Ethan nodded. "Then that's what we'll do."

"Thanks." Scarlett glanced around the empty room, more than ready to change the subject. "We have a lot of work to do here first. I can't wait to get into it. Fuel with a dark, sexy vibe? I like it. You told me you had some ideas for music. Tell me about them. Unless you think I'm a danger to your new venture. Leroy Simms could be stalking me as we speak. I wouldn't put anything past that psychopath." So much for a subject change.

"What does law enforcement say? Surely they've been in touch with you." Ethan was back to leaning against the bar.

"The Ranger I've talked to is pretty sure Simms is running as far from Austin as he can. It's the smart thing to do." Scarlett walked over to the door and picked up her backpack where Rhett had dropped it. "The man is not stupid, just mean, so I'm hoping he's in Mexico or Canada by now."

"It's where I'd go, if I had to run." Ethan frowned. "What are you doing?"

Scarlett pulled out her laptop and set it on the bar. "Password for the Wi-Fi?"

He gave it to her.

"I'm going to start looking for furniture. I like the idea of banquettes or sofas instead of ordinary tables and chairs. Give me the measurements you've made and let's figure out how much to order. I also need your budget." She began to rattle off questions, glad to get down to business. Obviously, Ethan wasn't going to fire her. She hoped he wouldn't regret it. She was determined to earn the exorbitant salary he was paying her by giving him an amazing bar at the lowest possible price. When she was immersed in costs and quantities, she could almost forget the problems waiting for her at the end of the day.

She felt safe here. Only a couple of people knew where she was right now, and one of them was a Texas Ranger. Mike had promised to have a patrol car from the Austin Police Department cruise Sixth Street, paying special attention to the area in front of the bar. Of course, every lawman in Texas was eager for the chance to put a bullet in cop killer Leroy Thomas Simms.

And then there was Rhett, who had managed, with Mike's assistance, to get his permit to carry his handgun yesterday while she was at work. Her brother was now armed. And would come when she texted him. She had nothing to worry about.

Ethan gave her a generous number to spend on furniture. He had deep pockets. She could fall for a guy with a killer grin and a sexy bar. That was the real danger here, getting involved with her new boss. When it was time for lunch, Ethan came out with a handgun looking ready to take on the world for her.

Another protective man. She should run like hell. But for some reason Ethan's attitude didn't bother Scarlett. Her former lover Chance Delaney would have bundled her out of town, never mind what she wanted. Ethan just quietly armed himself. Both men were masculine and had a competent air that appealed to her. But there was a big difference in how they handled her. Chance had always ordered her around, sure he knew what was best. Ethan just winked and held out his arm, waiting to see if she was sure she wanted to go out and face Sixth Street. Yes, her choice. Oh boy. Scarlett was pretty sure she was in trouble. This man was just about irresistible.

Chapter Eight

"This is a sweet setup."

"Sure is. But the owners will be back in a couple of days. While I'd like to cut those ass wipes, the smart play is to be settled in a new place by then." Leroy watched his woman walk around the living room and open the sliding doors and step out onto the balcony.

"Great view. Bet this place costs big bucks."

"No kidding." Leroy couldn't take his eyes off the way her short shorts cupped her ass. Her hair was down, just the way he liked it, and her hips swayed when she walked. One thing he'd always admired about her was the way she could change her look from slut to saint. The people she worked with wouldn't know her if they ran into her in the elevator.

She turned and pursed full lips painted bright red. "I guess you think you're coming to my place. Leroy, I can't let you do that. I don't want us connected, especially now that you killed a cop."

"I know you're not crying for one of them. But you're right. Give me some ideas. I need a place to stay." He moved in and slid his arms around her. He was gonna do her in that king-sized bed soon. He knew she wanted it as much as he did. Arriving in those skimpy clothes had sent that message. They'd always had the hots for each other. Ever since…

"I've been thinking about it. Tell you later." She smiled. "I've been waiting for you."

"Yeah, right. You expect me to believe that? How many men have you had while I've been locked up? Huh, *querida*?" He squeezed her ass. She laughed and stepped back.

"A few. What are you going to do about it, Lee? Cut me like you did that blonde?" She thumped him on the chest. "Try to toss me over this balcony and I promise to take you with me."

"Baby, why would I do that? You're my ticket to the big bucks, aren't you?" He did back her up until she was pressed against the railing. He pushed, holding on to her hair. If she didn't want to go over, it was on her. Her eyes were bright with excitement. Yeah, danger turned her on. He craved it too. They shoved against each other.

"Careful, Lee. I do know where the money is, and don't you forget it." She raised her chin and stared at him, daring him to hurt her. When he let go, she strutted toward the bedroom.

It didn't take Leroy long to show her what her other men couldn't give her. By the time he finally lit one of the cigarettes she'd brought him, she was smiling lazily.

"I missed you—and that, Lee." She ran her hand over his chest. "I'm sorry I can't take you home with me, but neither of us is stupid. Being seen together could ruin everything."

"I know that." He stared at the ceiling. *She* knew he could tell the cops all about his woman with the great connections. Then where would she be? "Get me a beer. I've got an idea." She'd brought him a six-pack of Lone Star and the smokes after he'd emailed her his location. It had taken her a few days to find a good time. She was going to take the laptop with her when she left. Something about the fact that he'd used it for that email worried her. Leroy knew he'd been careful, sending it to the secret account she'd used with Isaac Crane. He sure as hell hadn't signed his name. But his woman was cautious. If she thought the laptop had to go, then what did he care? She'd brought him a burner phone to take its place.

He watched her walk out of the room. She was older now, sure, but just as hot today as she'd been in high school and even smarter. He'd used some of his booster club haul back then to pay for her to get rid of their baby. She hadn't wanted to be tied down at sixteen any more than he had. They'd stayed in touch through the years—on again, off again lovers. When the chance for a big score had come along, she'd remembered him and made sure he was hired as part of Crane's crew. She'd even negotiated his cut. He'd done the job expecting a big payday.

Except the payday hadn't come. He was pretty sure she'd got most of hers up front. And that's why he'd called her. He needed money if he was going to disappear. Lots of it. So he'd get what was owed him, one way or another. It would be too bad if he had to get ugly with her, but he'd do what was necessary. Because no one stiffed Leroy Simms and got away with it.

Chapter Nine

Ethan could tell by Scarlett's reaction that she didn't know what to make of his visitor. The big guy looked like what he was—the leader of a motorcycle gang. Albert Madison insisted it was a riding club. Whatever. Ethan didn't stop to explain, just escorted Albert into his office and closed the door.

"You didn't introduce us." Albert shrugged out of his leather jacket, then looked around. "What's with you and furniture? First the bar is empty, and now you only have one chair in your fucking office?" He stretched, then finally settled on a corner of the desk. "I should stand anyway, it was a long ride from Houston."

"How the hell am I supposed to explain you to my new manager? Don't you own a car?" Ethan was beginning to wonder if Albert had been a wise choice. On the positive side, he didn't look like your typical private investigator. If she saw him, Mama wouldn't spot him as someone hired to check on her and drag her back to the hospital.

Albert had driven up on a loud Harley, which was parked in the alley behind the bar. He was sporting enough tattoos to be a walking ad for the parlor next door. Albert's club was a group of veterans from various branches of the service who enjoyed the open road and who helped each other and returning vets with PTSD. The Blue Star Brothers weren't saints, but they weren't thugs, either.

"Give me a break, Calhoun. Women like me, once they get to know me. Tell her the truth. I'm a potential investor in the bar." He looked around. "Looks like you need one." Albert stood and began to pace.

"Whoa. I'm trying to make this on my own. I don't need investors telling me how to run things." Though Ethan couldn't forget what his mother had said. Mama had always been a very sharp businesswoman. Even his daddy had admitted as much.

"Never go all-in if you can spread the risk." Albert winked. "I like Austin. Come up here frequently. But we'll discuss that later. Now, what's going on in your family? Billy told me your mother escaped from the nuthouse. That stay was court-ordered. Am I right?"

"Yes. We prefer 'mental hospital' to 'nuthouse'." Ethan sat behind the desk. He had a big check ready for the PI. "Here's a retainer. Let me tell you what I hope we can accomplish."

"She's a fugitive. I checked into the situation, your ma's got to go back. And the woman who escaped with her is bad news." Albert glanced at the check, nodded, and folded it before slipping it into an inside pocket of his jacket.

Ethan knew Albert took on investigations because he liked the work, not because he needed the money. He worked part-time for Ethan's brother-in-law, Billy Pagan. Billy had told him Albert was a millionaire with property all over Houston. Yes, he certainly had the money to invest in the bar. He was a brilliant man with a curiosity that made him love puzzles. Well, Ethan had one for him.

"She won't go willingly. My sisters and I want her back inside, Albert. We hope to separate her from that woman she's with first. I agree, Lisa Davenport is trouble and so unstable she makes my mother look like sweetness and light. Of course, you have to find them first." Ethan passed a paper across the desk. "Mama did give me the number of the burner phone she's using. Will that help?"

"Sure will." Albert picked up the saddlebags he'd brought in from the alley. "I can probably get a location with it. Why don't you call Ma right now? See how she's doing. Ask her where she's staying."

"You sure that's necessary? She'll want to know how I'm coming on the money she needs. And procuring a fake passport for her and Lisa. They want to leave the country. Some place with no extradition treaty. Not South America."

"Tell her Andorra looks good. Beautiful scenery, jet-setters love it, and you've got a line on a sweet little mountain chalet." Albert pulled out a laptop and fired it up. "Give me your chair. I'll be damned if I'll stand here like an idiot and run this program."

Ethan jumped up. "Tell me when you're ready for me to call."

"Give me a minute. What's the password to your Wi-Fi?" He settled into the desk chair and went to work.

Ethan told him, then watched this huge man, who looked like he could single-handedly take down ten men in a cage fight, type with fingers that were surprisingly nimble. "What should I tell her about the passport?"

"It takes days to get that done and you'll need fresh photos. We can use that problem to arrange a meet. Plus I'm sure they'll want more cash. You didn't give them a credit card, did you?" Albert stopped typing long enough to look up.

"No, I didn't trust either one of them not to go nuts with it." Ethan had big credit limits. He could charge a car on any one of them.

"Too bad. It's a great way to trace their movements, but you're right, it could get damn expensive." Albert typed a few more words. "Okay, call her. Then keep her on the phone until I give you a signal. All we're doing this time is trying to pinpoint a location in case she refuses to tell you where they're staying. Then I'll take a look-see. I can hire a crew to snatch them when I know where they are and how they're set up."

"They are both capable of violence, especially Lisa, Albert. Be careful." Ethan felt a little foolish warning big, bulky Albert about two women who together might not weigh as much as the biker did. But he knew his mother. She was unpredictable. If she'd gotten hold of a weapon, she wouldn't hesitate to use it. And Lisa's history of lashing out made her even more of a threat. At least his mother tended to plan her assaults. He told Albert as much.

"No worries, my man. This is a fact-finding mission today. If I actually run into the girls, the most I'll do is buy them drinks. Like I said, women like me. It's the Madison charm. My daddy's been married five times." He shrugged. "His charm tends to wear thin after the third year. Which may be why I haven't pulled the trigger with my lady yet." He grimaced, then stared at the computer screen. "Never mind. I'm all set here. Make the call."

Ethan dialed his mother's number. She picked up on the second ring.

"Ethan, baby, tell me the good news."

"I'm working on it, Mama, trying to get what you want. Where are you staying?" Ethan couldn't stand still, and so he began to pace the perimeter of the small room.

"Lisa says we shouldn't tell you that."

"Seriously? When I'm the one paying?" He listened to her yell at Lisa, who told her to just do as she said.

"Sorry, son. Lisa has things figured out. I'm just going along with her."

"I can't believe you're letting her call the shots, Mama. Is she threatening you?"

"No, but she got us out of that place. I owe her, Ethan. Now, when can we get some more money? Everything's so expensive! I told you that little dab of cash wouldn't last long."

"Soon. I found out that I'm not going to be able to get you a passport without a new photo, Mama. I can take your picture and give you more cash then." Ethan told her what Albert had said about Andorra.

"That sounds wonderful, Ethan. But don't forget about Lisa. You get her papers too."

"No, Mama. This is costing me a bundle. Lisa's on her own." Ethan felt like he needed to make that clear up front. If he was lucky, Mama would decide to ditch the woman.

"Shut your damn mouth and do what I say! Listen and listen good, boy. Lisa helped me work up the courage to get out of there. I owe her this."

"But I don't. I don't think she did you any favors, either. It didn't take courage to escape, it was foolishness. Now you're in big trouble, with the law after you." Ethan had heard her voice rise. It was a sure sign she was losing control.

"Screw the law!"

"Mama, calm down. It's going to take time anyway. I'll call you tomorrow. Stay put. I'm working on it." Ethan saw Albert finally give him a thumbs-up.

"Don't let me down, Ethan, or you'll be sorry."

"Threatening me, Mama? Remember, I'm the one with access to cash." Ethan hung up on her. Damn, but he was sick of her emotional blackmail. He'd spent too many years tiptoeing around her mood swings.

"You got the location?" He faced Albert.

"Sure did. This Lisa is smart. If you decide to call the cops, your mama and Lisa are toast." The big man gestured for him to look at the computer screen. "See here? They're at the Longhorn Airport Inn near the airport, Bergstrom. Not a bad choice. It's a busy place, where people come and go all the time. No one will pay attention to two women who might be waiting to take a flight. Unfortunately, it will be impossible to grab them there without causing a dustup."

"You going out there?" Ethan just wanted this over and done. He'd already been on the phone with both his sisters. They were as upset as he was. They'd volunteered to come help, but all he needed were the two of them adding to his stress. They'd never agreed about what to do with Mama. Shannon would try to take charge, Megan would fight her, and they'd both insist that their baby brother leave it to them. Nope. Mama had come to him, and he was going to handle this. Mama still saw him as her little boy who would do whatever she needed. He hoped he could use that to his advantage. Because, surprise! He was not jumping to Mama's tune, not this time.

Albert shut down his computer. "On my way. I have to say, this Lisa Davenport is going to make this difficult. From what I know of your family, Calhoun, it's probably not your mother's idea to shack up at a bargain motel. Obviously, the Davenport chick has had to disappear before, and she knew what to do. The Longhorn is cheap, because it's not a chain, and it has an attached restaurant/lounge. It's a good place to lie low. I'll see if I can run into them in the bar there."

"You need pictures of them? I've got—"

"Billy gave me all the background. Including pics." Albert smiled. "I'm surprised your mama didn't remember you have pictures." He picked up the computer. "Of course, she sure wouldn't want to use the one they took at the police station."

"No, of course not." Ethan felt tired and discouraged. When his mother had tried to kill his half-sister, Cassidy, it had been the last straw as far as the family was concerned. It was one thing to deal with mood swings, but a whole other thing to have to bail your mother out of jail for attempted murder. The sad truth that the wealthy rarely paid fully for their crimes was the only reason his mother wasn't stuck in prison serving decades for what she'd done.

"Ethan"—Albert slapped him on the shoulder, jarring Ethan from his dismal thoughts—"we'll figure this out, I promise, and I'll call you with a report. I might even check in at the motel. We'll see how it goes." He grabbed his jacket and saddlebags. "Think about the investment. I'd like to own a piece of a bar. But work up a proposal first. I'm gonna want facts and figures."

"I can do that. If I decide I need a partner." Ethan shook off his bad mood. Albert's solid presence and competency gave him hope he'd get Mama back where she belonged without blowback.

"Spread the risk, if you can, that's my motto." Albert's smile was amused. "Now introduce me to your new manager. I hope to hell you didn't hire her just for her great rack."

Ethan was speechless. But not for long. "Wait a damn minute. Where is this attitude coming from? Did Billy say something to you?"

"Not Billy. His wife, your sweet sister, whom I would run off to Mexico with if I wasn't crazy about Pagan's paralegal, might have mentioned your checkered past." Albert stared at him, for once totally serious. "A little joyriding as a kid doesn't bother me. Neither does bed-hopping. But I won't invest unless I know you're serious about this deal and mean to stick it out. Shannon said you were a big help when Calhoun Petroleum was in trouble, but that you bailed as soon as the inheritance was in the bag."

"I bailed, as you put it, because the oil business was my daddy's dream, not mine. Shannon knows that. I want to make it on my own. Yes, I'm starting with Daddy's money, but I plan to make that money grow." Ethan sure as hell didn't like the fact that his sister had been talking about him to Albert. "Listen, I may be Shannon's little brother, but I'm an adult now with more on my mind than great racks. Come on out and meet Scarlett to judge for yourself. She's already showing me she's an organizational wizard. By this time next week, the bar will be full of furniture and almost ready to open, thanks to her."

"Good to know." Albert stuffed his laptop into one of his saddlebags. "I'll take your word for it. Right now I want to hit the ground running. If your mother is as sharp as her baby boy, she might already be planning to move to new digs. I'd best get over to the Longhorn and see what I can find out."

"Thanks, Albert." Ethan shook his hand. "Getting Mama back where she belongs will allow me to concentrate on the bar opening. I sure will give the investment opportunity some thought. Scarlett is a terrific bargain hunter, but I'm already finding out that this bar is costing far more than I'd imagined it would." He walked Albert out to where Scarlett was working on her laptop. "I'll work up a prospectus. Run those numbers for you."

"Good." Albert stopped next to the bar. "Miss Scarlett, I'm Albert Madison, a family friend of Ethan's from Houston." He glanced at her computer screen. "Sorry if I'm interrupting."

Scarlett scooted off the bar stool and extended her hand. "No, that's all right. How do you do?"

"I'm swell. I see you're on the Tex-Mall website. That's a good one. I recently furnished some condos and used them. For paint, try…" He picked up a pad and pen then jotted down some information. "I buy and rehab property in Houston. Trial and error has helped me find good suppliers."

"Thanks, Mr. Madison. This will be a big help." Scarlett gave him a dazzling smile. "I'm determined to stay under budget on this. The bathrooms in particular need work. I don't suppose you know any plumbers here in Austin."

"Happens I do, and call me Albert. I've got a network of veterans who do excellent work and will give you a discount on my say-so." Albert wrote down another name and number. "There you go. Be sure to mention my name. Now I've got to jet." He saluted Ethan. "Later, pal."

Ethan watched him stride out the back door. He followed him and locked the door.

"That was great. We need to get the plumber in right away." Scarlett picked up her phone.

Ethan stopped her with his hand on hers. "Can it wait until after lunch?" He was hungry and had a lot to think about. A partner in the bar? But obviously Albert could be a real asset. He'd just proved that.

"Let me call and try to set up an appointment. This guy will probably have to work us into his schedule." She looked for permission.

"You're right. But the mention of Albert's name will work wonders. See if it doesn't." Ethan waited while she made the call. Sure enough, the man was fully booked until she mentioned Albert. Then he was suddenly free that very evening.

"That's perfect." She smiled and hung up. "He'll be here at six. Do I need to hang around, or will you do it?"

"I live upstairs. It's no hardship for me to be here and see what he says. I'll get an estimate. Of course, I have no idea what would be reasonable." Ethan was beginning to realize how out of his depth he was. Drinks and music, he could handle. But stuff like plumbing? He'd never even used a plunger.

"Maybe your friend Albert could look over the estimate. Sounds like he has the kind of experience to know if we're being ripped off or not." Scarlett was using a search engine. "Oh, if you ask what a bathroom remodel should cost, it can go from hundreds to thousands."

"Yeah, I'll see if Albert will check it out. He's interested in investing in the bar. But he wants a formal prospectus. You know how to do one of those?"

"I might." She shut the laptop and stood. "Why don't we discuss it over lunch?" She looked around the bar. "The ladies' room here is the pits. Let's find a nice, busy restaurant close by with a clean restroom." She frowned down at her hands. "I need to wash my hands before I eat."

"That settles it. We get our bathrooms fixed first thing." Ethan usually went upstairs to use the facilities. He certainly hadn't checked out the ladies' room here. "It's bad?"

"Hideous. If I want to know who can't get it up or I need to brush up on the Kama Sutra, there are names, phone numbers and drawings on the bathroom walls." Scarlett shuddered.

"Women do that? I'd expect it in the men's room, but I thought ladies…"

Scarlett laughed. "Stayed ladylike? You know that saying about a woman scorned?" Her cheeks were rosy. "Let's just say some of those drawings are anything but flattering. You'd need a magnifying glass to see some of those private parts. And whoever Luke is?" She rolled her eyes. "Well, no woman is going near him. He's rumored to have more venereal diseases than a Tijuana—"

"Stop!" Ethan put a finger over her mouth. "There's a tattoo artist next door, Luke Ramos. He strikes me as quite the ladies' man." He laughed until he had to wipe tears from his eyes. "I can't wait to tell him this."

"Hey, ask him if he knows what happened to our condom machine. Someone ripped it open with a crowbar. Then had an orgy that ended with bare footprints on a wall above one of the toilets." Scarlett shuddered. "There's also ample evidence that desperate lovers made use of the sinks and the floor. In a public bathroom!" She picked up her purse and set it on the bar. "Let's just say I will never use the facilities in there until it has been gutted and completely redone."

"Can't blame you." Ethan liked the way her eyes were shining as she touched up her lipstick and ran a brush through her hair. Getting ready to go to lunch. "It's certainly not my idea of a romantic setup." He waited until she was done, then walked her to the door, his keys ready. "What would you say is? Romantic."

"Hmm. Let me think about it. Later. When the vision of the bathroom orgy isn't fresh in my mind." She waited until he was outside, then stepped behind him, looking both ways before she grasped his arm. "How far do we have to walk?"

"Half a block. Best burgers in Austin. How's that?" Ethan locked the door behind them. "It's guaranteed to be crowded at"—he glanced at his watch—"one o'clock on a Tuesday."

"Okay, then." Scarlett finally seemed to relax when an Austin police car cruised past. "Let's go. I'm starved."

Ethan was careful to walk next to the curb, keeping his eyes peeled for the man whose mug shot he'd seen on the news. He hadn't really paid attention before now, but he vaguely remembered the guy was medium height and build and had dark hair. Unfortunately, the only thing outstanding about him had been his surly look. He was sure Scarlett would recognize her attacker though. He was glad when they arrived at the burger joint and stepped inside without incident. Yes, it was crowded, but he'd made friends with the owner and he managed to score a booth in a back corner. Only when they were seated with a menu in front of Scarlett like a shield, did her shoulders come down from around her ears. The woman had been terrified just to walk down the street.

That helped Ethan decide something. Whether Albert partnered in the bar or not, once this matter of his mother was settled, he was going to hire the PI to do whatever he could to help find this Simms character. He couldn't stand to see Scarlett terrified. Not for another day.

Chapter Ten

"So how did it go with Casey?" Scarlett smiled at her brother. After she'd texted him, he had come to pick her up looking like he'd been outside all day. His hair was windblown, and he was sunburned. Then there was his grin. She knew the signs. He was crushing on a new woman. He dropped to the couch with a groan.

"It went." He picked up the remote. "Any news on the asshole?"

She snatched the remote and threw it on the coffee table. "Don't change the subject. I want details. What did you two do all day?" The last thing Scarlett wanted or needed was to talk about her issues. Rhett looked happy. She could use some good news. She'd gotten a text from Mike keeping her up-to-date. Simms was still out there.

"We rented bikes and rode along the lake near the bar. Then we stopped and had lunch at a food truck. Seems Austin is big on those. She introduced me to *tacos al carbon*. I like them even better than enchiladas. Never had them in Boston." He leaned his head back against the sofa cushions. "Casey is quite a woman. I was worn out by the time she got through with me."

"Oh?" Scarlett hit him in the ribs with her elbow. "What does that mean?"

"Not what you're thinking. Unfortunately." He reached for the bottle of water he'd grabbed as soon as they'd hit the door. "We went from the bike riding to a walk up a freaking mountain. She called it a hill. Anyway, the view from the top was worth it. I did get a kiss up there. But that's all I got." He smiled, obviously remembering. "This could be something, Scar. We talked for hours, just sitting up there staring down at the lake. Under normal circumstances, I'd ask her out to dinner. This is her only full day off this week."

"Why don't you? But promise me you'll shower first before you see her again." She slapped at him when he raised his arm and waved a pit in her face. "Stop it!" Brothers. But he was happy, and she was glad. "Make her introduce you to Texas barbecue, Austin is famous for it. I'll be fine here. I've got sandwich makings in the fridge if I get hungry later. I probably won't. Ethan took me out for a big lunch. I even had a chocolate milk shake."

"You went out with him. To a restaurant. Weren't you scared to walk outside?" Rhett got serious.

"I told him what I was going through first. He kept his eyes open and even has a handgun. He wants to protect me, Rhett, just like you do. Isn't that great?" Scarlett still couldn't believe a man who was basically a stranger not only trusted her to help him set up his business, but he also seemed determined to try to keep her safe.

"Yes, it is. I liked him right away. But maybe I should stay in. Keep my eyes on you like Ethan did." He frowned. "That asshole is still out there. I haven't forgotten that."

"I'm safe here in my fortress, Rhett. If you're really into Casey, see if she'll go out with you again. I'll be fine. I'll put my gun on the coffee table while I watch a movie if that makes you feel better."

"It should make *you* feel better. Are you sure you're okay alone?" When Scarlett nodded and shoved him off the couch, Rhett got up and pulled out his phone. It was obvious he was anxious to set up his date.

"Have a good time tonight. Forget all about me. I promise I'll be fine." Scarlett was rewarded with a quick smile before he was talking on the phone. He laughed as he walked toward the bathroom. So he was going out. She got up and tried to decide if she really wanted that sandwich. It was almost time for the news, but she really didn't want to hear the latest from some talking head. Instead, she grabbed her phone off the bar, took it into her bedroom, and closed the door.

"Mike, I'm sorry to bother you, but I wondered if you have any more of an update on Simms than what you said in your text." She sat on the bed.

"I wish I had something to tell you, Scarlett, but maybe this is a case of no news is good news." Mike was in a noisy place. "Let me step outside. I'm in a restaurant. I took my family out to dinner."

"Oh, God, I'm sorry to keep bothering you." Scarlett flopped back on the queen-sized bed. "I can talk to you tomorrow."

"No, I'm outside now. I want to hear your concerns."

Mike was such a good guy. Scarlett knew he had a pregnant wife and child waiting for him, but he was determined to take time for her.

"Answer me honestly. Do you really think Simms is out of Austin?"

"Why do you ask?"

"Because I'm sick of hiding in my apartment and skulking around town like I'm the one who's on the lam. If he's truly gone, then I should be free to drive down to my new job when I feel like it. Like tonight." Scarlett really wanted to see what that plumber had to say about the restrooms. She had ideas about how they should look and needed cost and time estimates for the changes she wanted to make. It was killing her to just sit here and let Ethan handle it. It had been obvious to her, when she'd handed him a list of questions for the plumber before she left, that he didn't have a clue about such things as washerless faucets and vessel sinks.

"I get what you're saying. My best guess is that he's gone. There have been absolutely no sightings of Simms since he killed that cop, and we have every law enforcement agency within miles of here on high alert. But he's dangerous, Scarlett. I'd feel better if you didn't take any chances as long as he's loose. I can't guarantee he hasn't gone to ground somewhere in town. Stay inside and don't take chances." Mike spoke to someone else. "Listen, my food's getting cold. And my wife's getting hot. Know what I mean?"

"Yes. Thanks, Mike. I know there are no guarantees." Scarlett wished this was over. Could she really just stay here and hide? What if Simms was across the border and they never found him? She made a decision that had her stomach churning but, damn it, she had never been a coward. "I appreciate the advice. I will be careful. But I can't stay trapped here on the off-chance Simms might come after me. It would be a stupid move on his part even if he is holed up in Austin. Right?"

"He may be just that stupid, Scarlett. If you insist on going out, keep your eyes open and stay cautious. Call me if you see anything suspicious. Understand?" With one more request to just lock herself in her apartment and wait out Simms's capture, Mike ended the call.

Scarlett dropped the phone on her bedspread. She knew it was a risk, but she had to go on living. Leroy Simms had already taken way too much from her. He was not going to take her freedom too. She'd wait to leave until after Rhett was gone, though. No reason to get him in a lather about her taking off. She'd finally calmed down enough to think things through. Why would a man on the run from the law take a chance on settling an old score? He'd killed a cop. Her testimony in a kidnapping was nothing to Simms now. Scarlett was finally putting things into perspective. She would be the last thing on Knife Guy's mind. He was looking for a ride out of town, not petty revenge.

She got up and gathered a fresh set of clothes, then opened the bedroom door. When she got to the bathroom, she remembered why sharing a home with Rhett was such a pain. The toilet seat was up, there were wet towels on the floor, and he'd left the cap off the shampoo—what was left of it. She thought about screaming at him but decided to save it for another day. For a while there, she'd forgotten who she was. Scarlett Hall was a strong, independent woman. She was through wimping out and being scared of bogeymen. She did flinch, though, when Rhett banged on the bathroom door.

"I walked the dog. Now I'm leaving and setting the alarm."

"Have fun! Stay out as late as you want or don't come home at all. Whatever. I'll be fine."

He didn't answer her. Had he even heard? Didn't matter. Scarlett wiped away the condensation on the mirror and brushed out her hair. She needed to hurry if she was going to get to the bar before the plumber left. But that didn't mean she wasn't going to look her best. She and Anna called it putting on war paint. She needed makeup to hide the evidence of her recent sleepless nights. The outfit she'd chosen was too casual for work, but this was after hours. The blue print top dipped low and clung enough but not too much. Her jean shorts showed off her legs, and the sandals made her glad she'd recently gotten a pedicure.

If Ethan continued to flirt, she was ready for him. She couldn't wait to show Ethan and the plumber her ideas for a dynamite ladies' room, then get cost estimates. Scarlett grabbed her purse and her laptop and headed for the door. Then she stopped. Her stomach churned, and she had to take a steadying breath. YoYo jumped around her feet, and she gave him a treat to get him out of her way.

Stupid. You can do this. But it took her three tries to get the code right to deactivate the alarm. Then she had to unlock the door, all the dead bolts. *Now, turn the knob and step outside.* Why was she still so scared? Scarlett leaned her forehead against the door. It was getting late, almost six thirty. If she didn't move, she'd miss the plumber, and then what? There'd be no point in going. *Suck. It. Up.*

She jerked open the door and stepped outside. The night air was cool and crisp. It felt wonderful, almost chilly. Shorts had been a risk. Did she need to change? But if she went inside again, even for a sweater, she knew she'd never get back out here. Oh, hell, no. She turned, locked the door with her keys and set the alarm. Before she could change her mind, she ran down the stairs. She'd done it. For the first time in days, she was defying her fears. She hit her key fob and unlocked her car, tossing the laptop on the passenger seat along with her purse. Quickly locking herself inside, she leaned back, then grinned, slapping the steering wheel before she started the car.

All right then, the old Scarlett was back. Ethan Calhoun had better watch out. She was in the mood to do something dangerous.

* * * *

"I've made contact, Ethan. This isn't going to be easy." Albert sounded like he was standing beside a freeway, cars and trucks rumbling by. Then it was obvious a jet was flying over, and there was no conversation until it must have reached a higher altitude.

"Where the hell are you? Go inside where I can hear you." Ethan was losing patience. He hoped he wasn't being charged by the hour.

"Can't. The women are in the lounge. I tried to get a room, but there's not going to be anything until later. That Lisa chick indicated I could bunk in with them, but I made an excuse." Albert had to wait out another jet takeoff. "Sorry, but you can't pay me enough to cheat on my lady."

"Fine. I assume you're buying them drinks, figuring out our next move." Ethan had to like Albert's ethics if not his choice of places to make a call. Damn it, how many planes were taking off per hour there?

"Oh, yeah, I'm buying. Well, you are. This goes on my expense account. And, believe me, those two can knock 'em back. Top shelf too. Let me tell you, Lisa Davenport scares the hell out of me. It's the eyes, my man. Nobody home. Well, nobody with a conscience." Albert cursed. "Hold on, one of them is coming out."

Ethan heard him speak to someone. Was it his mother? Albert was too young for her. He was closer to Lisa's age, around thirty-five. So Lisa was a psychopath. No surprise. Her temper, along with her tendency to destroy things when her anger got the better of her, had made him wonder about that. Why in the hell had his mother hooked up with her? Missy Calhoun had her mood swings, and she certainly had no problem inventing her own version of the truth, but she could be loving and a good mother, at least when she was on her meds.

"Sure, I could eat, but I want to look at the menu first. Tell him to put it on my tab. I'm still trying to get a room. Let me finish this call to my boss and I'll be in." Albert finally got back on the phone after another delay for a plane taking off. "Lisa came out to see if I wanted to eat dinner with them. You heard me. I'm buying them dinner. She's sticking to your ma like glue. Never lets her out of her sight. Well, except she just did, didn't she?" Albert chuckled. "Okay, that gave me an idea. I can work with this.

Davenport wants money, any way she can get it. If she thinks a man can pay her way, she'll move on from Mama Calhoun, see if she don't."

"Good. Keep me posted, Albert." Ethan heard a knock on the door and glanced at his monitors. It was the plumber, if he could go by the tool kit and the logo on the man's work shirt. He hung up and walked to the alley door, then pulled it open. "Glad you could make it."

"Sorry I'm a little late. Wreck on the loop held me up." The middle-aged man walked inside. "Rex Reagan." He shook his hand. He was short and walked with a limp, had a Marine Corps tattoo on his forearm and a shaved head.

"No problem, I'm just glad you could come on such short notice."

"The lady who called said Albert Madison recommended me. That was all I needed to hear." He looked around with narrowed eyes. "So you're rehabbing this place? Good to know. I used to come to this bar back before I joined the service. When I got out, it had closed. Now look at it. What do you have in mind?"

Ethan told him about the secret bar concept while walking him toward the ladies' room.

"That's cool. I've been to a couple of those secret bars here in town. There's one in an old firehouse. Get me buzzed and I'm sliding down the pole like I'm a kid again." The plumber laughed, then stepped through the door into the bathroom. "Well, this isn't a laughing matter. Someone trashed the hell out of this." He shook his head. "Broke the sinks with a sledgehammer, looks like. That's just pure meanness."

"I never even came in here until my manager told me about it today. I got the building at a bargain price. Now I know why. It was really the location I was after." Ethan tried to ignore the reek coming out of the stopped-up toilets. No wonder Scarlett refused to come in here. He'd been pretty damn stupid now that he saw what a mess it was. He could have negotiated an even lower price for the building.

"Yep. Sixth Street is booming. Don't know how long this sat vacant, but this is clearly vandalism." Rex set his tool kit outside the door, obviously able to ignore the smells as he threw open stall doors and looked the place over.

Ethan handed the man Scarlett's list. "My manager has some ideas about what we need in here. Here's a list she made."

Rex looked it over, then pulled out an electronic tablet. "What about the men's room?"

"I don't care much about it as long as it's functional and the door's well marked." Ethan felt in the way as Rex got out a measuring tape.

"My thoughts exactly." The plumber smiled. "This is a good list. She even wrote down your budget. It'll be tough to stick to it, though. Costs are up. Especially on anything coming from overseas."

"See what you can do." Ethan heard a knock on the front door. "Someone's here. I'll be right back." He left Rex to his work. A glance at the monitors, and he hurried to the front door. "What are you doing here? And where's your bodyguard?"

Scarlett rushed inside. "Am I in time to meet with the plumber?"

"He just got here. He's in the ladies' room." Ethan stopped her with a hand on her wrist. "Answer me, Scarlett. Why are you alone?" He looked out the window, but her brother was nowhere in sight.

"I'm sick of my paranoia. It's foolish. Think about it, Ethan. Simms killed a cop. He has much bigger worries than testimony from me. Or even revenge for my attitude when he was captured. The guy is running for his life now. Every cop in Texas is looking for him with an itchy trigger finger."

"True." Ethan let go and looked her over. "I see you got rid of the work clothes."

"Yes. But I am here to work." She smiled. "Can I go talk to the plumber now? I have some bathrooms I want to show him." She waved her laptop. "Women need a great bathroom. We hang out in there. It must be pretty and have enough space for women to discuss who they danced with or whether they're going home with the guy or not."

"You're kidding. You'd go into the bathroom and tell a perfect stranger you're thinking of hooking up with a guy you just met on the dance floor?"

"It happens. Women bond over the craziest things. I once asked a total stranger to help me pick out my prom dress. Which is a major decision when you're sixteen." Scarlett patted Ethan's cheek. "Admit it, you'll never understand women."

"You're right about that. Get in there and consult with the plumber. But keep the budget in mind. He's already making noises about cost overruns and he hasn't even touched a pipe yet." Ethan watched her hurry toward the bathroom. Damn, she looked good. The shorts hugged her butt, and that blue top looked crazy-perfect on her. Did women know they were buying stuff to match their eyes? Of course, they did. His sisters had told him that.

Men didn't think that way. If he did, all he'd own would be brown shirts. He looked down. He'd showered after work too. Did Scarlett like him in a yellow shirt? For all he knew, it made him look like a fucking school bus.

Chapter Eleven

Leroy almost didn't recognize himself in the mirror. And he sure as hell didn't think a cop would know him. Damn, it felt funny to be slick on top. They'd put his hair in a trash bag and would toss it somewhere far away. The disposable razor too. He was pretty sure the cops would figure out he'd been in the apartment hiding as soon as those yahoos got back from their trip, but he wasn't going to make it easy for them to connect the dots. So he and his woman wiped down everything he'd touched and bagged his beer cans. Even ran the dishwasher on the hot cycle so it would steam off any fingerprints from the dishes and utensils he'd used.

Then he had the pleasure of tearing the condo apart, making it look like a robbery. Computer was missing, of course. He couldn't take the big screen TV, too noticeable in the elevator, but he did find a nice stash of jewelry behind a book on a shelf in the office. Couldn't pawn it anytime soon, but later it might bring a few bucks. Then he put on the costume that completed his transformation.

"My God, your own mama wouldn't know you, Lee." His woman rubbed his newly shaved head just before she stabbed a gold loop into his ear. "There, that's perfect."

"Ouch! You enjoyed that a little too much." He slapped her bottom. "But you're right. That did it. I look like a fucking Parrothead." Leroy grinned. His new mustache itched like hell, but he resisted the urge to scratch it. "You ever go see Jimmy Buffett?"

"Margaritaville?" She sang a few bars, then giggled and handed him a pair of flip-flops. "You're right. You have the look down pat, baby."

Leroy wasn't going for a low profile. Hell, no. In his colorful Hawaiian shirt and cargo shorts, he was making sure he looked as different from the man who'd run out of the jail as he could. The woman was right. His own mama, God bless her, wouldn't know him. He slipped on sunglasses he'd found in a drawer. He was ready to move on, and he had figured out where to go.

"You sure that apartment is still available?"

"He paid for a year. Crane was very careful about things like that. He used cash and had me pick up the key for him." She grinned, clearly admiring his new look as she slid her hand into the back of his shorts. "Of course, I made a copy before I gave him his key. I'm always looking to the future. You never know what might happen. With Crane dead, it's all yours."

He turned and faced her. "Yes, I do know how you plan, so I know you have Crane's money."

"We can talk about that later, can't we?" She tugged at his shorts. "Look at you, skin and bones. Let's go and hit a drive-through for burgers."

Leroy knew she was trying to distract him, and it worked. He couldn't eat jailhouse shit. A fresh burger and fries made his mouth water. Of course, the shorts were loose and about to fall to the carpet. The asshole who lived here could afford to lose a few pounds. The wardrobe Leroy had packed into a duffel would be big everywhere. He sure as hell didn't take any of the asshole's underwear.

"Fine. Let's go. At least you agreed to give me a ride to the apartment." He dug his fingers into her hair. "But I'm not forgetting about the money. You hear me?" He waited until she nodded before he let her go and picked up the duffel. They were good together, had been since high school. It would be a shame if he had to hurt her to get what he wanted.

Chapter Twelve

"You think I can't tell when I'm being stalled, Ethan?" Missy had shown up on his doorstep with Lisa not five minutes after Scarlett left with the plumber to look at sinks and faucets at a local supplier.

He had stalled them for three days. So he shouldn't have been surprised when Mama got tired of waiting. Damn, though, that had been a close call. How would he explain his mother to Scarlett? Mama was wild-eyed. And Lisa? The woman pissed him off as she strutted into the bar like she had the right. No bat today, but she'd scrounged up a purse that could pack a punch. His hand twitched. He'd grown up forbidden to hit a woman, but here was an exception. Yeah, he wanted to smack the shit out of her and end this thing.

Mama still wore what she'd escaped in, and she looked the worse for wear. He shouldn't feel guilty about that, but he did. He'd been stingy with the cash. Of course, she hadn't been able to shop for clothes. At least the hospital had let her dress in her own wardrobe. If she'd been roaming the town in scrubs... Lisa? She could wear a burlap sack for all he cared.

Ethan felt a headache coming on. Bad enough that workmen were busy in the bathrooms, ripping out the old plumbing fixtures. The noise was deafening. Now they were undoubtedly noticing he had company.

"Mama, come into my office. You two are going to be seen." Ethan pulled his mother toward the room just as one of the plumbing crew came out carrying pieces of porcelain sink.

"Maybe I want to watch." Lisa checked out the man who filled out his work shirt with bulging muscles.

"Girl, Ethan's right. Come on." Mama grabbed Lisa's arm. "Are you forgetting what we're doing here?"

"No. But relax, Missy, and fix us a drink. We're not exactly on the local news, you know. We were lucky. Here all they talk about is that cop killer." Lisa smiled as another man came out with a toilet. "Bet that's heavy!" she called out to him.

"Sure is." He stopped in his tracks and looked her over with a grin. "Smells like, uh, you know. Best stay upwind." He winked and went on outside, passing the other man who was coming back inside.

Ethan shook his head and gave up on the office. If Lisa got caught, he would be happy to see her go, but he needed his mother safely back in the hospital first.

"We're here for our money, Ethan. The motel wants some more cash or a credit card." Missy pulled a bottle of her favorite bourbon out from behind the bar. "You could give me one of those, you know. Don't you trust me?" Mama had bided her time until her money had run out, and she was obviously getting desperate.

Ethan didn't bother to answer that. "I wasn't stalling you, Mama. I'm trying to get this business going. I had meetings lined up today and workers here. I couldn't just drop everything and do your bidding." Ethan actually had found he had little to do with Scarlett taking the reins on most of the ordering. He'd been spending time on his computer, checking out the other secret bars in town and approving his new manager's choices. That was about it.

"Listen to me. If it wasn't for a nice man Lisa met at the motel, we would have been kicked out of there two days ago. He let us put the room on his credit card. Of course, we had to promise to pay him back. We pretended we were waiting for a relative to come in at the airport with our cash." His mother splashed bourbon into two glasses and slid one down the bar to Lisa. "Good thing I hooked up with her. Lisa could charm—"

"I get the picture, Mama." Ethan pulled out his wallet. He'd been expecting this, thanks to a call from Albert the night before, and he had made a run to the bank. "Speaking of, while you're here, let me take those photos for the passports. Take turns standing against a wall. They're gutting the bathrooms, and there's plain drywall in the men's room."

His mother paused as she counted the hundreds he'd handed her. "This is more like it. Photos? What do you think, Lisa?" She glanced at the woman who sipped her drink and walked around the bar.

"Now? Look at my roots! We need to go to a salon first. I have to get my color refreshed before anyone snaps a picture of me. Missy, you could stand a touch-up yourself." She stuck her head into the ladies' room and came back out again. "No mirrors yet, and he was right, it does stink in there. You have a long way to go before opening, Ethan."

"I know that. It's why I don't have time to worry about your problems." He pulled out his phone. "Now, are we going to do this or not?"

"Not." His mother shook her head. "Lisa's right. We'll find a local place. You know none of the hairdressers here will have any idea we're on the run. We'll get beautified and then come back." She put her empty glass on the bar. "Give us a while."

"I know how you are at a beauty shop." He saw her frown down at her nails and then check her cash again. Yeah, she'd get the full treatment. "It'll take you hours, and it's late afternoon now. You'll have to come back tomorrow. And don't just drop in. I'm expecting a new investor. Text me when you want to meet and we'll set it up." Ethan waved them toward the door. "Who is this guy paying for the motel? You sure he isn't an undercover cop? Don't tell him about me. I'll be damned if I go to jail for aiding and abetting a fugitive."

"Two fugitives." Lisa gave him a hard look. "Keep that in mind if you're thinking to screw us over, Ethan."

"Now, Lisa, Ethan's helping his mama. Just relax. Albert's a nice man. I think he's got a thing for you. He may be taking it slow, but why else would he have offered his credit card for our room?"

"I do have a way with men." Lisa smiled and watched the plumber's helper carry another toilet out the door.

Missy poked at one of the heavy boxes full of urinals and toilets waiting to be installed. "A new investor? So you did take my advice. That's better than a loan. Good boy." She patted Ethan's cheek. "I hope you do well here, I really do. But get your priorities in order, son. We need to get the hell out of here before the law comes sniffing around. You know what I'm saying?"

"Believe me, I want you gone as fast as possible." Ethan let them out the back. He was pretty sure Albert had followed them, and he wasn't surprised when a few minutes later the man tapped on his front door.

"You get their pictures?" Albert studied the bar, as if looking for progress in the restoration. "How'd it go?"

"They're headed for a beauty shop. I'll get a text when they're ready to meet for a photo session tomorrow."

Ethan handed Albert the file folder full of facts and figures that Scarlett had helped him prepare. He did need a partner, and he would like Albert's input on some of the bids he'd gotten for paint and flooring.

"What's this?" Albert set the folder on the bar and began flipping through pages.

"I'm taking your advice. It's become apparent to me that I probably shouldn't do this on my own. You'll see a proposed budget, what we hope to make the first year, and the overhead, including the number of employees we plan to hire and the salaries they'll be making. I see the wisdom of bringing in an investor, Albert, and you have the kind of experience with remodeling that would come in handy about now." Ethan stopped short of admitting he was feeling a little desperate. Money was flowing out too damn fast, and a date for the opening was getting further away every time he got a contractor's bid and timeline. It seemed like no one was in a hurry to get work done except him.

Albert whistled. "You have some pretty expensive taste, Ethan. This bartender and chef? What's so special about them?"

Ethan explained his rationale for bringing them in from successful places nearby and giving the brother and sister team a chance to work together. He'd introduced them to Scarlett, and they were already setting up interviews with the local media outlets.

"You're paying your new manager a healthy sum." Albert pulled out a sheet with the plumber's estimate. "I'm sure she's worth it, though. I got a call from Rex. He says she asked all the right questions and had some good ideas for the bathrooms. She even found some bargains on the Internet for fixtures he could use."

"Scarlett's great. She'll be back pretty soon." Ethan had known her for less than a week, but they'd clicked. After she'd finally settled down from her panic, she'd proved to be a dynamo. She came in early, worked late, and seemed determined to save him money. Good thing, since he hadn't planned on this project taking quite so much of his inheritance. "Take your time and think it over, Albert. How about a report on Mama and her running buddy? Didn't you see a chance to take my mother while you were out there enjoying steak dinners and top-shelf bourbon at my expense?"

"I told you, Lisa sticks to Missy's side. If I was willing to sleep with Lisa, it might be different, but I'm not." Albert shook his head. "I should have rented a car and followed them to this beauty shop. I have to admit the Harley doesn't make a good vehicle for trailing anyone."

"Even I could have figured that out." Ethan dug in his pocket. "I have an extra car, an SUV. It's garaged down the block and across the street, under those condos." He described it down to the license number. "Use it while you're here. You can put the Harley in its spot."

"An extra car." Albert grinned. "I forget you're a rich guy, son of a billionaire. Of course, you have an extra car. Your daddy had one of the best collections of sports cars I ever saw."

"Which in his will he insisted be sold at auction. Broke my heart. That was the penalty for my joyriding as a kid." He laughed. "So the first thing I did when I came into my inheritance was to buy back the Porsche I drove through our neighbor's lawn when I was fourteen. I'm sure Daddy rolled over in his grave." Ethan heard a noise at the back door and saw on the monitors that Scarlett and Rex were back.

Albert jingled the car keys. "Thanks for the ride. That's a nice building across the street. You should get some customers from there once you're open. Put out flyers offering the residents a discount." He greeted Scarlett before she ducked into the ladies' room to check on progress. "I'll look at these papers and get back to you. Think I'd better drive around and see if the ladies are at one of the shops nearby after I change out my wheels. Tomorrow go to the bank and open a small account with a few thousand in it. Then get Ma a debit card. If she gives me the slip, I can track her by what she spends on that."

"Good idea. Wish I'd done it sooner." Ethan had to admire the way Albert thought as the big man stopped to speak to Rex, then headed out. Their conversation had given him an idea.

"A successful shopping trip." Scarlett smiled as she set her purse on the bar. "We ordered all the sinks and countertops, then shopped for the faucets." She opened the laptop she'd left on the bar. "We even came in under budget."

"Fantastic." Ethan wanted to pull her into his arms and spin her around the room in celebration, the way he would with one of his sisters. But he didn't feel brotherly with Scarlett.

Stay practical. "When will all the stuff be delivered?"

Rex came out of the bathroom, frowning down at a puddle near the door. "Monday. We should be able to install everything next week if we don't come up with a serious plumbing issue before then." He stalked back into the ladies' room. "Where the hell did that water come from?" He kept talking as the door slammed.

"Uh-oh." Scarlett lost her joyful smile. "Let's hope that was just a spill, nothing serious."

"Right." Ethan looked up the number he needed and made a call. Voice mail. He left a message. "Where have you been parking lately?"

"What?" She stopped whatever she'd been doing on the computer. "In the lot next to the park. A few blocks over. Why?"

"That's a hell of a walk. Doesn't that freak you out?" Ethan could imagine that it did, especially the two nights she'd stayed in the bar until after dark. "Can't your brother pick you up?"

Scarlett was biting her lip, a sure sign it had done more than freak her out. She'd been acting tough, but he knew Simms was still out there. The local news barely mentioned the manhunt anymore, but it was still going on.

"No. I told him not to bother. He's seeing a lot of Casey. They have dinner together every night. Then…" She smiled. "Well, let's just say I'm pretty sure they've progressed to the next level."

"Good for Rhett." Ethan couldn't help thinking he hadn't even progressed to first base with Scarlett. He looked away from that damn lip he wanted to bite himself. She wore red today. He'd already noticed her top matched her toenails, which peeked out from her sandals. Sexy feet. Small, delicate. His own size twelves could be used to stomp out forest fires.

"I'm happy for him. I can handle driving myself to work and back. I have pepper spray, and I'm thinking about buying a gun. Really. I can take classes in shooting, whatever it takes to get a license." She was gripping her knees through her jeans. Like the idea of it was already making her tense.

"That takes time." He laid his hand on her shoulder. She was so freaking delicate. The bones under his hand would break easily if some creep grabbed her. Pepper spray. How long would it take for her to even find it in that purse she carried? No, she would have it on her key chain. But still… His phone rang. "Give me a minute."

His call was being returned. It didn't take long to make the arrangements. He knew from experience that throwing money at a problem was frequently the easiest way to solve it. He really did need a partner in this bar. Albert would probably call him crazy for this "business expense."

"Did I just hear you arrange for a parking space?" Scarlett jumped off her bar stool. "Where is it?"

"Why don't you let me show you?" Ethan grinned and grabbed her hand. "Come on. Rex can hold down the fort here. I gave him a key yesterday, so I can tell him to lock up when he's done. No need to set the alarm. I doubt anyone is going to walk off with a toilet."

"You mean we're not coming back?" She followed him to the bathroom, where he met Rex at the door.

"You got here early, Scarlett. I think you can knock off for the day." Ethan got a report from the plumber. So far the puddle seemed to be merely a spill from a careless hand. No new problems. Rex was going to leave with his crew in another hour. Ethan glanced inside the bathroom, pleased with the progress. Even the smell was almost gone. He wasn't surprised when he bumped into Scarlett, who was peering over his shoulder.

"Looks good, doesn't it?" She said the same to Rex.

"Good? It has a long way to go to get there, but at least it's almost empty." Ethan eased her toward the front door. "Grab your purse. You're right. We aren't coming back tonight."

She did pick it up, staying close as he unlocked the front door. "I can't thank you enough for this, Ethan. You have no idea how hard that walk to and from the parking lot has been. Last night it was so dark..." She shuddered. "I hate that I'm still so paranoid. You know Simms is probably drinking tequila in Cancun by now. But I keep remembering..."

"Of course you do." Ethan pulled her outside. "Look, we still have a police patrol." He locked the door behind him as a cruiser went past them and then moved on down the street. "Look over there at the high-rise condo building. That's where you'll be parking."

"That close?" Her eyes widened.

"There's a parking garage underground. More than enough spaces for the residents. I arranged for two spots for my personal vehicles when I moved in over the bar. You heard me on the phone. I just added three more. For you, the chef, and the bartender. We'll call them a perk of your jobs. Tax write-offs for me. I grew up hearing my daddy talk about tax write-offs. I figured, why not?"

"Fantastic." Scarlett kept her hand in his as they walked down the street to the traffic light on the corner. It was a long block. When the light changed, they hurried across. She was bumped by a man rushing the other way.

"Oh, sorry," she said. He didn't say a word, just kept going.

"Asshole." Ethan pulled her toward the concrete steps that led down to the parking garage. The bald guy could have at least apologized for almost knocking over a woman. Instead, he'd just kept going, apparently more concerned with holding on to his sunglasses as he dashed across the street. Probably headed for the liquor store at the end of the block. It was one of those places where you could buy smokes, a few groceries, and of course, alcohol. There wasn't another convenience store like that anywhere close. The condos and Ethan's apartments were close to downtown, but not to any kind of shopping unless you wanted to walk blocks the other direction to the big Whole Foods grocery store.

"Which spot will be mine?" Scarlett had already forgotten her brush with rudeness. She was in the garage and looking around. "Oh, there's the kind of car my brother likes." She pointed to Ethan's Porsche.

"That's mine. What do you think? Do you like it?" Ethan waited for the verdict.

"Are you kidding? It's great. What is it so I can tell Rhett?"

"A 1957 Porsche 356 Speedster. Completely restored to its original condition." Ethan patted the shiny racing-yellow hood with pride. A man did have his passions, and cars were one of his.

"I may have to ask you to write that down for me. Can we go for a ride?" Scarlett laughed at what he knew was his surprised look.

"Of course. And not a lame ride around the block either. I'd like to take you out to dinner. There's a great restaurant out by Lake Travis with a killer sunset view. The drive out there will give me a chance to show off what this baby can do." He decided then and there he was making a move tonight. He'd waited long enough to get closer to Scarlett.

"Can I go dressed like this?" She frowned down at her jeans.

"Of course you can. You look great. I thought blue was your color. Now I think red might be." Ethan pulled his keys from his pocket. No fancy keyless entry for a vintage car.

"Really. After a compliment like that, I'm all yours." She dropped into the leather bucket seat and touched the dash with all the proper reverence Ethan could have hoped for. "And you'd better put the top down. I love convertibles."

Ethan got busy dealing with the cloth top. *She was all his.* It was the kind of offhand comment that meant nothing, but had his thoughts going in only one direction. He reminded her to fasten the old-fashioned lap belt, then started the car. She laughed, obviously delighted with the roar of its powerful engine as they drove out of the parking garage and turned onto Sixth Street.

Ethan noticed the asshole standing in front of the liquor store with a brown paper bag in his arms. The man watched them drive down the street. Ethan just resisted the urge to shoot him the finger. Not necessary. Clearly the poor fool was getting an eyeful of a very lucky man with a beautiful woman beside him in a car that cost a damn fortune.

The light turned green, Ethan shifted gears, and the car leaped forward. Scarlett let her blond hair blow in the breeze while her laughter filled the car. Could the asshole hear it? Didn't matter. Nothing mattered but the night ahead. The weather was perfect, cool and clear. They'd get to the restaurant in time for a spectacular sunset. A delicious dinner, a few drinks, and then… Well, Ethan had a few ideas for dessert.

Chapter Thirteen

"Where'd the beer come from?"

"Where do you think? I had to go get it. There's a package store down the street." Leroy popped the top and caught the cold foam before it could spill over. "You took your sweet time coming by. I was out of everything. Nobody noticed me. I was in and out in minutes."

"You took a big chance, Lee." She stopped and looked at the screen on the laptop they'd found when they moved him into the apartment. "What's this? Why are you looking up Scarlett Hall?"

"I saw her today." Leroy settled onto the cheap sofa. The apartment had obviously come furnished, but it wasn't much compared to the place where he'd holed up before. The TV was small, the refrigerator had been empty, and the cable was basic. Shit, the only good thing about it was the fast Wi-Fi and the laptop. Not that he really cared about stuff like that.

"What do you mean, you saw her?" His woman plopped down beside him. "From the balcony?"

"Yeah, sure. She was pulling weeds in that fucking ditch." Leroy took a long pull from his beer. That was another thing he hated about this apartment. Crane had gone cheap. This unit faced the back, overlooking a concrete culvert and alley. No view at all. It had one dinky bedroom with a queen-sized bed that had a mattress little better than what they gave you in lockup.

The woman pinched his arm. "Look at me, Lee. Where the fuck did you see Scarlett Hall?"

"Watch it. You take a chunk out of me again and I'll show you what pain is." Leroy pulled the knife he'd found in the kitchen out of his pocket.

It wasn't much, but the paring knife had sharpened up pretty good. She had fear in her eyes. Good.

"Sorry, baby." She leaned over and kissed the spot where she'd left a red mark. "I just want you to be safe, you know that." She moved closer and pressed her breast against the same arm. "Now, tell me everything. You know I hate that bitch."

"Not sure why. Unless maybe you're jealous." He kept the knife out. He'd sure like to check out Miss Scarlett's ass. See how his work had held up. Damn, but he wanted to finish what he'd started.

"Lee!" She moved back, out of reach. "Get serious now. Where'd you see her?"

"I ran into her when I went out for beer and cigs." He smiled at the way her eyes widened. Yeah, that jolted her. She even glanced at the door, like maybe the cops would arrive any minute and she'd be caught here, with him. "Don't worry, she didn't recognize me. I told you this disguise would hold up." He laughed and set the knife on the coffee table. "It's genius. I crossed the street, ran right into her, and she never even put two and two together."

"You didn't say anything, did you?" She stood, like maybe she was thinking about taking off.

Leroy was on his feet instantly. "You really don't respect me, do you?" He grabbed her arms. "Do I have to teach you a lesson? I'm thinkin' it's overdue." He jerked her to him. "I know you've been holding out on me. I saw the way you looked when you spotted that laptop of Crane's. It's got the key to getting his money, doesn't it?"

"Now, Lee. Of course I respect you. Look at how you got away from the cops, right under their noses." She pressed against him.

"The laptop, woman. Tell me the fucking truth." He knew he was hurting her. Good. She was definitely planning to cut him out of the big payoff, and he wasn't going to stand for it.

"Yes! He's got money stashed in a few places. It's still there. I know how to get us into those accounts." She licked her lips. "But we can't just show up and make a withdrawal. Not like you could at a bank here. You can't pass for Crane, baby. He was a freak, tall as a basketball player. Much as I love you, I can't see you fooling those bank officials."

"Then go ahead and move the money so we can get to it ourselves. You know you can do it." He dragged her over to the computer sitting on the cheap dining room table. Damn it, he hated computers. They made him feel stupid. He wasn't dumb. He *had* outsmarted the cops. And he'd fooled a lot of people a lot of times. It took brains to do that. But sit him down in front of one of these fucking machines and he just...

"It's not that easy, Lee." She fell into the chair in front of it. "I admit we got lucky here. He obviously had planned to come back and either take the laptop with him or destroy it. It was password protected, but I figured out what his password was." She smiled up at him. "Don't get jealous now, but Isaac and I had a few rolls in the hay. He told me some stuff. The man wasn't much in the sack, but he was a fucking genius with technology."

"Jealous? Baby, you could fuck a kangaroo and I wouldn't care, as long as it got us the money we need to get the hell out of this town and set up for life. Tell me you managed that."

She frowned. Of course she wanted him jealous. Women. Leroy didn't like playing their games. But she did have an advantage here, being the computer-savvy one. She'd worn something low cut so he'd see down her top and get distracted by her breasts. It wasn't working this time. "Go ahead, keep talking. You always were smart as shit. What did he tell you while you were taking him to paradise between the sheets?" He stood behind her and concentrated on the screen. She was tapping away, and soon a bank site came up. The Caymans. Of course. He didn't ask questions, just watched her work.

"That he had managed to squirrel away a bundle in advance from an overseas buyer and put it here. Millions, Lee. He'd already sold some other shit he'd stolen from a government agency he used to work for. Government secrets. Maybe a nerve gas. The man was pure evil." She wriggled in her seat. Was it because evil turned her on? Wouldn't surprise him.

"How many millions?" Leroy wasn't sure what she was doing on the computer, and he didn't care. Crane could have sold his own grandma to a drug kingpin and he wouldn't have cared. Not if it brought in millions.

"No idea. But listen. I put in my alias and the new social security number I bought to set up my own account down there. I had to be careful and moved a million over first. Last fall. That was small for Isaac. He didn't miss it, and the bank didn't check with him for such a small sum." She leaned back so her head rested against him. "Can you believe it?"

Small? A million was small? Leroy refused to show how impressed he was. What kind of idiot didn't miss a million bucks? "Then what?" He shoved her head away. She was still trying to take his mind off of business and what she was doing. No way in hell.

"Isaac was really into planning that robbery. He let me take care of the details. All he could think about was Anna Delaney and her program."

"Yeah. He was obsessed with her and it." Leroy couldn't imagine letting a woman screw with his head that much.

"Look, Lee. I moved some more money right before you pulled the job." She showed him a screen where there was a balance of two million in her account. "Went through like a charm."

"Where's my name in all of this?" Leroy pressed his hands down on her shoulders, hard. "All I see is you getting rich. Me? I got nothing."

"When we leave here and go to the Caymans, I can put your name on everything. We need to get you a new fake ID and the shit that goes with it. Now, watch this." She began typing. "I'm going to try a bigger transfer. If I'm right, they'll send an email to this computer, asking for permission from Crane to complete it." She wriggled in her seat again. This was definitely turning her on. "I can confirm from here. Then..." She paused, as if holding her breath. "Holy shit, Lee! We just got twenty million more in that account!"

Leroy dragged her to her feet. "Like I said. My name isn't on a fucking thing." Twenty million. Twenty-two million. By God. She was filthy rich—and she could leave here and never look back. "Do I need to remind you that I can tell the cops exactly who helped Crane from the inside at that tech company? You try to walk away from me, lady, and I get caught? You might as well kiss your own free ass good-bye."

"Lee, calm down. I'm not going to forget you. We're in this together, baby."

He looked her in the eyes. But he knew she could lie with a straight face and never blink. "Remember who took all the risks?"

"You, Lee. Every time." She leaned against him and kissed him, pressing close.

Leroy was hard. Just the thought of all that money had made him that way. Yeah, it was clearly a package deal. He had to keep this woman on a short leash. No problem. If he went down, she was going down right along with him. Let her try to dump him and go off to her island bank without him. She wouldn't live to spend a penny of Crane's money.

"I sent a letter to my mama. With details. I die? It's all in there. You understand what I'm saying?" Leroy knew he'd said the right thing when her body stiffened. Yeah, she'd thought about taking him out. She had put down that dweeb at her job. Cops thought he'd murdered the computer nerd because she'd used a knife. Yeah, she had planned it that way so it would come back to him if he was caught. Leroy had enough sins of his own without taking on hers. He was going to make sure she knew that. "Mama won't open the letter unless I'm dead. But then all bets are off. You hear me?"

"You always were smarter than people gave you credit for, Lee." She kept her arms around him but now her nails dug in, just enough to hurt.

"And don't you forget it. Now you know we need to leave town, go to the coast, and get a boat to take us there, to that bank." Leroy picked her up and carried her to the bedroom.

"Let's tie up a few loose ends here first, Lee." She bounced when he dropped her on the bed.

"What do you have in mind?" He pulled off his shirt, then dropped his pants. She was already wriggling out of her shorts. The T-shirt was next.

"Scarlett Hall. I don't like the fact that she's so close. You need to get rid of her. She might think about it later and realize it was you she bumped into. Give them a new description. We can't afford that if the cops come looking in this area." She smiled up at him. "Maybe you could bring her up here. I'd love to help you do her."

"A three-way?" God, but he loved this woman, even if he didn't trust her.

"I don't know about that, but I want to be the one to kill her. You have no idea how much I hate the bitch. She came in and tore apart the office I'd worked so hard to put together. I had it just the way I liked it. Friends in spots ready to do just what I told them to do." She frowned. "She called us disorganized. Can you believe it? Me? Disorganized?"

"No, baby, she was wrong. You've always had your shit together. That bitch has to go. I'll hand you the knife myself." Leroy figured Scarlett Hall, witness, was history. But first, he wanted to complete the job of carving his initials into her body. Maybe do a few more things to Hall's plump backside. Then he'd tell the bitch now digging her nails into him and urging him closer that she could finish Hall off. Yep, sounded like a plan. He'd have even more to hold over his woman to keep her in line.

Sure, she acted like he was a sex god now. Probably had done that with Crane, too. He didn't give a shit, of course he didn't. Leroy pounded into her until he was satisfied. Was she? Who the hell cared? He needed to teach Ramona a lesson. She was definitely getting a little too full of herself. He wanted his name on those bank accounts. Soon. No more excuses.

He rolled off of her and reached for a cigarette. When she gave him a look then reached down to touch herself, he slapped her hand. "You left me waiting. Now you can wait. Tell me about a new ID. Where you're going to get it and when it'll be ready." He rolled toward her, the lit cigarette less than an inch from her nipple. "I mean it, Ramona. We're getting this settled right now. Half that money is mine. I want to see you fix this before we leave here."

She inhaled so that her nipple actually touched the tip of that cigarette. Her face hardened as she took the pain, watching Leroy's face. The standoff lasted for a long moment.

"Don't fucking threaten me, Lee. You know what my daddy did to me. I've taken a lot worse than what you can dish out."

"Yeah. I remember." He pulled the cig back and took a draw, blowing the smoke away from her.

She stared at him for a long minute. "Unless you took an advanced computer course in lockup, you have no clue how to get into that bank account. Did you?"

"Okay. I need you. I could get out of town without Crane's millions, but it would be hard and I'd end up doing shit work across the border somewhere just to survive." Leroy gave her a hard stare of his own. "I contacted you for my payday. But that doesn't mean I'll stand for having my balls busted over it. Money won't do either of us any good if you make me lose my temper. Remember what happens if I do?" Leroy reached for his knife, never far from his right hand. He'd left it on the nightstand.

"Yeah." She ran her fingers over his fist. "We need to work together. You think I want to go on the run by myself? What fun is that? Bonnie without her Clyde?"

"This isn't some movie, woman. I need a fake ID, passport, you know what it takes to start over." Leroy let his fingers relax on the knife.

"Don't worry. I can get papers for you in a few days. Believe it or not, I've been working on them." She smiled and stretched. "Are we good now? You gonna kiss it and make it better?"

Leroy knew his bluff had been called. He sure as hell couldn't leave here without the ID, and she had the key to the only way he could get to the money. What did she need him for? He put out the cigarette and leaned over her. Muscle. That was all he was good for. And fucking. So he did what he did best. He reached for her, aiming to please. Damn her. Why did she have to be so smart?

Chapter Fourteen

Scarlett licked the salt off the rim of her second margarita. The evening couldn't have been more perfect. Ethan treated her like a princess. She felt like one too. First, there had been the drive in that fabulous car. With a brother who worshiped fast sports cars, she'd known she was riding in something special. The valet had even parked the car right in front of the restaurant. The car was obviously expensive, a status symbol.

She wished she wore something besides jeans and a red silk shirt. But she fit right in with the crowd here. Ethan had scored a table next to the railing with a view of the lake, just in time for them to watch the sun sinking below the horizon. The colors in the sky had been spectacular. Now it was dark and lights twinkled across the water. A waiter had come to light the candle on their table to give it an intimate glow. To top it all off, a guitar player wandered through the crowd playing music designed to put lovers in the mood. It didn't hurt that the drinks were strong and the food service was slow.

"Two drinks is my limit." She studied Ethan over the rim of the glass.

"Good to know. I want you fully aware when I make my move." He grinned and gestured to the guitar player who was way too close. He murmured something to him in Spanish, then thrust a large bill into his hand. The guy moved away with a "*Gracias.*"

"What was that about? I was enjoying the music." Scarlett leaned forward. "Did you bribe him to go away?"

"He was playing in my ear." Ethan picked up his drink. Nothing fancy for him, a Mexican beer in the bottle.

"Obviously you speak Spanish." She smiled at him. "He kept singing '*Besame.*' What does that mean?"

"Kiss me." He set down his drink and leaned forward. "I'm all for it, but I didn't need a heavy-handed guitar player making my moves for me." Scarlett gazed into his eyes. Kiss him. Yes, she wanted to. He looked strong and mysterious in the low light. And the way he studied her, with his eyes on her lips, drew her closer until she was leaning against the table.

"What are you waiting for?" She pushed her glass out of the way when he reached for her. He slid his warm, firm hands into her hair. His thumbs settled just behind her ears and eased her toward him. The candle... She shoved it next to her glass and licked her lips.

"Guess the guitar player does get the credit." Then he closed the distance between them, covering her mouth with his. He seemed to take her measure at first, finding how they fit. When she leaned in a bit more, that was all the encouragement he needed. He pressed forward, taking her mouth hungrily while she braced her elbows on the table, her hands wrapped around his wrists. When he finally drew back, she let go. Reluctantly.

"Salty." He licked his own lips, then smiled.

"Mmm." Scarlett couldn't form words. He'd blown her away. Here she was, doing it again. She had a pattern. Didn't bother to deny it. Falling hard and falling fast. This man could kiss, and he made her feel... Yeah, she wanted him bad.

"Dessert?" A waiter had appeared at Ethan's side.

"What do you think, Scarlett?" He looked at her with a gleam in his eyes. What was he really asking?

"We have *flan*, *sopapillas*, a delicious *tres leches* cake..." The waiter was in selling mode.

"Couldn't eat another bite." Scarlett picked up her glass. "I'm about ready to leave. If that's all right with you, Ethan."

"Sure, just bring us the check." He never took his eyes off of her as she downed the rest of her drink and licked salt off her lips again.

The waiter had the check ready. Obviously he'd noticed the romantic interlude and had anticipated their quick exit. Ethan glanced at the bill, dropped some cash on the table, then stood.

"I'm ready if you are."

Ready? Scarlett thought about that. She knew it was her call. He'd made the first move. The next was on her. If she played this the way she usually did, she'd end up in his bed. Yes, she was usually pretty quick to go there. And she was throbbing just from that world-class kiss. She wanted more. But he was her boss. Sleeping with him would complicate things. Maybe she should slow this down. At least talk it out first. Good idea. She grabbed her purse and walked with him to his car.

"Thanks for a lovely evening." She settled back into the leather seat and waited while he put the key into the ignition.

"Is it over?" He didn't turn on the motor yet. The valet had scurried off to retrieve another customer's car. "That's your decision. Totally." He did lean over and kiss her again.

Scarlett couldn't catch her breath. Her decision. Then he kissed her like that. So that all she could do was feel and taste him. Beer and man and the warmth of his chest under her hands. She could actually feel the thump of his heart under her palm beneath his soft cotton shirt. Then he pulled back too soon with a satisfied smile and started the car.

They were in front of a busy restaurant. Not the time or place to do this. This? What was she thinking? Where had "slow" gone? And what about the talking? Scarlett fell back into her seat and fumbled with her seat belt. She wasn't thinking at all, and she sure as hell had no idea what to say.

He shifted gears expertly as he drove down the hills toward downtown again. The wind was chillier now and Scarlett shivered, some of the heat from his kisses vanishing as reality slammed into her. She should be smarter than this. She couldn't just let her emotions rule her. Sure, she wanted him, but having him was only going to make things awkward at work. She had to slow this down. Now.

When he reached for her hand and set it on his hard thigh, she planned to jerk it away. But it felt so right there. He was so entirely masculine. Every time he used his leg to shift a gear or accelerate, she could feel the muscles in his leg ripple under her fingers. So incredibly hot.

The pathetic truth was that Scarlett Hall was a sucker for a hot guy who could kiss like a dream. She'd had a bad three months. She now wore a beautiful tattoo and was horny as hell. Damn it, if she wanted to get laid, maybe she should. They could talk this out afterward. Ethan had been pretty up front about things, hadn't he? Yes, he had. He would be fair at work, she knew it. She sucked in a breath of cool air. Good grief! Was she seriously talking herself into this?

Of course she was. She studied him in the lights from the vintage dashboard. Handsome, with the kind of cheekbones and firm nose that could be on the cover of a romance novel. She deserved a man like this making love to her. She'd *suffered*. After what Knife Guy had done to her, a really good time in bed would go a long way toward healing her. So why deny herself?

There you go, Scarlett. Decision made. She pulled her phone from her purse and sent her brother a text. She wouldn't be home tonight. Not to worry. She was with Ethan. Please take care of the dog. Now all she had to do was make sure she and Ethan were on the same page. She put the phone away and laid her hand on his thigh again, this time a little bit higher. He glanced at her and grinned. Oh, yeah, he'd gotten the message. All systems go.

By the time they'd pulled into his parking spot under the condo building, Scarlett was practically squirming in her seat. After he turned off the car engine, they sat there for a moment.

"I didn't ask. I can drive you to your car." Ethan turned to her. "If that's what you want."

"Um, no. I was thinking maybe we could go to your place." He was making her say it, damn him. "For a nightcap. I'd like to see your apartment." She realized she was gripping his thigh a little firmly. She let go. "Unless you'd rather not—"

"I would love for you to see my place." He picked up her hand and held it. "It could use a woman's touch. I moved in and took it as it was. Furnished and actually kind of sad. About the only thing I bought was a new bed. I have a thing about sleeping on a good bed." He let go and climbed out of the car. Then he began putting the top up on the car.

Scarlett sat there. Decorating advice. Now he was taking care of his stupid car. She was being silly. Of course they were on the same page. He was giving her time to be sure about this decision. Well, she'd come this far, she had no intention of turning back now. She opened the door and climbed out. It was a low-slung car, and a graceful exit was impossible.

"Here, let me help you." He pulled her out and up against him. "We both know why you're coming to my place." He wrapped his arms around her. "At least I hope to hell we both know why."

Scarlett felt him against her, as hard and as wanting as she was. She ran her hands through his windblown hair, straightening it. "You want my advice on bedspreads and—" He covered her mouth with his. It was a deep and hungry kiss that left no doubt in her mind that he could give a damn about bedspreads. She held on to his shoulders, on tiptoe because he was tall and she couldn't get enough of him. Finally he set her down and leaned her against his car.

"I think we've wasted enough time down here."

"You're right." She turned around to grab her purse. "I texted Rhett that I wouldn't be home tonight."

"I like the way you think, woman." He locked the car, then took her hand. "I don't know about you, but I really don't need a nightcap."

"No, I've had enough alcohol tonight." She had to skip to keep up with him since he was walking fast as he headed up the stairs to the street level. "Ethan, you know this will change everything."

"I think I'm mature enough to handle it." He stopped at the corner. There was little traffic, but one of the few cars on the road was a police cruiser moving slowly down the street. It stopped for the light, waiting while they crossed. "What about you?"

"We'll see how this goes. For now I can't think past the next few hours." Scarlett waved at the policeman as they walked in front of his car. "I know, not very mature at all."

"I can promise you this, Scarlett." Ethan stopped on the other side of the street before heading toward the bar and the apartments upstairs. "If this ends with you deciding to dump me on my butt, I won't hold it against you. You're a terrific manager. I know that. Your job has nothing to do with this." He leaned down and kissed her again.

Scarlett pulled back and tugged him down the sidewalk. "Good to know. Now, can we hurry? I've been hibernating for months now. You're about to get the results of that long dry spell, mister. So brace yourself."

Ethan laughed and picked her up, holding her against his chest as he literally ran the last block, before heading down the alley to the stairs for the apartment units. By the time they got to the door he had to unlock, Scarlett was laughing so hard, she was afraid she was going to wet herself. He put her down, got the door open, then stopped to unlock his own apartment door. In answer to her breathless question, he pointed to his bathroom and she had to make a run for it. Not a romantic way to start what she was sure was going to be an amazing night.

Scarlett came out of the bathroom with her hair brushed and a smile on her face. Ethan couldn't take his eyes off of her.

"So this is where you live. Give me a tour."

"It won't take long." He was embarrassed to admit he'd settled for such a shit apartment. He should have rented one of the nicer units across the street until he could redo this one. Compared to the mansion in Houston where he'd grown up, it was crap. The floors were covered in a worn brown carpet and the kitchen was barely functional. Of course, what did he care? As long as there was a coffeemaker, a fridge with ice-cold beer, and a microwave, he was set. She'd already seen the bathroom with the scarred tub and the plastic shower curtain. At least the toilet flushed on command, but the faucet in the sink dripped.

"I admit I'm surprised. After riding in that fabulous car, I expected more of a bachelor pad." She sat on the faux leather sofa. "I see you managed to get a big-screen TV in here."

"A new bed and a decent TV. A guy has his standards. I moved in right before the Super Bowl." Ethan walked into the kitchen and came out with two bottles of water. He passed one to her and sat. He had a feeling she wanted to talk.

"This is going to complicate things." She twisted off the top and took a drink. Then she looked around, like for a coaster, before finally setting the bottle on the surface of the scarred coffee table.

"It will only be complicated if we make it so." Ethan really wanted to bypass this and go straight to the good stuff. Her blouse was unbuttoned to the point that cleavage showed. Had she done that in the bathroom? Yep. She'd worked all day around those workmen with not a bit of skin showing. "You're doing a great job. I don't want to lose you now that I see how you run things." He set down his own bottle. "Look at me. If we don't work out, I am not one of those jerks who will make you pay if you decide to dump me. I swear it. I can even have it formalized. A contract, if you like." He smiled. "Hey, my brother-in-law is a hotshot lawyer in Houston. I'll have him draw up a formal employment contract. Lay out your terms, and we'll get it all in writing."

"I'd like that." She laughed. "Surprised you, didn't I?"

She really had. Most women, when they got to the point of coming to his place, not that he'd brought anyone *here*, weren't as coolly calculating as Scarlett Hall.

"Clearly you're able to compartmentalize your priorities—business on one side of your brain"—he moved closer and slid a hand into her open blouse—"pleasure on another." His fingers brushed the edge of her bra. "I admire that. Very much. Will you take my word that the contract will be forthcoming?"

She eased closer, the movement pushing his hand inside her bra cup. "Yes, I believe I will."

Ethan bit back a groan at the feel of soft warm flesh under his hand. She was perfect. When she grasped his wrist and urged him to keep going, he found her nipple and covered it. He kissed her then, while he dealt with the rest of the buttons on her blouse.

She finally pulled back. "Ethan." Her voice was breathy. "We didn't finish the tour."

"What?" He looked down and saw a lacy black bra. God. Front clasp. He loved a bra with an easy front clasp. He inhaled warm woman with a touch of a fragrance that reminded him of an expensive perfume counter. Flowery but not too much. He realized she was watching him.

"The tour, Ethan. Don't you have a bedroom?"

"Two." He got the bra open and there they were, two of the prettiest breasts he'd ever seen. He just looked his fill before he realized she was waiting. "Oh, yes. Come on." He stood, painfully aware of how hard he was. She knew. She trailed her hand over his bulging zipper.

"Lead the way." She didn't bother to close the blouse or the bra. She just walked like a queen, her shoulders back and those incredible breasts on display. She didn't even seem to mind that he'd turned on the overhead lights when they'd come in. Not shy. Good to know.

"This one. The other is full of junk for the bar. I stored it up here. Decorations. You can look at it all later. See what you think." *Shut the fuck up.* Ethan flipped on the light in his bedroom. Had he made his bed? Hell, no. Clean sheets? Housekeeper came on Thursday. This was Friday. Good enough. He jerked off his shirt and tossed it toward the laundry basket in the corner.

"In a hurry?" She shrugged out of her blouse and hung it on the closet doorknob. Bra was next. Then she stood there, topless.

The sight almost brought Ethan to his knees. Why the hell not? He fell at her feet and went to work on the button at her waist. Jeans were always tough. Hers were a little loose, thank God, and they came open easily. Nothing to the zipper. Behind it? Tiny black lace panties. He leaned forward and traced the lace edge with his tongue. Smooth skin like satin. He almost groaned with pleasure. Her hands landed in his hair, and he felt her stomach contract when he touched her.

"Ethan!"

"You like that?" He grinned up at her. "Don't answer. If I can't tell, I'm a moron." He pulled down her jeans, then got them tangled in her sandals. Yes, he was a moron. She held on to his shoulders while he got each shoe off before he could toss aside those heavy jeans. Shorts. He liked her better in shorts. He'd tell her so as soon as he came up for air. Because right now he was determined to kiss his way back up to those pale thighs. The lacy panties were in the way. But that was okay. He'd get rid of them soon enough. He slid his hands around to cup her ass. Curvy, just right. She was damp, and the way she was moving against his tongue told him all he needed to know. He pulled down the panties with his teeth.

"You're making me wild." She gasped when he finally licked inside her. "I haven't even seen you yet."

He rocked back on his heels. "You will. After I make you come." He walked her back to the bed and set her on the edge, then opened her legs so he could do what he knew would get her out of control. He couldn't wait to give her pleasure. She was so damn sweet and eager. She moved against him and called his name while he held her, savoring the way she clenched and grabbed his hair.

He was breathing like he'd run for miles by the time she lost it completely, screaming his name. He kissed a path up her stomach, then stood so he could pick her up. God, he loved the fact that she was so small. Carrying her to the bed, he felt all man, a giant. Compared to some of his friends, he was pretty much a runt at six-two. She clutched him, kissing his chest, his neck, wherever she could place her mouth. He felt her trembling. He'd done that.

She lay in the middle of the bed, her cheeks flushed and her eyes glazed. "I owe you one, Ethan."

"I'll hold you to that." He toed off his shoes and dropped his pants. Then he came down beside her and kissed her breasts, first one, then the other, loving the shape and feel of them. He was giving her time to find herself again. She'd trusted him. Some women shied away from totally giving themselves. Not Scarlett. When she finally began running her hands over his body, it was with a sigh of pleasure, as if she'd never seen anything so fine.

"You are just too much, Ethan Calhoun. Now it's my turn." She shoved him onto his back. He let her, of course. She started exploring him, kissing a path from one spot to the next until he knew he was close to losing control.

"Scarlett, I want this to last." He groaned when she stroked his cock, then made love to it with her mouth. "Condoms, pants pocket."

"Not the bedside table?" She sat up and smiled at him.

"You're the first woman I've brought to this hovel." He watched as she bounced off the bed and bent over to pick up his jeans. "Stop. I see your tattoo. It's a beauty." He rolled toward her. "Will you let me…"

She froze, her hand full of the condoms he'd bought that morning in a burst of optimism. "Kiss it and make it better?"

"Nothing can make it better, I know that." He climbed out of bed and pulled her into his arms. "Fuck that bastard. I'm sorry I said anything. We were having a good time, and now—"

"Now nothing." She looked down to where he was still as hard as the bedpost. Then she ripped open the condom. "I will not let that man take one more thing from me." She handed him the condom. "Now, get on that bed and take care of business. Lie back and let's finish what we started."

She blinked back what could have been tears. But she obviously wasn't about to let them fall. "You hear me?"

"Damn right." Ethan dropped back on the bed and got ready for her. She was soon on top of him, sighing as she made sure he was all the way inside her. He thought he'd never felt anything like it. She was so tight, so right. He waited for her to move, even though he was so damn far gone he would probably ruin things with one or two pumps.

She leaned over and kissed him, mouth open, tongue inside, and eyes on his. Then she sat up and moved, gingerly at first, like maybe she was a little out of practice. Ethan grabbed her hips and helped her along. He used what he was surprised to discover was an iron will to make this last for her. He wanted to feel her tighten around him. Hoped to see her lose it again. But she was concentrating, her eyes closed as if this was something she had to force herself to endure.

What was she thinking? Was she back there reliving that nightmare, the time when that bastard had cut her? No, hell, no. He needed her to forget, to see *him* and know she was safe. Know that he'd never hurt her.

"Scarlett! Look at me." He ran his hands up her sides and quit moving, though it just about killed him. "It's Ethan. I'm here for you. Please relax. We can stop if you want. I swear to God I will never cause you pain."

Her eyes popped open. "You can't promise that." She stayed where she was, her fingers splayed on his chest.

"You're right. We're human. I may do something stupid. Say the wrong thing. Hurt your feelings. I'm a man. Clueless about women. My sisters have told me that." He let go of her. This was on her now. How this would go. *If* it would go. He realized sweat had popped out on his brow. Yeah, he was hurting. *Suck it up.*

"Listen to me, Scarlett. I swear I will never lay a hand on you or cause you physical pain. I am not that man. What do you call him? Knife Guy. He's an animal. I am not. Don't mix us up in your mind. I want you. I admire you. But I will not use you or abuse you. Understand?" He held his breath. This was that important to him. *She* was that important to him.

She took a shuddering breath. Okay, maybe he was an animal too, because he couldn't take his eyes off how her rose-tipped breasts moved. But he quickly looked up at her face. Tears ran down her cheeks. She was biting her lip again. That thing she did. He'd tasted it now, had even bit it lightly too as they'd kissed. Her lips were full and fit perfectly against his mouth.

"You can't let him ruin this for you." His voice was husky. His whole body ached from the effort to stay still and wait for her to decide what came next. He was inside her, so hard he thought he might burst. God give him strength.

"You're right." She opened her eyes and looked down at him. "Thank you." She fell over on top of him, holding him so tightly her nails dug into his biceps.

"Do you believe me?" He was very careful how *he* held *her*, not too tight, but firmly. So she'd know he was serious about protecting her and keeping her safe.

"Yes. I know you won't hurt me. Not physically."

"And I'll do my damnedest not to hurt you any other way." He rolled them to their sides so they were facing each other. Forget the lovemaking. It was over and done. He needed to get rid of that condom. He brushed her hair back from her forehead, feeling unexpectedly tender toward her. "Like I said, I may screw up. I have a history."

"So do I. Love 'em and leave 'em." She managed a small laugh.

"Would be nice to break that habit." He meant it. Go figure.

"I agree. Time to grow up. I'm even older than you are. Saw it on your driver's license."

"You're kidding. I'm messing with an older woman?" He ran a finger between her brows. "So that's why you have a wrinkle here."

She slapped at his hand. "Only two years, Ethan. I'm thirty."

"I have a sister your age. An older sister." He laughed when she slapped at him again and missed. "She'd love you. Megan is just as feisty as you are."

"Feisty. I like that description." She rubbed her breasts against his chest. "I blew this, didn't I?"

"No. But if you're interested in blowing something…" Ethan got a swat on his bare butt for that remark. "Okay, forget I said that. How about a shower? It's not a great one, but the water's hot. And I do want a closer look at Casey's work. Flowers. Very pretty." He managed to distract Scarlett as he raced her to the bathroom. Somehow he was going to make this night end right. But if he ever got a chance to meet Leroy Simms in a dark alley, he was going to tear that son of a bitch apart for what he'd done to Scarlett.

Chapter Fifteen

Scarlett woke up in a man's arms for the first time in months. It felt good. Right. But how did Ethan feel about last night after she'd had a meltdown about her tattoo and acted like a crazy person?

She held perfectly still, afraid to wake him. Once he realized who he held, he'd probably start easing her toward the door. Nice knowing you. Your job is safe, but it'll be awkward as hell. Damn it. Why couldn't she just *get over it*? Ethan had told her when they'd first met that he really didn't need more drama in his life.

She got up her nerve, rolled over, and looked at him. Of course he was awake. He stared at her with deep brown eyes the color of a chocolate bar. She did love chocolate. With wild hair and warm skin, he was beautiful to her. His arm pressed against hers, but he didn't try to make a move even though she could tell he wanted to. Sex. Was that all he was after? He had one of those morning erections that just begged to be accommodated. She reached out and found one of the unused condoms from last night next to her on the bed, then handed it to him with a smile. Why not?

"Seriously?" He ran a tongue over his teeth. "Before I brush my teeth?"

"Just don't kiss me. I find the idea kind of hot." She ran her hands over his chest. It was a smooth chest, not hairy. Her preferred type. She gave in to the urge to lick one of his nipples while he dealt with the condom. He obviously didn't need to be asked twice. Then she pulled him on top of her.

"I'm sorry I messed up last night." Saying it made her feel a little better. So did the weight of his body, fitting so perfectly, despite their height difference.

"Forget it. I'm about to get my happy ending. Right?" He slid into her, making her gasp with pleasure.

"Now, it's my understanding that a happy ending—"

"Shut up and wrap your legs around me." He reached for something in his nightstand drawer, which made their position a little weird but kind of delicious.

"What are you doing?" She got her ankles locked behind him. Oh, yes. This was perfect.

"Breath mints. Chew one fast. I want to kiss the hell out of you." He pushed a mint into her mouth and popped one into his own.

Scarlett chewed. Peppermint. When she inhaled, her eyes watered. Very strong peppermint. Before she could think much about it, his mouth claimed hers. Mmm. This with kissing was much better. He began to move, one of his hands already finding her breast. He was definitely a boob guy. Hers were sensitive, and the pressure of his fingers on her nipple made her clench deep inside. She ran her hands down his back and gripped his butt. Lean, hard. She hadn't seen Ethan work out, but he must get exercise somewhere. He was ripped.

He sat up, his face taut as he reached down between them and found just the right spot. His thumb pressed and he moved faster, clearly as excited as she was. God, this was good. Then thought fled and she just absorbed sensation after sensation.

"Ethan! Please!"

He kept moving that thumb, bending over to tease her breast with his lips at the same time. It was more than enough to push her over the edge. Pleasure swamped her, flowing through her until she could swear she saw stars. Her toes curled, and she dug her nails into his backside. Was that sound really coming from her? She buried her face in his neck when he collapsed on top of her. Heart pounding, thighs still tensing from the aftershocks, she could only hold on while she tried to figure out what the hell had just happened. She was surrounded by a peppermint haze, his heavy breathing in her ear.

She opened her eyes and looked up. An ancient ceiling fan wobbled drunkenly, a cheap three-bulb light dangling from it. They'd left the lights on all night. He'd done that for her, because he knew she was still recovering from her attack. When had she told him she couldn't sleep in the dark? She hadn't. He'd guessed.

She ran her fingers through his silky hair. What an exceptional man. Most men would have run like hell when she'd freaked out like she had last night. Ethan had been warm, understanding. About everything. He had even promised to get a contract drawn up to make her feel better about sleeping with the boss. Or had that been an empty promise to get her into his bed? She wasn't about to bring that up now. Not when she felt so perfectly boneless.

"It's Saturday. We're not working." He rolled onto his back, beside her, then looked over and smiled. "Except for one thing. I've been checking out the websites for the other secret bars in town. I think it's our duty to visit them personally. Tonight. What do you think?"

"I love that idea." She leaned over and kissed his stomach. "I need to go home and change clothes, of course." She looked around. Where was her purse? No sign of a clock. His cell phone was on the nightstand. She picked it up and saw it was close to noon. "Look at the time. Are you hungry?"

"I could eat. There's nothing here. I don't cook." He got up, taking his cell from her. "I'm actually expecting a call or text sometime today. Family thing. We can grab a bite, then I'll take you home, well, to your car anyway. I can pick you up at your place around eight tonight, if that's all right. We might need to skip dinner. I'll let you know. No idea how this family thing's going to play out."

"I'll give you my address." Scarlett realized he was the first person outside of her family whom she'd trusted with her new location besides Mike. Her stomach fluttered a little while she rattled off the address. Ridiculous. Of course she had no qualms about Ethan coming to her apartment. She told him how to get there. "I'll buzz you in when you get to the gate. I have some pretty serious security. You understand why."

"Yes. I'm glad you have a good setup." He typed the address into his phone. "Let's get dressed and head out. I've got a text here that I need to answer. Sorry if all this sounds mysterious. Trust me, you don't want to know all the family drama I have going on."

Didn't she? What could be such a big deal that he couldn't tell her? It was annoying, but who didn't have a secret or two?

Scarlett let it go. They'd had a wonderful time, and she really, really liked this man. She wasn't about to ruin it by becoming a pushy nag about things that he clearly thought were none of her business.

She rolled out of bed and spotted her bra and blouse still hanging from the doorknob. Her jeans were in a wad on the floor under them, along with her panties. That made her smile. Ethan was a wonderful lover, generous and clever. She had let him take the lead. Maybe she'd turn the tables after their tour of secret bars tonight. She couldn't wait.

"I have to take another quick shower. Alone." She patted Ethan's butt as she headed for his bathroom. He didn't object, just stood frowning over his phone. That family drama he was so worried about? Too bad. But she was going to have to put it out of her mind. She detoured to the living room and grabbed her own phone. A text from Rhett. Thumbs-up. That made her grin, and she sent him an emoji of a happy dance. Then she did a rinse off in the shower and dug in her purse for her emergency stash of makeup and tiny travel toothbrush.

Lunch? It would have to be casual. She stuck her panties in her purse and went commando. The bra went into the spacious bag as well. The way Ethan's eyes followed her when she emerged from the bathroom showed her she'd made the right choice. He dashed into the room after her and closed the door. She heard the shower running while she headed into the kitchen. Coffee. It was easy to find the resources since the place was almost empty. She soon had two cups ready and was sipping a mug by the time Ethan emerged set to go.

"You are a woman without equal." He poured the other cup and took a drink. "I needed that."

"You realize this kitchen is a disgrace."

"I know. My sister says these appliances are from the seventies. She called this color Harvest Gold." He frowned. "I hope you didn't want cream or sugar."

"No, black is fine." She shook her head. "What I meant was that you have empty cupboards. Come on, Ethan. Couldn't you at least buy a box of cereal and a gallon of milk?"

He shrugged. "Okay, I'm spoiled. I grew up with a housekeeper who fixed me breakfast every morning. You should taste Janie's blueberry pancakes."

"My mother makes terrific pancakes too, but that didn't mean I couldn't learn to fend for myself when I left home." Scarlett opened his refrigerator. "Beer and water. Seriously?"

"You want to take care of me?" He grinned. "I admit it's been a pain to go out for every meal. Feel free to fill my pantry and refrigerator."

"No thanks." She realized she'd walked right into that one. "You offered lunch. That burger place was pretty good and it's close."

"Works for me. They know me well there." He drained his cup and moved closer. "I like you in that blouse without a bra." He ran his hands over her breasts, making her shiver. "Sexy. You sure you're hungry?"

"Starving. Let's go, Calhoun." She backed up, running into the Formica countertop.

He moved even closer. "You leave off the panties too?"

"What do you think?" She pressed her hands against his chest.

"I think I'd like to find out." He unzipped her jeans and slipped his hand inside. "Yes, indeed. The lady is going commando." He kissed her then, slowly, as if savoring her coffee flavor. "I've lost my appetite...for a burger."

Scarlett slid her own hand down to his waistband and inside. Yes, she'd managed to turn him on and then some. This was new and so hot, she wasn't about to waste it. She opened his zipper and pushed his jeans down to his knees.

"What do you have an appetite for, mister?" She laughed and put her hands behind her, jumping up on the counter.

"Guess." He jerked off her jeans with a quick movement and tossed them aside. Then he touched her with sure fingers.

"Really?" She shivered as he delved deep, making her want more.

"Really." His eyes were dark as he moved in, lifting her so she had to hold on to him as he drove inside her. "This is going to be fast. Can you take it?"

"I can take anything you dish out, Calhoun." She squeezed her knees together, shocked at how much she wanted him, how wild and fantastic it felt to be uninhibited like this. "Make it good or you'll be sorry."

"Good? I'll make it great or die trying." He carried her over to the nearest wall and braced her there before he began to move.

Scarlett just held on and let it happen. No, not let it happen, *made* it happen. She was as eager and as in control as he was, biting his neck and pushing against him. God, but this was amazing. *He* was amazing. She was so over her head this time. She couldn't imagine letting him go.

* * * *

Ethan couldn't believe his mother wanted to meet at a busy mall on a Saturday. And at Neiman's. She was taking a big chance that she would be recognized. Her pals traveled the state going to charity events. It was entirely possible one of them might pop into the expensive store to pick up something at the last minute before one of their "galas."

He parked the car and walked inside. No sign of Albert, but then that was probably a good thing. He rode the escalator up to women's sportswear, where his mother had texted him to meet. Damn it, he wanted to strangle her.

"Bring your credit card." Apparently she needed a new wardrobe before she could get her picture taken. He stepped off onto the floor that even smelled like a pampered woman. Lisa had her hands full of clothes and stopped in front of the entrance to a dressing room when she saw him.

"She'll be out in a minute." She smiled and looked him over. "What's the matter, Ethan? Don't you like shopping?"

"Not particularly. And I'm sure as hell not buying all of that. Put half of it back." He said it quietly, ignoring Lisa's dirty look as she hung a few items on a rack in front of the dressing room. He didn't love shopping. He'd spent his childhood on velvet chairs waiting for his mother and sisters to make their selections. It took patience and an electronic device to keep him happy, because there was no rushing the process. He sat in one of the predictably comfortable chairs and glanced at a fellow sufferer. Thank God he didn't recognize the man. They exchanged pained looks after Lisa disappeared through a doorway.

"She your wife?" The man put his phone aside.

"No. My mother is in there. I was told to meet her here and bring a credit card." Ethan pulled out his own phone. The last thing he needed was a conversation with a nosy stranger. If the man had heard what he'd said to Lisa, he wasn't showing signs of it.

"The women have been in there awhile. Got the saleslady hopping." The man smiled. "My Peg is buying something special for our dinner tonight. It's our anniversary. Thirty-five years."

"Congratulations." Ethan nodded. "Is this her?" A woman came out in a red dress. "Now, that's a pretty picture."

"Sure is." The man jumped to his feet. "Get that one, Peg. You look as beautiful as the day I met you." He walked around her, then zipped her up. "Not too tight, is it?"

"No, honey. It's perfect. But the cost…" She showed him the ticket under her arm, and he winced.

"You're worth it, baby." He kissed her cheek. "Get it. We'll just forget about going to that fancy restaurant." He hummed a few bars and twirled her around. "I'll grill some burgers, we'll put on some tunes and have a special night, just the two of us."

Ethan couldn't believe it. He'd never had to consider the cost of anything. And the way the couple looked at each other . . . They honestly didn't care where they spent the evening, as long as they were together. He got up and pulled out his wallet.

"Thirty-five years together deserves a nice dinner out. It's on me." Ethan handed the man two one-hundred-dollar bills.

"I couldn't." The man flushed. His wife was already back in the dressing room.

"Sure you could. Just do me a favor. Give me your email address. I'm opening a bar in a few weeks. Fuel. It's going to be one of those secret bars. Come see me then and have a drink and a dance. Your wife can wear that pretty dress again. Bring some friends and then help me spread the word if you have a good time." Ethan shook his head when the man tried to hand him back the money. "I'm serious. You two stuck it out for the long haul.

It's a good reminder to me that it's possible." He saw his mother had come to the door of the dressing area. "Mama! You about done?"

"Yes. Ethan, I heard what you said to this man." His mother frowned at the stranger. "He's right, mister. His daddy and I had a bad marriage and went through a messy divorce. No wonder he hasn't been able to keep a decent long-term relationship." She patted Ethan on the shoulder.

"Now, Mama. I'm not blaming you and Daddy. I just haven't found the right woman yet." Then he remembered waking up this morning with Scarlett. No, it was way too soon to remember how right that had felt.

His mother kept talking to the man next to him. "Pride is a good thing. But if Ethan wants to give you and your wife something, take it. My boy is a fine, generous man, and thanks to his daddy's nose for oil, he can sure afford it." Mama smiled, looking pretty in a new outfit in her favorite color of bright blue.

"Well, then. Thank you, Ethan. I'm Doug, and my wife is Peggy Carruthers." He shook Ethan's hand. Then he turned to Missy. "We have two boys. We're as proud of them as you are of yours, ma'am." The man smiled when his wife came out holding the red dress on a hanger. "We both thank you." He dug in his pocket and pulled out a business card. "My email is on that. I've been retired for a while now and do part-time website work. If you need anything like that, look me up. I'll be sure to watch for that email. We'll come to your bar and tell all our friends about it." He whispered in his wife's ear. She laughed and gave Ethan a hug.

"Thank you! This *is* a special day." She dragged her husband over to the counter, waving at Ethan before they got busy paying for her dress.

"Lisa had better watch what she picked out. I don't mind spending on you, Mama, but—" Ethan felt his temporary good mood vanish.

"We needed clothes, Ethan. Keep a tally. I'll pay you back." His mother smiled. "That was a nice thing you just did for those folks. I'm proud of you." She hugged him.

"Thanks, Mama. But we need to hurry this along."

"One more stop, then we can go." She looked down at her feet. She'd escaped the hospital wearing tennis shoes. "We have to hit the shoe salon."

"You realize how dangerous this is?" Ethan was losing patience.

"Don't be silly. Who would I know here in Austin?" Mama turned to greet the saleswoman loaded down with her choices. "Did you get everything?"

"Yes, ma'am." She glanced at Ethan. "You must be her son. She said you would be paying today."

"Of course." Ethan handed her his credit card. He couldn't begin to calculate what this would cost. Didn't matter. He wanted to get out of there as fast as possible. "Where's Lisa?"

"I'm here." She had her arms full and had changed into jeans and a red top. "I finally feel human again."

Would it kill her to say thank you? Obviously. "Speed up. I can't wait to get out of here. Shoes next, then we need to get those pictures taken."

"Fine. Whatever." Lisa stalked over to the counter and dumped her selections. "We wouldn't have to involve you if you trusted us with a credit card."

"Trust you? Not happening. But Monday, I'll get Mama a debit card. With a reasonable limit." Ethan waited while the clerk worked in slow motion. He had a little sticker shock at the total, but just let it go. He'd grown up coming to this store, and he knew quality cost money. He'd suggested they drop Lisa off at a discount store for her clothes or shoes, but his mother had started to throw one of her temper fits, so he'd backed off. They arranged to pick up everything at customer service and headed downstairs to the shoe department.

"Mrs. Calhoun!" The euphoric exclamation could have been heard halfway to Houston.

"Charles!" Missy was smothered in a warm embrace by a man who wore a white carnation on his lapel. He could have just come from a wedding except he wore a discreet name tag under a puff of white satin in the breast pocket of his gray-and-white pin-striped suit. "What are you doing working here?" She smiled and settled into a love seat.

"I moved last fall, darling. After that horrible hurricane wiped out my home in Houston. None of that nasty weather here in Austin." He got introduced to Lisa, who was going by a fake name, Lauren.

"I am so sorry to hear that, Charles. That you lost your home. Maybe the commission from a big sale to me will help you recover." Mama waved her hand toward the closest display. "I need shoes, and you certainly know what I like. I lost everything too, through a little misunderstanding."

"Darling, I will take care of you. And your friend?" Charles looked at Lisa, who was not about to get far from Missy. He correctly guessed Lisa's shoe size, making both women laugh.

"Dear Charles, you are such a genius. Sandals, pumps. We both want at least five pairs." Missy squeezed his hand, then gestured at Ethan. "This is my son, he will pay for everything."

Ethan stepped up to Charles and pressed a large bill into his hand. "I'm really sorry about your losses in Houston, man. Now, do me a favor, will you?"

"Anything, Mr. Calhoun." The money disappeared into the pocket of an Italian suit tailored to perfection.

"Miss Lauren will get two pair, Charles, from your sale rack. My mother can have five, whatever she wants." Ethan gave the salesman a man-to-man look. Dear Charles was clearly on the ball. He winked, understanding perfectly.

"Of course. As you wish, Mr. Calhoun. Can I offer you some refreshment? A glass of wine perhaps?" Charles eyed Ethan. "Adore your shoes. If you wish to check out Gucci's spring line, the boutique is across the way. Or you can sit anywhere and make yourself comfortable. This may take a while. We want our ladies to choose carefully. Mrs. Calhoun is a special client. I must make sure her selections are right for her."

"Do your thing, Charles. I'll stay out of the way." Ethan shook his head. What next, the Calhoun name announced over the public address system? If "Dear Charles" said the words "Mrs. Calhoun" one more time, he was going to be choking on a spring sandal.

Ethan moved a few rows away, behind a potted plant, and hoped to hell he couldn't be seen if someone else came along who remembered that Mama was supposed to be locked up in a mental hospital. He waved away the offer of a drink, but of course the women accepted glasses of white wine while Charles scurried off to find them the "perfect shoes." Ethan texted Albert that he was going to be at the bar in an hour to take their pictures. He wanted to know where the hell Albert was anyway.

Apparently the PI had been busy. He had arranged for the rooms at the Longhorn to be assigned to someone else because of "prior reservations." Missy and Lisa would have to move. He was going to "help" them settle into a new place that was more isolated with less traffic. That would make it easier for him to capture one or both of them and get them back where they belonged. Ethan breathed a sigh of relief. Then he heard excited chatter and his mother's name.

"Missy Calhoun! As I live and breathe!" A well-dressed woman and her two friends surrounded his mother, their gazes avid. "I'm calling 9-1-1 right now. You're supposed to be locked up, last I heard." The woman dug in her leather bag for her phone.

His mother rose to her feet and grabbed a high-heeled shoe from the nearest display. "Mary Louise, put that phone away now or you'll need it to call an ambulance." She took aim. "Elaine, Marie. Step away. Mary Louise will meet you in the purse department. Clearly she needs to update her spring bag." She brandished her shoe while she gripped Mary Louise's arm.

Ethan started to get up. What the hell was this? To his relief, Mary Louise shoved her phone in her purse and the other women scurried away.

"Let me go!" Mary Louise looked down at his mother's grip on her. "You think I don't know what's going on? There was an article in the Houston paper. You escaped from the looney bin. The cops are looking for you."

Ethan wondered if he should get into the middle of this. What could he say? Mary Louise was right. To his relief, his mother did let the woman go. And Mary Louise had kept her voice down. Lisa was on the other side of the large shoe department, deep into the sales rack. After shooting him a "Go to hell" look, she'd realized she was going to have to make the best of it.

"Don't believe everything you read, Mary Louise. As you can see, I'm perfectly fine. In Austin updating my shoe wardrobe for the spring." She looked Mary Louise up and down. "Honey, we all need an update from time to time." Mama had kicked her tennis shoes under a chair out of sight and stood in her bare feet, her toenails painted a bright pink.

Ethan slumped in his seat. If Mama pulled this off, it would be a miracle. At least she hadn't added that she was visiting her son here.

"I don't believe you. You just threatened me. And I remember the scene you made at the country club during that last style show for charity. At the boutique afterward, you ripped a dress right in half trying to get it for yourself. You were out of control, Missy. I heard—"

"Really, Mary Louise, stop right now. I don't have time for your third-hand gossip." Missy glanced toward where Mary Louise's pals hovered near the purses then brought the high heel up near Mary Louise's face again. "I wouldn't be spreading it around, either, if I were you. I have a story or two of my own I could tell. About Harold. I hear your husband bought a new condo in downtown Austin recently. That will be convenient for him and his new little filly. While you're at the lake house here."

Mary Louise's face reddened. "Shut your mouth. He keeps his horses at our ranch."

"You know it's not a horse I'm talking about, don't you, Mary Louise?" Missy smiled. "I bet your gal pals know her. Redhead? Gives a good ride, I've heard. On the rodeo committee with old Harold." Missy put down the shoe. "Call the girls over and we can have a gabfest if that's what you want."

"No time." Mary Louise hugged her purse and glanced toward her friends. "I just remembered I have an appointment to get a mani-pedi this afternoon. Pretty pink on your toes, Missy. But a little bright, don't you think? Maybe I'll see you in Houston." She turned on her heel and walked away.

As soon as she was out of sight, Ethan got up. "What was that about? I thought you were done for sure."

Missy smiled as Charles staggered out of the back room with a huge stack of shoeboxes. "Don't ever underestimate me, son. Mary Louise's husband, Harold, has a mistress. She pretends he doesn't. The last thing she wants to hear is an update on his horsing around." She laughed, then plucked a gold sandal out of a box and slipped it on. "Knowledge is power, Ethan. Don't ever forget that." She smiled and walked around the room. "Charles, these are perfect!"

Ethan went back to his seat. It was easy to forget that his mother was a formidable woman. This had been a good reminder. But she'd been seen now, and by one of the biggest gossips in Houston. Missy had humiliated the woman in front of her friends too. It wouldn't take long for Mary Louise to hit the Internet and realize she'd been right—Missy didn't belong in Austin. The urge to gossip was always hard to resist, and the desire to get revenge even harder to let go. The shit would hit the fan.

They had to move and fast.

Chapter Sixteen

"Have you lost your mind? You went to a tattoo parlor?"

Leroy didn't bother to answer her. His heart was still racing from the near-miss at the place. Who would have figured that a cop would be in there getting his own tattoo? Damn, but it had felt good to fool the law like that. He'd been lying there with his shirt off while the artist, named Luke, had been working on his tat. It was perfect—red heart around his newly pierced nipple with Ramona's name spelled out over the top. When the cop had walked in, Leroy had almost jumped off the table and ruined everything. But he had nerves of steel. Hell, yes, he did. So he stayed there, under the needle, with a cop just feet away.

"Calm down, baby. Nothing happened. I keep telling you, this disguise is golden." Leroy pulled her in and tried to give her a kiss to distract her. She wasn't having it. "He never even looked my way."

"You told them my name." She shoved away from him. "Damn it, Lee, how many times do I have to tell you that we can't afford to be connected?"

"I'm getting sick of this." He stalked to the kitchen and pulled a beer out of the fridge. At least she'd remembered to bring him a new case of Lone Star. If he didn't know better, he'd think she was planning to ditch him. Time to remind her of how things stood. He took a deep drink, then wiped his mouth with the back of his hand.

"You're sick of this? What about me? I'm out there having to act like everything is cool while you sit on your ass drinking beer and watching baseball. I took all the risk—" She gasped when he grabbed her arm and flung her onto the couch.

"Oh? *You* took all the risk? Who almost died in a shootout with the cops, and then was hauled off to jail?"

He wasn't getting through to her. She just sat there, watching him and rubbing her arm.

"I hate being locked up, Ramona. Hate it." It was a weakness that he didn't expose to just anyone, and he probably shouldn't be telling her this now. Ramona might use it against him later. "I had to kill a cop to get out of that hellhole. You know what will happen to me if I get caught now?"

"You loved killing him. Don't deny it." She raised her chin, daring him to say otherwise.

"Yeah, maybe I did. Because I'm good with a knife, and don't you forget it." Leroy stood over her. He was so mad he was shaking, beer sloshing out of the can and spilling onto her. She sat still for it because she was smart enough to know you didn't cross him when he was this pissed. "Then there was that asshole Isaac Crane. Do you think you did me a favor, setting me up to listen to that nutcase for days and weeks on end while he plotted his get-rich scheme that fell the hell apart?" He took a drink, daring her to get up. "All you did was some fancy computer work and a few pity fucks with the guy."

"That's what you think." She was mad now too, her chest rising and falling as she stared up at him. "I had to sweet-talk people at work and pretend to be someone I'm not for years, Lee. You can't imagine how hard that is." She tried to get up, but he pushed her down again. "And about those pity fucks. I'd like to see you lying under a sweaty pig like that, a man who thought he was God's gift so he didn't bother to do much more than…"

"I've heard enough." Leroy fell onto the couch beside her. He wasn't about to go down that path. He'd gone to jail the first time young and good-looking. Still had nightmares about those years. "So you had it rough. That's over. Crane's dead. And no one will know you're the Ramona on my chest. I sure didn't give that tattoo artist my real name and I paid cash." He'd calmed down. "The Crane job cost us both, but it'll be worth it in the long run. We'll soon be gone, with money enough to buy an island somewhere."

"What would we do on a damn island?" She grabbed his beer from him and took a swallow. "I want bright lights, people. Besides, I have plans for some of that money."

"What plans? They include me?" This was what he'd been waiting for. He'd been in a holding pattern here. Time to lay it all out there. Ramona had better be careful. If she tried to cut him out of the payday…

"Sort of." She reached for her phone on the coffee table. "I want to show you something. Why I have to keep my name out of this. Promise you won't get mad."

"You know I can't promise that." He finished the beer and crushed the empty can in one fist, in case she needed reminding that he was powerful. Making him mad wasn't smart. But he did need her to get to the money. "What have you got there?"

She held out her phone. There was a picture of a young man in a football uniform. He was kneeling, his helmet on one knee. Classic pose for a high school jock.

"Who the fuck is that?"

"Tommy, our son." She touched the phone, then ran her finger across the screen. "Look at all the pictures."

"Hold up. What do you mean 'our son'?" Leroy took her phone and studied the pictures. Tall boy, dark hair and eyes. Did he look like him? "I paid for you to get rid of our kid right after you told me I knocked you up."

"I know that. But my mom and grandma got wind of the pregnancy. I was sick as a dog every morning. My ma's not stupid. She knew we were humping like bunnies back then." She leaned into the corner of the couch while he scrolled back through a bunch of pictures until he was staring at a toddler with a toy truck. "You try getting rid of a kid when two women are waving rosaries in your face and praying over you."

She jumped up and wagged her finger in his face. "'Abortion is a sin, Ramona. You'll go to hell, Ramona. *Madre de Dios*, you will kill *Abuela* if you do this.'" Her voice had been full of the Spanish accent her mother had never gotten rid of. "You see what I put up with? They wouldn't drive me to Corpus for it, either. You know our Podunk town didn't have a doctor who would do it." She sighed and sat again. "I was stuck, Lee, and, I admit it, they got to me. So I popped out the kid. Ma and Gran helped raise him. He's graduating high school this May." She gestured to the phone. "Look at him. He's good-looking. Smart, too."

"No shit." Leroy threw her phone in her lap and stood. "You named him Tommy?"

"After you, Lee. But he's got my name, Delgado, since I wasn't married." She watched him as he paced the floor. "He's clever, athletic. Reminds me of you when we were in high school. He's going to college, Lee. Already has a scholarship. But it's not enough to pay for everything. This money we're getting will take care of the rest with plenty left over for us to do whatever we want."

"Shut up, I can't think." He had a son. He grabbed her phone again, paging through those pictures. And she'd never told him. Eighteen years between them, and she'd never thought he'd want to know? He stared down at her. Of course she'd kept it from him. He'd spent a couple of stretches in prison, years trapped in a cell. What kind of role model would that make him for a smart boy?

"You don't need to think, Lee. Tommy's mine. He has a bright future. He sure as hell doesn't need a cop killer showing up and claiming to be his father. You know what that would do to him?" She was up, facing him and full of defiance.

It was all Leroy could do not to slam her against the wall. Why had she told him this now? To torture him? And to make sure he didn't go near the boy. Ramona had a mean streak in her, and she was probably enjoying this. Well, she'd met her match.

"Maybe I want to see him. Invite him to help me pull my next job. His old man could show him the ropes. Did you at least teach him how to shoot? How to use a knife?" He almost smiled when her face went white.

"You stay away from him, Leroy, or you'll never see a damn dime of that money. The only reason I'm telling you now is so you understand why I have to keep my name out of this. You crossed a line with that tattoo. If you're caught…" She stepped up until they were toe to toe. "Damn you!"

"And here I thought you'd like it." Leroy really wanted to hurt her. "I put a fucking heart around it."

"Eighteen years too late for that, Lee. Our boy is going places, will do great things. He doesn't know who his father is. I made up shit about a man in my past and he let it go. My ma and grandma are doing a fine job with him. Neither of us needs to ruin his life with our baggage."

"I don't know about that." Leroy pulled her close with his hand in her hair. "You let the cat out of the bag, Ramona. It's not that easy to get it back in. I'm thinking I should have a chance to see the boy." He looked her straight in the eyes. "What does he think you do here in Austin? Is he happy that his ma left him to go to work so far away?"

"He understands. I send money home every payday. You know how our town was. There's no decent work there. Teenagers don't care about much beyond their next meal and new pair of jeans. Leave the boy alone and I'll make sure you and me end up rich. He'll have a good education and will be well taken care of. He'll be better off if he never sees either of us again." She traced the heart outline with her fingertip. "Look at you, claiming you love me. If you mean it, prove it. Do this for me. Tommy doesn't need his father showing up now, he's doing fine without one."

"Maybe I have lost my fucking mind. I never should have gone to the tattoo parlor." He knew she was right about that, as much as he hated to admit it.

"I could give you another baby, if you're so hot to have a family." She rubbed against him.

"Are you kidding? I don't want a brat running around. I'm looking forward to adult fun and games." Leroy realized he meant that. He'd never wanted a family. Didn't want the responsibility or the ties that came with kids. He hated the fact that she'd hidden this boy, but it was probably for the best. He'd been free to live his life the way he wanted. No strings. Her family was decent, religious, and had surely done right by the boy. If it gave him a little pang that he'd missed something, well, that was just foolishness on his part.

"One thing, Ramona. I want you to promise me something." He didn't like being manipulated, and he'd make her pay for it, one way or another.

"What's that?" She was smart enough to look worried.

"I want Tommy to know my mom and grandmother. That he has more family. You can tell him I'm dead, I don't care. But this will tickle my mom to death. To look at that boy is like looking in the mirror. I broke her heart so many times, and you know it. She deserves a grandson she can be proud of. Tommy is a chance to give her something fine from me." He slid his hands around her neck.

"Lee, I don't know—"

He tightened his grip until she gasped. "I'm not asking, I'm telling. Promise, Ramona. You know my folks are good people. They deserved better than me. In fact, I'm calling my mother tonight and telling her that Tommy Delgado is my son. It's a small town, and I'm sure Ma knows your mother. She'll be able to track him down easily. It's out of your hands."

"Please don't." Her eyes filled with tears.

"'Please'. I like it when you beg. But I'm doing it. For the boy. So get used to the idea. Maybe make a call of your own." Leroy gave her neck a final warning squeeze before he leaned down to kiss her. She turned her head away. So what? He picked her up and carried her to the bed. Keeping something that big from him? She deserved to be punished. If she thought fucking Isaac Crane had been bad, she was going to find out that a pissed-off Leroy Thomas Simms was twenty times worse.

Then he heard her sob. Damn it, why did he have to love her? She sure as hell didn't love him, not and pull this kind of shit. He couldn't stand it, though, that sad sound. He held her until she settled down. They'd both been so young when they'd made Tommy. How could he blame her for a decision that had been so important? He could blame her for keeping it from him, though. She let him make slow love to her until she finally started kissing him back. But he knew she was thinking hard. He'd have to watch himself around her. She wasn't happy with him. And Ramona Delgado could be a dangerous woman.

Chapter Seventeen

Scarlett was walking the dog when her cell phone buzzed in her pocket. Mike was calling her.

"Tell me they finally captured Leroy Simms." She stopped while YoYo sniffed a likely bush.

"I wish I could. I do have some news, though."

"You sound serious. Why do I think this is bad news?" She saw that YoYo was finally finished and headed back toward her apartment. She'd feel safer inside with the door locked.

"We discovered that a condo near the courthouse had been broken into after Simms escaped. It took some doing, but we finally found DNA that proves he was using it as a hideout while the couple that lives there was out of town." Mike cleared his throat. "They just got back a couple of days ago. That means Simms has probably been hanging around Austin this entire time, Scarlett. He could still be close."

"Damn it." She fumbled her keys but finally got her door unlocked and stepped inside. Of course Rhett wasn't around. He was so into Casey that he'd booked a tattoo and had her doing that circle of flames around his bicep. It was ironic that her tough big brother was afraid of needles. What a man would do for love... *Focus.*

"We've kept up the patrols down Sixth Street."

"Yes, I noticed." She locked the door behind her and set the alarm. Scarlett couldn't believe she'd actually relaxed the past few days. With no sightings of the cop killer, it had been easy to believe that he was long gone. "I appreciate that."

"You still carrying the pepper spray?"

"Of course." She hadn't had it with her just now, though. Really, she should be safe in this apartment complex. Only her brother, Mike, and Ethan knew where she lived. Thank God she'd quit Zenon. "I'd planned to go out tonight with Ethan Calhoun, my new boss. He owns the bar next to Amuse Tattoos where I'm working now. We want to check out our competition before we open, but if you think I shouldn't go out, maybe I'll cancel."

"I wouldn't blame you if you did. I take it as a good sign, though, that Simms hasn't made a move on you in the week since the escape. Believe me, we've been watching your old apartment and Zenon for signs of him. So I hope that means he doesn't have you on his radar. His first priority has got to be to get out of town. He's obviously holing up, waiting for the manhunt to cool off so he can run. Could be transportation is an issue, or money. Still, the safest thing might be for you to stay in. Lie low. Your decision, of course." Mike was obviously in his car and the radio blasted a command. "Look, I've got to go. I told you this so you could stay on your toes. We found evidence that Simms took some casual clothes—shorts, Hawaiian shirts—from that apartment. Clearly he's changed his look. We're going through surveillance tapes at the condo building now, trying to find out what else he might have used as a disguise."

"Just what we need, Simms incognito. I could have run into him on the street and not even known it." Scarlett's stomach flipped. God, she had seen a man in a gaudy shirt recently. But no way could he be Knife Guy. He'd looked nothing like him. Great, now anyone she saw in a floral print shirt would be on her personal suspect list. This was going to drive her crazy.

She glanced at her kitchen clock. If she was going out, she needed to get moving. It would be too cowardly to cancel just because her stomach was in a knot and her imagination was running worst-case scenarios in her head. Besides, she really wanted to see Ethan. And those bars.

"If you do go out, keep your eyes open. If you think you see him, call 9-1-1. Whatever you do, don't try to confront the bastard. Don't let Ethan try that, either. We know how dangerous Simms is."

"Got it." Scarlett realized Mike had ended the call. She probably should have told him that Ethan had a handgun. But he wouldn't bring it tonight. It was against the law to take a handgun into a bar in Texas, even with a permit. Ethan had explained that to her days ago.

She wasn't going to overreact to Mike's news. Simms wouldn't go to a trendy bar. She'd calm her nerves by concentrating on the evening ahead. She wanted to look special for Ethan. She had thought about running to the closest mall and buying a new dress, something short and flirty. Why the hell not? Leroy Simms wouldn't hang out in a woman's dress shop in a busy mall, either. She grabbed her car keys and unlocked her front door again. The alarm blared, making her jump. Stupid. She quickly turned it off, then answered the ringing phone. She gave her password, then assured the operator that it had been her own dumb mistake that had set off the alarm. It was reassuring that the alarm company was on the ball. She refused to turn back into a scared little girl. New dress, fresh coat of paint on her nails, and something different with her hair were the plans for the day. Scarlett smiled as she ran down the stairs to her car. She wanted to knock Ethan right out of his Gucci loafers.

* * * *

"You took long enough to get here." Ethan had been pacing the floor in the bar, waiting for his mother and Lisa. He'd texted Albert, and they'd decided that this might be the time and place to capture the women and get this over with. Unfortunately, nothing seemed to come together. Rex the plumber had shown up with an unexpected delivery along with his crew to install the parts. So there went the intervention. And now Albert had let him know that the crew he would need to make sure Mama and Lisa got transported back to the mental hospital wasn't going to be available until tomorrow anyway.

"We wanted to take the clothes back to the motel, Ethan. And you won't believe what happened when we got there." Mama told him how they'd lost their room at the Longhorn. Luckily their new friend Albert had found another motel for all of them since he'd had to move too. While she'd shared all of this, she reached for the bourbon. "I need a drink. Lisa?"

"Sure." Lisa waved at Rex and his men. "I see the hunks are back. Working on a Saturday. That's overtime, Ethan."

"I want to open soon, so I'm willing to pay it." Ethan frowned at his mother. "Are you developing a drinking problem, Mama? Every time you come in here, you go straight for the booze."

"Well, what if I do like a drink now and then?" She poured herself a double, then one for Lisa. "Maybe I'm coming down from all those drugs they pumped into me at the hospital." Mama sniffed. "I felt drunk half the time. I'm pretty sure they did that so I wouldn't cause trouble."

"You're probably right." Ethan didn't like the sound of that. But he remembered Mama's mood swings and her horrific tantrums. It would be tempting to control her with a cocktail of tranquilizers. "You got therapy too, didn't you?"

"Ha! If you can call sitting in a circle whining about how bad life treated you, therapy." Mama sipped her drink. "I'm telling you, son. They used drugs to turn us into zombies. So they wouldn't have to deal with us. Can you understand now why I had to get out of there?"

"I'm sorry. If you end up back there, I'll—"

"Shut up! I'm never going back." She slammed her glass down on the bar. "You can't make me." Her eyes were wild. "Tell him, Lisa. We won't go back. I'd rather die than be treated like that again."

"She's right." Lisa strolled around the bar and picked up the bottle of bourbon. She splashed more into both of their glasses. "If you're thinking of a double cross, Ethan, think again. Missy's right. We won't go back." Her eyes were hard. "You hear me?"

"Relax. Did I say anything about forcing the issue? I got you here to take your pictures. You both look great. Let's find a spot with a plain background and get this over with." Ethan gestured to where the drywall had been replaced but not painted yet. "Here's good."

"Freshen your lipstick, Missy." Lisa handed his mother her purse. "Ethan, are you just going to use your phone for the pictures? Will that work for the passports?"

"Sure, why not? It's not like I'm going to the official passport office. The guy who is doing this said to email him the photos." He waited while Lisa renewed her own red lipstick. He hadn't been lying about one thing. They both looked good, especially Lisa. Her hair had been lightened, and she wore a red knit top that made her skin glow. His mother waited her turn, fluffing her hair until she was satisfied that she looked her best. Then they had to check out the photos, carefully deleting any they didn't like.

They began to gather their things to leave when there was a pounding on the door.

"Who the hell is that?" Lisa ran to the window and pulled back one edge of the heavy drapery. "Holy shit! It's a big black cop. Ethan, what have you done?"

"We could go out the back." Mama grabbed her purse.

"Wait! He could have a partner covering it." Lisa pulled a gun out of her purse. "Ethan, get rid of him."

Ethan backed away from her. "Where did you get a gun, Lisa?"

"Never mind that. I said get rid of him." She waved the gun at him.

"I didn't call the cops. Just stay quiet and out of sight. And for God's sake, put that gun away." He looked around. At least the plumber and his crew were still in the bathroom with the door closed. "I'll see what he wants. Go into my office." He gestured at it.

"I'm going to be listening to every word you say. And the gun stays out." Lisa kept it pointed at him.

"Lisa, stop that. My son is not going to turn us in." Missy moved to stand right beside her. "I didn't pay for that gun for you to use it on him. What if one of the plumbers sees you with it? They'll know we're guilty of something."

Ethan wasn't surprised Mama had bought the gun. Of course she had. What surprised him was that she wasn't the one holding it. At least she was backing him in this. "Relax, both of you. I'm going to step outside. I'll leave the door cracked so you can hear me. But be ready to get in the office if he needs to come in for some reason." More pounding on the door.

"Coming!" Ethan shouted as he threw the dead bolt. Yes, it was a large black Texas Ranger, complete with cowboy hat. "How can I help you, Officer?"

"Are you Ethan Calhoun?" The man stepped back when Ethan moved outside and kept the door almost closed behind him.

"Yes, I am. This is my bar, but we're not open yet." Ethan smiled. "I'd invite you in, but they're doing work in here and it's pretty noisy. Dusty, too." Thank God the plumbers cooperated, banging on some pipes just then.

"That's okay. I'm Mike Taylor, a Texas Ranger. I'm actually here as a friend of Scarlett Hall. She said she works for you." The man was big and intimidating, even though he was smiling as he held out his hand.

Ethan shook that hand, glad the handshake didn't turn into one of those tests of strength. "Nice to meet you. Have you been working on the cop killer case? She told me all about Leroy Simms and her ordeal. She's sure been upset that the man is still on the loose."

"We all are upset, to put it mildly. That's why I'm here." Mike leaned against the stone façade next to the door.

Damn it, Ethan should be able to invite Mike in, offer him a cold drink. He was glad this big man, who exuded confidence, was looking out for Scarlett. But of course Ethan could almost feel Lisa breathing on the other side of the door. It wouldn't take much to push the volatile woman over the edge. Cop killer. He didn't doubt Lisa could turn into one if she lost her temper.

"Any leads on Simms and his whereabouts?"

"We found evidence that he's been hiding here in the city, not that far away as a matter of fact. In a downtown condo. Apparently he's developed some kind of disguise. If he's looking to start a new life somewhere, I'm pretty sure he needs more money than what he could get from the few things he stole from that condo. He might have a source for cash here or is looking for one. We checked for known associates in the area and came up empty." Mike rested one hand on his holster. "I've warned Scarlett's boss at Zenon and he's surrounded by armed guards. I'd say he or his daughter would be the most likely targets if kidnapping for ransom was Simms's next play."

"You think he'd take Scarlett? Try to squeeze money out of her? Or because she taunted him when he was captured?" Ethan realized his gun was upstairs on the kitchen counter. A lot of good it would do him there. Then again, what would have happened if he'd pulled it out and confronted Lisa? A standoff? Or would one of them have ended up dead or wounded?

"It would be a stupid move. But I wouldn't put anything past him. She just told me you two are planning to go out tonight." Mike was studying him, sizing him up.

"You think she should stay in? I want her to be safe." He looked the Ranger in the eyes. He'd never meant anything more.

"I'd like her to stay in hiding. I know Scarlett is scared of Simms, and for good reason. He threatened her once, but he's got much bigger problems now than revenge for her testimony against him or a few taunts. He needs a way out of town. Scarlett's just a working woman, not someone he could tap for the kind of big bucks he'd need to start a new life. But I wanted you to be aware of the potential danger to her in case she decides to go out anyway. She has this puny canister of pepper spray." Mike shook his head. "Thinks that makes her a badass."

"By the time she got it aimed, he'd have her on the ground." Ethan shoved his hands in his pockets, pretty sure they were shaking at the thought of Scarlett facing off against a knife-wielding monster like Simms.

"Exactly." Mike leaned in. "I'm hoping you will take protecting her seriously. Not that I want you to do my job. Just keep your eyes open when you're together. Stay alert to your surroundings, things like that."

"I get it. I don't want to take Simms on, certainly not with Scarlett right there in the middle of things. Give me your number. If I think she's being followed, see anything suspicious, I'll let you know." Ethan took the card the Ranger handed him. "Thanks. I have a permit to carry concealed, but we're going into bars." Ethan knew why it wasn't wise to take a gun into a place that sold alcohol, but it was damn inconvenient under these circumstances.

"Good to know." Mike glanced up and down the street. "Not a bad idea to keep it close when you're not bar hopping. No law officer would blame you if you put a bullet in Simms. I'm pretty sure Scarlett would recognize him if she saw him, even disguised. But always call 9-1-1 first if you think you see him. I'd never ask a man not sworn to do it, to take on a bad actor like Simms, and I'm not asking you to do it now. He's damn dangerous."

"I appreciate that, Mike." Ethan heard a crash from inside the bar. "I'll be sure to keep my eyes open tonight and every time I'm with Scarlett." He pulled out his own business card. "Can you email me the picture you have of Simms? I want to refresh my memory. In case we do happen to come across him. Since you say he might still be downtown."

"Sure will." Mike told him about the stolen clothes. "He could have taken those things to throw us off. I don't know. Just stay close to her. Simms threw out a lot of threats when he was arrested, some of them aimed at Scarlett. I dismiss most of that as tough talk, but I'd rather be safe than sorry. Know what I mean?"

"I sure do." Ethan clasped Mike's hand. "Hawaiian shirt and shorts. Funny. We saw a guy like that yesterday. Right across the street. But then there are people like that everywhere with the weather heating up. Not a bad notion for a disguise."

"No one ever said Simms was stupid. That's the problem. It's made him hard to catch. But we'll get him." Mike took off his cowboy hat and wiped his forehead, then looked across the street. "Was it near those condos? He broke into one condominium, so it might be a pattern of his."

"Yes. But this guy was bald. I remember Simms as having a full head of dark hair." Ethan heard another crash. "I'd better get back in there. So far this construction crew has been a good one. But every crash sounds like money to me."

"Nice to meet you, Ethan. Scarlett is special to me." Mike gave him another searching look. "Just so you know."

"Why is that?" Ethan sized up the man. "You must meet a lot of victims in your line of work."

"Too many." Mike straightened to his full height, which was intimidating as hell. "I walked her through what she assured me was the worst day of her life. Saw her fall apart, then pull herself back together again like a real trouper. I admire her guts."

"That all there is to it?" Ethan stood his ground when Mike seemed to loom over him.

"I'm married, bud. There's nothing between us but a friendship. Her best friend is marrying my best friend in a few months. We'll both be connected then. Forever, if our pals are lucky. You got any more questions?" He stopped short of poking Ethan in the chest, but he seemed like he wanted to do it.

"No, I'm good. Just want to say, Scarlett's special to me too." Ethan held out his hand. To his relief, Mike shook it again. Then he watched the Ranger cross the street, jaywalking. Not that anyone would dare say a word to the huge man who looked like he could bench-press a Toyota.

"Is he gone?" Lisa grabbed the back of Ethan's shirt and pulled him back inside.

"Obviously." Ethan shut the door behind him. "What was all that noise?"

"Your mama is having one of her fits. Can you calm her down?" Lisa glanced at the bar. Shattered glasses littered the floor around it. "Sometimes I wonder why I decided to tie myself to her."

"Feel free to move on, anytime." Ethan knew she'd never let go of his mother's money. Lisa didn't say a word, just frowned when his mother picked up another glass and hurled it to the floor. "What set her off?" Ethan had been a witness to plenty of these temper tantrums. Something had pushed Mama over the edge.

"Everything. Nothing. She's your mother. Deal with her." Lisa had the gun out of sight, but she clutched her purse like it might be in there.

Ethan walked over to his mother and put his arm around her. She'd quit throwing things and started sobbing, leaning into his shoulder.

"Ethan, I'm so sorry." She held on to him. "I never should have brought that bitch into this."

"Now, Mama, what's got you in such a state?" Ethan glared at Lisa. Her smile made him pick up an empty tumbler and make a show of aiming it at her. She ducked, which pleased him even though he didn't throw it. Mama was right. What a stone-cold bitch.

"She threatened you." Mama shuddered. "Here you helped us, financed us, and she would just shoot you down? You know she would."

"Oh, get over it, Missy. I put the gun away. You know you'd never have escaped from that hospital without me, so stop your whining." Lisa stomped to the back door. "Let's get out of here. Albert texted me the address of that new motel. You want to risk losing another room?"

"Treat my mother right, Lisa, or you won't get a passport. You hear me? Or another damn dime." Ethan handed his mother a dish towel so she could wipe her eyes. "Mama, you don't have to go with her if you don't want to. I can find you a place by yourself."

His mother pushed away from him. "No, I'm okay now." She stared at Lisa. "Promise me you won't do that again. Aim a gun at Ethan. He's our ticket out of here. And my precious boy. You hear me?"

"Loud and clear. Sorry, Ethan. Missy isn't the only one with a temper, you know." Lisa had obviously remembered where the money was coming from. She frowned when more banging came from the bathroom. "Now, let's go. We've said enough with those hunky workers nearby. I realize now that I never should have pulled my weapon out around them. That was stupid." She held out her hand. "Come on, Missy. Albert says the new motel is next door to a nice restaurant and he's buying."

"I hope it's better than the last one. I'm sick of steak." Missy threw down the towel and picked up her purse. "Steak tough as shoe leather anyway."

"It's a seafood place. I've got a craving for fried shrimp. What do you say?"

"Yes! Or crab cakes. Now you're talking." Missy hurried to the door, suddenly in a good mood again. She stopped. "Wait. What did the cop want? Did he ask about us?"

Lisa smiled before Ethan could answer. "It sounded to me like your baby boy has a new girlfriend. The cop is a friend of hers. Right, Ethan?"

"Really? You have a girlfriend?" Mama was excited. "Tell me about her."

"She's my new manager, not really a girlfriend. I'm just getting to know her." Ethan couldn't count the number of women who'd been scared off by his mother's interference and wild mood swings. What would Scarlett think about his current family situation? He didn't want to test their new relationship by sharing any of this yet.

"I hope she's good to you." Mama kissed his cheek. "You deserve a nice girl." She sighed, then headed for the door. "Now, you be sure to call when you have our passports ready. Put a rush on them." She waved and was gone.

Ethan slumped against the bar. He should be used to dealing with his mother by now, but it always took a toll. Would she ever be well again? He remembered times as a child when Missy had been warm, loving, like his friends' mothers. Then Daddy had started neglecting her and … Hell, it would be easy to blame others for Mama's problems. Fact was, she had made everyone around her miserable for years. There could be no quick fix for that.

He got out a broom and swept up broken glass. It wasn't the first time he'd had to clean up after one of his mother's spells, but he hoped to God it would be the last.

Chapter Eighteen

"Right on time and dressed up. I like what I see." Scarlett looked Ethan up and down. He was so handsome in gray pants, a white silk shirt, and black blazer. Yes, he had on those Gucci loafers and no socks. Was any man sexier? Not that she could remember.

"You look beautiful." Ethan pulled Scarlett in and kissed her. "You smell good, too."

"She's clearly trying to impress you. Don't disappoint her." Rhett came out of his bedroom with a suitcase. "Sorry, am I interrupting?"

"You are, but that's okay. We can pick up again as soon as you leave." Scarlett laughed at the look on her brother's face. "What time is your flight?"

"I've got a couple of hours." He sat in the middle of the couch. "Time enough to play big brother if necessary."

"You want a financial statement? Or how about a copy of the contract promising I won't fire your sister if this relationship goes south? I've already got my lawyer working on that." Ethan kept his arms around Scarlett. If he was intimidated by Rhett's big brother act, he didn't show it.

"Both of those will be fine. I'll expect them to hit my in-box by the time I get back from Houston." Rhett grinned. "Quit staring daggers at me, Ladybug."

Scarlett eased out of Ethan's arms. "And you quit being a jerk. I'm too old for you to pull this crap." She did like the fact that Ethan was following through on that contract, though. "Surely you didn't make your lawyer work on a weekend." She looked up at her boss, who also happened to be her very hot lover.

"He's my brother-in-law. My sister just gave him a son. He'll do whatever makes her happy. Right now, she owes me for handling the family drama

I've told you about, Scarlett. He'll go into his office tomorrow and draw up that contract if I tell him to rush it." Ethan slid his arm around her waist again, then looked down. "Who is this ball of fur jumping around my feet?"

"That's YoYo. I'm going to have to be home tonight to make sure he's taken out later." Scarlett liked the possessiveness of his arm pulling her closer, but of course he hadn't told her a damn thing about his family drama, except that it was ongoing. "He's just visiting for a few weeks. He belongs to my best friend, who is in Boston for a family visit. If we come here after the bars close, that'll work."

"Last night I took care of him"—Rhett leaned forward, elbows on his knees—"since my sister didn't come home." He frowned. "I hope you two are practicing—"

"Rhett!" Scarlett was mortified. "That's enough. Go pick up Casey. Does her brother hassle you like this when you two sleep over?"

"Sure. Where do you think I got the idea?" Rhett stood and collected his small suitcase. "Relax, Ethan. I'm enjoying watching my sister's face turn red."

"Did she tell you that guy who cut her is probably still in town?" Ethan glanced at Scarlett's cheeks.

"Wait. Simms is still in Austin?" Rhett dropped his suitcase and grabbed Scarlett's arm.

"Mike seems to think so. They recently found evidence that he'd been hiding downtown." She deliberately hadn't told Rhett. He had a book signing in Houston, and she didn't want him to cancel it.

"I can stay if you're afraid to be alone here." Her brother let go of her, but he was frowning. "I can always reschedule the signing."

"No, I'll be fine. Mike doesn't think Simms has any interest in me."

"I'd be happy to stay here tonight. If that suits Scarlett." Ethan glanced at Rhett.

"How are you going to protect her if she needs you?" Rhett picked up the dog, who was whining at their serious tones. "For all I know, you have about as much killer instinct as this mutt here."

Ethan reached out for the dog, who was happy to come to him and snuggle. "You don't know me. I sure as hell don't know you. But I have a handgun and can shoot the head off a rattlesnake from a hundred yards away." He ruffled the dog's fur.

"We're not expecting rattlesnakes, Calhoun." Rhett did look impressed. "Question is, how do you feel about taking on this asshole who hurt my sister?"

"I grew up hunting. I love dogs and women. Hate bastards like Simms, who maimed Scarlett just to be cruel. Frankly, I think an asshole like that needs to be put down and put down hard." Ethan suddenly had a Texas twang in his voice as he set the dog on the floor and reached for Scarlett. "I'll be honest with you, Rhett. I've never shot a man, but if he comes after someone I care about? Well, I wouldn't hesitate to blow him to hell. How about you?"

"I feel the same." Rhett held out his hand. "I'll leave Scarlett with you then. Let's hope you have nothing to worry about."

"Good grief. Would you two stop this?" Scarlett was set aside while the men shook hands like they were sealing a deal. What? To guard her with their lives? Dear God, it had better not come to that.

"I have something to say about this." Scarlett liked the fact that the two men she cared about had come to some kind of understanding, but seriously? "We're going bar hopping. End of story. Then if I want him, I'll bring Ethan back here. If I'm not in the mood, I'm perfectly capable of locking myself in this apartment and sleeping alone. I've done it for a long, long time."

"Yeah, yeah. Big talk from a big girl. Let us pound our chests if we want to, Scar. But, in the mood or not, just promise me you'll take no chances." Rhett kissed her cheek.

"Oh, good grief. You know I won't."

"Okay, then. I'm going. Casey is probably already standing in front of the tattoo parlor waiting. I never saw anyone so punctual. No, scratch that. The woman is always early. Drives me crazy." He picked up his suitcase again. "We'll be back Monday night. Unless…"

"No, go ahead and stay that extra day. Explore Houston. You know you're going to put something from there into your book." Scarlett handed him the case that held his laptop. With Casey along, she doubted he would do a lick of work, but he always took it with him. "Have fun! Don't worry about me. I'll be fine."

"She will be." Ethan held the door open, closing and locking it as soon as Rhett stepped outside. "He'll be gone two nights?"

"Yes." Scarlett walked into the kitchen to make sure YoYo had plenty of kibble and water. "You really don't have to babysit me, Ethan."

"I wouldn't call it babysitting. Not with what I have in mind." He stood behind her and ran his hands around then up to cup her breasts. "Did I tell you how beautiful you look tonight?"

"I believe you did." She sighed and leaned against him. "I don't mind hearing it again." She'd bought the first dress she'd seen because it had been perfect. Deep blue, low cut with a short full skirt, it had fit right and was on sale. Then she'd found some fun sparkly earrings that Ethan was currently making swing with his tongue. "Mmm. Don't you dare mess up my makeup. We're leaving here and going to those bars. No detours to the bedroom."

"Are you sure? You know you wore this dress to get me stirred up. Mike paid me a visit today. Despite what you just said about Simms having a different agenda, he thinks we should stay in. Keep you safe. I could enjoy that." He ran the zipper down the back and slid a hand inside.

"I'm not letting you, both of you, make me a prisoner in my own home."

"Even if there are perks?" Ethan pushed the short sleeves down her arms so the bodice fell forward. "I love this kind of underwear, lacy and barely there, isn't it?" He turned her so he could look her over.

"Quit trying to distract me." He was right, of course. She'd pulled out a midnight blue set that she'd paid big bucks for. Totally worth it. He hummed his appreciation when he bent to kiss the slope of her breast exposed by the deep vee.

"I think it's working. Yeah, this is what I love. Open the bra clasp and it's like opening a present." He eased the top of the dress down to her waist, slipped the bra open with an expert hand, then grinned when her breasts popped free. "There. Absolutely perfect." He leaned down to kiss one nipple, pulling it into the heat of his mouth while he toyed with the other, his fingers clever and driving her crazy.

"God, Ethan, you are a wicked man. Keep going." Scarlett held him close, her fingers in his hair. She shivered at the pleasure pulsing through her. Her knees almost gave way. How long could she stand there when he was making her melt? If she lifted her skirt and dragged his hand where she wanted it…

"Nope. I'm taking you at your word. You say you want to prove you're not scared. So we need to go out. You have your own agenda. Plans for this evening that some murderous asshole is not going to spoil." He let her go. "We have to hit those bars and check out the competition. I can't disappoint my manager, who is doing such an excellent job." He carefully pulled the bra closed and fastened it. Then he lifted the dress back into place, turning her so he could zip her up again. "Unless you've changed your mind?"

Damn him, he looked calm and unaffected while she was shaky with need. Scarlett moved closer, pressing against him. Yes, he wanted her too. But he was willing to wait. She had to admire that, even though she was really, really tempted to drag him to her bedroom and have her way with him, agenda be damned. Hmm. Maybe he was bluffing, hoping she'd change her mind and stay in.

"Nope. A little anticipation never hurt anyone. Know what I mean?" She trailed her hand across his chest as she brushed past him, then walked to the bathroom, where she glanced in the mirror. Color high and her lipstick was long gone. She grabbed a tube of pink out of a drawer and slapped it on, then fetched her evening bag from her bedroom. Ethan was in the living room, talking to YoYo, who sat in his lap and looked up at him with doggy adoration.

"I tell you, my man, I cannot pretend to understand women. I can see someone evil fixed you so you'll never have the pleasure of really being with one." Ethan rubbed the dog's ears. "I'm sorry for you, pal. Because making love with the right woman can be heaven on earth. I'm just finding that out." He fell back on the couch and stared at the ceiling. "I'd better keep her safe or I'll never forgive myself. Because I have plans, bud. Let's hope I don't screw this up. Know what I mean? Shit. Guess not."

Scarlett leaned against the door and took a shuddery breath. He hoped *he* didn't screw this up? God. If only she could be the right woman for Ethan Calhoun. Because he kept doing things that were making her fall for him—sweet-talking the dog, standing tall like he'd risk his life to protect her. But he never told her what to do. He let her decide. Like tonight. Respecting her need to go out and face her fears.

Then there was what happened when he touched her. Being with him felt way too real and precious. Special. She had to hope that nothing would happen tonight to ruin what could be the best thing to ever come into her life.

Chapter Nineteen

"That's right, Ma, you have a grandson." Leroy could understand why his mother was having a hard time with this. He was still working through it himself. He'd made Ramona send those pictures to his phone so he could look at them again. Yeah, the boy was the spitting image of him at that age.

"Leroy, you know that girl was wild back then." Ma was afraid to hope. "Could be someone else's boy. If she's trying to get you to pay support—"

"It's not like that, Ma. She knows I'm in no position to have anything to do with the boy. Not after what I done. I'm sending you some pictures. Look at them on your computer. You'll see Tommy has to be mine." Leroy knew his mother's email address. Had used it to keep in touch with her over the years. Did Ramona think she was the only one sending money back home? He'd taken care of his ma and Gran. It was the least he could do. It sure wasn't their fault he'd turned to crime. They'd spent every Sunday in the Baptist church, praying he'd "straighten out" ever since his first run-in with the law. The fact that Tommy had been raised Catholic wouldn't set well with them. Too late to fix that.

"If you say so, Leroy. I'm so worried about you. We see the news down here. And there have been cops by asking about you." His mother sniffed, probably crying now. "I told them I didn't hear from you. I understand why you couldn't call before. Running, aren't you?" Now she sobbed. "Boy, why did you have to go and kill a cop? You know what they'll do to you?"

"I'm sorry, Ma. That this hurts you. I had to do it. They were locking me up. I can't—" Leroy took a breath. Not even Ma knew how those tight places made him crazy. "Well, I just lost it when they were dragging me back in chains. I'm not going back inside, I tell you that right now. If I get caught, I won't let them take me alive."

"Leroy! Don't talk like that!" Ma sobbed, and he couldn't calm her down.

He waited until he thought she could hear him. "Now, listen, Ma. I've got plans. I'll be coming into some big money soon so I can leave the country. I can send you a little right away. More later. You won't see me again, but don't worry. I'll be living large where cops won't be able to find me."

"Leroy, you're my only child. Never see you again? You sure that's what you have to do?" She just kept crying.

"It's that or the needle. Death row. That's where cop killers go, and you know it." Leroy waited out her wails of grief again. Damn it. He'd broken her heart for sure. Probably shouldn't have called her, but he wanted her to know her grandson. "Ma. Calm down. Remember why I called in the first place."

She finally pulled herself together enough to speak. "I'll look up the boy, this Tommy Delgado. If he's yours, I'll love him and make sure he knows you wanted him to know us. That he has more family. And that we're good people. Right, son?"

"Yes, Ma. You and Gran tell the boy I just found out about him. Ramona held that secret all these years." Leroy heard the cheap phone crack in his hand.

"Don't come here, no matter what, Leroy. Like I said, cops have been sniffing around us. Oh, son, I wish I could give you a hug. So does Gran. I know it."

"Listen, I got to go. If those cops come around again, you never heard from me."

"I know, Leroy. Please, please be careful. I love you. I wish Gran was here to tell you good-bye, but it's her bingo night. Can you call back again? Maybe when you get where you're going?" Her voice was shaking so bad Leroy had to strain to hear her.

"I'll try, Ma. I love you, too. Both of you. Thanks for everything you did over the years. I'm sorry I hurt you. It was sure nothin' you did, so don't go blamin' yourself for how I turned out. You hear me?"

"I've prayed on it, Leroy. I ask the Lord what I did wrong." She said it softly, her voice breaking.

"None of that now. I guess I'm what you call a bad seed. Can't seem to help myself. You want to cast blame, put it on my old man. That son of a bitch ran out on us, but not before he made sure I felt his fist and his belt." Oh, shit. This was sounding like a pity party. "Never mind that ancient history. I've got to go. You take care now. I'll send money through the usual channel. Right away." He ended the call before he started crying like a fucking baby. He stared down at the phone, tempted to throw it across the room. But he didn't have another one.

God, he couldn't believe he'd dragged up his daddy, that worthless piece of shit. Now Ma would be thinking she never should have married him. Put the blame on herself again. Maybe he could lay some of this at her door. Why did women have kids with mean bastards? Of course that was exactly what Ramona had done, wasn't it? Damn it to hell. No wonder she'd never told him about the kid. If he had been around the boy, who's to say he wouldn't have lost it like his old man had and walloped the kid?

Leroy dug in his pocket and counted his money. Ramona had been stingy, but he could send Mama a hundred right now. The liquor store had Western Union, and she'd pick up the money at the Piggly Wiggly, just like she always did. He checked the clock. He had fifteen minutes before they closed. If he hustled, he could make it. It was dark outside, a good time to go out on the street and blend in with all the folks hitting the bars and restaurants on a Saturday night. No one would give him a second glance.

He changed clothes, putting on the white dress shirt he'd stolen from the condo closet. The fool living there probably hadn't even noticed it was gone with more than a dozen just like it. Same thing with the dark pants. This outfit and a ball cap left behind by Isaac Crane gave him a new look, and that was what he was after. He'd also sprouted enough beard that Ramona had trimmed it into a neat goatee along with his mustache to make him look like a fucking pirate. She thought it was hot. He wasn't sure about that, but again, a new disguise was all right with him.

He strode across the street like he didn't have a care in the world. Inside the store he picked up cigs and a bottle of Jose Cuervo, then arranged to send the money. The clerk barely glanced at him, eager to count his till as the clock edged toward closing time. Back outside, Leroy sniffed the air. Steak was sizzling on a grill somewhere nearby, he could tell. Damn it, he wanted a decent dinner. Would it be risking his life to wander into a trendy restaurant and order a rib eye? But he didn't have enough money left to pay for it, or even a burger. Shit.

He pulled out his phone. "Where the hell are you?"

"Why? You missing me?" Ramona obviously wasn't taking him seriously.

"I'm sick of frozen dinners. Pick up some decent takeout and bring me more cash. You got an hour." He was starting to cross the street when a police car drove up. The cop inside gave him a good look, right in the eyes. Leroy ended the call and stopped. Yeah, he'd almost crossed against the light. The cop drove on, slowly. Nice to know the disguise had held up. The light changed, and Leroy walked back to his building.

The roar of a powerful engine drew him down the steps to the parking garage. Damn it, he needed wheels. The yellow Porsche that usually sat there was gone, and there was no sign of Scarlett Hall or her boyfriend. He'd seen them that one night, run into them on the street. Man, he'd itched to use his knife. But he knew better. He had to stay hidden awhile longer, and all the cops cruising up and down the street told him they had eyes on the Hall bitch.

The car coming into the garage was an expensive SUV, black with deeply tinted windows and fully loaded. While he watched, it stopped and a big man got out. The guy walked over to a gleaming Harley and backed it out of a parking spot. Then he jumped into the SUV, pulled it into the now empty space, and locked it.

Interesting. The man wore leathers and looked all biker. He stuck a helmet on his head before he started the Harley with a roar that made Leroy hard with envy. He'd never owned such a prime machine but had always wanted one. Damn it, with a little planning, maybe he could take down the big guy and make that Harley his own. But he'd come out without much more than the little knife. Ramona needed to bring him a gun, or at least a better knife. He just stood at the bottom of the steps and watched while the guy drove away. The garage still echoed with the sound of the powerful engine long after the biker drove away.

What the hell was he thinking? He couldn't pull a job like that now. Once he was away from here with millions of dollars, he could buy a dozen bikes. Porsches too. Yeah, he had to keep his eye on the long game. Leroy walked back up the steps and looked across the street. Still no sign of that looker Scarlett Hall. And no sign of Ramona. She drove a decent but ordinary white compact car that would probably have to serve to get them out of town. Soon. He was getting antsy.

The only thing holding them in town now were his fake papers. Ramona kept putting him off, telling him they weren't ready. Well, maybe he needed to get rough with her again. Because he'd had enough of hiding. Time to make a move before sheer boredom had him doing something stupid, like using his knife on someone just so he could ride a Harley and taunt the cops. Man, would that feel good. He ran back upstairs before he could give in to foolish urges. Eyes on the prize. He was too close to having everything he wanted to give in to bloodlust now.

Chapter Twenty

By the time they hit their third secret bar, Ethan had decided a couple of things. First, he was with the right woman. Scarlett was fun, beautiful, and never missed a detail. He saw her get out her phone again as they left the tiny place hidden behind a hotel in the middle of downtown Austin. She was taking notes by talking into a recording app. She'd also snapped pictures of the setup when she had the chance. Clever girl.

His note was that he fucking hated secret bars. Too bad that was going to cause a problem between him and his manager. A big problem. He walked beside her, keeping his eyes open for assholes with knives as they headed for his car. Scarlett was relaxed after three cocktails, and he was glad of that. She clearly trusted him to protect her. Would she still be happy with him after he shared his thoughts about their evening?

"What did you think of the last one?" She was so excited about the bar business, she almost danced in her high heels. The shoes along with her short skirt made her legs look a mile long, though he knew they weren't. But the effect was sexy. He'd had to glare at more than one guy who thought she might be fair game. No way in hell.

"Too small. And the drinks were weak. We sure won't try to pull that shit at Fuel. Customers won't return when they think they're overcharged for weak drinks. Which we were. And what was with that cart? I had to fight my way down the aisle when I went to the john. Seemed like a fire code violation to me." Ethan knew he sounded surly. But seriously? The setup had reminded him of those serving carts in an airplane. The waiters had even dressed like flight attendants. Considering how bad airline service was lately—peanuts, anyone?—he thought it was a dumb idea. Then they mixed your drink right there when they took your order, trying to hide the fact that the pour was light. That routine made it a problem if they didn't have what you asked for on hand. They didn't even stock his favorite brand of top-shelf bourbon. He was never landing there again, that was for sure.

"The concept was neat, but the execution was bad. You're right. The place was too small. No food, either. Pretzels don't count, even if they were some exotic flavor that tasted like they'd been dipped in mustard or cayenne pepper. Those choices were so obviously designed to make us thirsty so we'd order more drinks. Did you see the waiter's face when I asked for water?" She frowned, then spoke into her recorder as Ethan stopped and unlocked the car.

"That's why I hired the chef I did. I want people to linger. Enjoy the food, the music and drink too. He's assured me his bites are cheap to make but will go for top dollar." He leaned her against the car. "Guess what I want sounds more like a club, not just a bar."

"Full service, nothing wrong with that." She smiled up at him, running her hand over his shirt. "This was fun." Scarlett looked up and down the street, seemed to realize how dark it was, and her smile disappeared. "Guess we'd better go. It's getting late. Parking here is like every place downtown. A nightmare." They'd had to leave the car more than a block from the bar, and it wasn't under a streetlight.

Ethan gave up the idea of leaning in for a kiss and reached around her so he could unlock and open the car door. He helped her in. "It'll be the same for Fuel. Nothing I can do about that. People get off to fighting for parking spaces. It makes them think they're getting into the coolest bars if they have to walk a mile to get there and it's crowded as hell." Ethan enjoyed the flash of thigh as she settled into the low bucket seat. "Are we done now? Seen enough?"

"There's one more…" She looked up at him and smiled again. "Never mind. I can tell you've reached your limit."

"Thank you!" He slammed the car door and ran around to get in the driver's seat. "I'm sure YoYo's ready for a walk anyway. Think he'll do his business for me?" He started the car and locked the doors.

She leaned over and kissed his cheek. "After that male bonding I heard going on? I'm sure he'll do whatever you ask."

Ethan faced her. "You heard." He tried to remember what he'd said. Something stupid about the dog being fixed and… Distraction time. He leaned over and kissed her. Sweet and even better than he remembered. She held on to him and sighed into his mouth. Oh, man, did he wish they were already back at her place. Someone tapped on his window. He pulled back.

"What the hell?" He rolled down the window.

"You leaving? My boyfriend's trying to park." A woman stood there, obviously ready to hit the bar down the street.

"Sure. Move so I don't hit you. We're leaving now." Ethan maneuvered out of the space, ignoring the woman's wave and shouted thank-you.

"Popular place." Scarlett's hand landed on Ethan's zipper. "Just relax. We don't have far to go."

"What are you doing?" Ethan felt cool air on his cock, then her warm hand there. "Scarlett?" He needed to shift gears but her arm was in the way.

"I told you to relax." She moved so he could shift gears. "Is that better?"

Ethan couldn't think. Better? She'd managed to adjust her seat, sliding it back so she could put her body between… holy shit! Her mouth touched his cock and he almost ran a red light.

"God in heaven." He prayed the light stayed red for a long time while he gripped the steering wheel with one hand, the gearshift knob in his other hand so tightly his knuckles turned white.

"Mmm."

The light changed and the car behind him honked when he didn't move. So he shifted gears again, doing it from memory because he sure as hell couldn't figure out what made the car go forward or how he was driving without plowing into the sidewalk.

"Scarlett, stop or I'm going to kill us." He sounded like he was being strangled. Maybe he was. The woman was evil and wonderful and he could swear his eyes were crossing. Automatic transmission. Why the hell hadn't he taken back his SUV with the automatic transmission away from Albert?

She popped up and was suddenly sitting in her own bucket seat again, a devilish grin on her face. "Why, Ethan Calhoun, I thought you had more self-control than that." She reached over, carefully tucked him in, and zipped him up. "Sorry if I underestimated you."

"You will pay for this." Ethan shifted into second, then third, was into fourth and risking a ticket as he sped toward her apartment. When they got to her gate, he punched in the code from memory. She took forever to take care of her extreme security and all those dead bolts at her door while he watched. She just smiled, cool as could be. Of course she was enjoying his pain. A woman feeling her power. Fine. He admitted it, she had him on the ropes. It was all he could do not to pick her up and carry her to bed as soon as they were inside. But there was that damn cute dog, dancing around like he was about to wet the floor.

Without a word, Ethan put him on a leash and headed outside. Men together. It helped him cool off and plan the next step. Yeah, he needed to talk to Scarlett about this idea of hers. He didn't want a secret bar. The whole idea didn't appeal to him after what he'd seen tonight. He wanted bright lights, everything open and lines out the door like he'd seen at bars down the street. There sure weren't lines at those places hidden like they were a damn mystery. His epiphany was going to be hard for Scarlett to take. At least until the killer was caught.

He and YoYo had a long talk about women. His conscience might hurt him, but he was going to wait until Monday to bring up the bar thing. He was going to use this weekend for lovemaking and developing a relationship with Scarlett. The thought jolted him. Was he serious? Seemed so. And what about his mother and her issues? He'd have to tell Scarlett about Mama, the whole thing. Because tomorrow he'd probably have to meet Mama and maybe help Albert get her hauled back to Fairhaven. Shit. He really didn't want to talk to Scarlett about Mama at all.

"Let's go, YoYo. I'm going to shut the bedroom door. You cannot come in. No three-ways. Get it?" He walked the dog upstairs, pretty sure the pup was tired enough to sleep through whatever commotion he and Scarlett made. And he planned to make a lot of it. He entered the apartment smiling.

"Tell me this, Scarlett. Would you have pulled that trick in the car if I'd had the top down?" He laughed at the look on her face, then chased her into the bedroom. Yes, he was with the right woman.

Chapter Twenty-One

"I'm really sorry about that, Ethan." Scarlett had listened to his confession about his mother and her mental health problems over breakfast. It had certainly killed her appetite. The implications of what he was dealing with were staggering. What was she supposed to say next? Ethan drizzled maple syrup on his pancakes and dug in.

"Thanks. Hey, you were right. You did learn how to fend for yourself." He took a bite. "Delicious. Did your mom teach you how to make these?" He kept eating. Obviously unburdening himself had given him an appetite.

"No, those are from a mix. I don't pretend to be the domestic goddess she is, though I do make a killer corn bread." Scarlett got up and brought the coffeepot over to refill their cups. "What are you going to do if the police get wind of your involvement? Aren't you in trouble if that happens?" Her stomach churned at the thought.

"Of course I am!" He laid down his fork. "I've been going crazy ever since she walked through the door." He took her hand across the table. "It helps to have someone to talk to about it. My sisters offered to help, but were glad that I got it dumped in my lap. I told them to stay in Houston. One of us in potential trouble with the law is enough. At least Shannon is married to the sharpest lawyer I know, Billy Pagan. He's the one drawing up that employment contract for you. I can only pray that getting Mama back to Fairhaven will help me avoid criminal charges for aiding and abetting."

"Ethan!" Scarlett squeezed his hand. She couldn't bear the thought that he might go to jail. And not just because she'd bet her future career on him. No, she'd fallen for him. He was everything she'd been looking for—strong, kind, and so wonderfully protective. Not that she'd ever thought protection was something she needed. And yet it was soothing to have his arms around her, his body next to hers in bed at night, and his reassurances that she wasn't going to have to face anything alone. She could just sink into...

No, this wasn't like her. She was obviously still letting her PTSD or whatever it was dictate her actions or reactions.

"I'm hoping this will get settled today." Ethan polished off his pancakes. "Albert has his crew together. The men have vehicles big enough to handle taking the women to Houston and the hospital, even if they're sedated."

"My God!" Scarlett tried to imagine it. "Are you going to wrestle them to the ground and shoot them with tranquilizers? Can you do that to your own mother?"

"If I have to." Ethan laid down his fork. "I don't know. The entire operation will be complicated. Believe me, I don't want you anywhere near this. The woman who escaped with Mama, who I'm pretty sure was the mastermind of the whole thing, is armed and very dangerous." Ethan picked up his fork again and speared a sausage link. "We'd like to spin it that Mama was her hostage if it comes to that."

"She has a gun?" That put a new complication on what he was facing.

"Unfortunately. That's one reason why we would like to separate her from my mother." Ethan frowned. "She needs Mama for her money. Once we capture them, I'm going to try my damnedest to get Lisa transferred to a different facility, well away from Mama."

"I'd like to keep her separate from you!" Scarlett couldn't believe he could eat after saying something like that. "Seriously, Ethan, how can you sit there calmly knowing what's ahead of you? And I'm supposed to what? Just wait here while you go out and risk your life?"

"You sound like you care." He watched her closely.

"Of course I care!" She tried to blink back sudden tears. Damn it, she loved him. PTSD or not, she couldn't imagine losing him. "Don't you dare get yourself killed by this psycho bitch."

"I don't plan to." He threw down his napkin and got up from the table. "Don't you dare sit there and cry over me." He walked around and pulled her to her feet. "Baby, please." He kissed her wet cheeks. "I'll be careful, I promise. Albert is a licensed private investigator now, but he served in the army, several tours in Afghanistan. All of his men are trained to take down people like that bitch Lisa. I hope it can be done without firing a shot. It may be that we have to call in the police. Whatever it takes. But I sure don't plan to get hurt. Or let my mother get hurt. Do you believe me?"

"I'm trying." Scarlett leaned against him, felt his strong arms around her, and fought for control. She was terrified. She'd seen firsthand what could happen when people with weapons got involved in a situation. Ethan thought he would be all right. He couldn't be sure. There *were* no guarantees. The day she'd been taken hostage had been an ordinary Sunday, just like this one. She'd left Anna's apartment, and her life had been changed forever in a matter of moments. Because of a psychopath's warped plan. You never knew what waited for you on the other side of a door.

"God, Scarlett, you're shaking. Please, calm down." He picked her up and walked over to the couch, then sat down with her in his lap. YoYo jumped up beside them, whining at the emotion clouding the atmosphere in the room.

"Don't go. Let Albert handle it." She looked up at him. "I have a bad feeling about this." She kissed his chin, his cheeks, his mouth. "Please. I don't want to lose you."

"You won't." He just held her until his phone vibrated in his pocket. "I have to get this."

"Of course." Scarlett moved over to sit beside him. She hated what she'd become: clingy and demanding. This had to stop right now. He was obviously talking to his mother. She heard him call her Mama and arrange to meet her at the bar later. By the time he ended the call, she'd pulled herself together. She wasn't about to become another problem he had to handle.

"You'd better call Albert and get him over there with his men." Scarlett had been holding the dog. She leaned over to set him on the floor. "Don't forget to strap on your gun. I guess it's loaded. That Lisa sounds like a rattlesnake you may need to shoot."

"I hope it doesn't come to that, but yes, I'm calling him now. Of course my gun's loaded. I promised your brother and Mike I'd keep it that way." He put his arm around her. "You sound like you've calmed down."

"I have. Sorry if I was stressing you out. I won't do it again. You have enough to deal with." She looked over her shoulder at the mess in the kitchen, his empty plate and the barely touched food on hers. "I can heat up the rest of the pancakes if you're still hungry. Fry up some more sausage."

"I've had plenty. Thanks for breakfast. You can't convince me you're not a domestic goddess." Ethan pulled her against him. "You're right to be concerned. Thanks for that too. I guess it's finally hitting me. What we'll have to do to get Mama and Lisa into our custody and back where they belong. It won't be pretty. Scratch that. It'll be ugly and possibly damn dangerous." He stared up at the ceiling. "I probably should have called the police the minute Mama showed up at the bar."

"I understand why you didn't." Scarlett rested her head on his shoulder. "She's your mother. No matter what she's put you through, you can't forget that. I'm sure you have lots of good memories. How could you just turn the woman who raised you over to the police?"

"You're right. But this misguided attempt to help her could very well send me to jail." He rubbed his cheek against her hair. "It was damn stupid of me to try to pull this off. I can only hope Albert knows what the hell he's doing."

"Not stupid. Impulsive, maybe. Hopefully that brother-in-law of yours can make sure you come out all right if this goes in front of a judge." Scarlett heard her own phone buzz from where it sat next to her plate. "Now I'm getting a call. If you're sure you don't want more to eat, then you'd better go." She ran to grab her phone. "It's Mike. Maybe they finally caught Simms. I'd love some good news right now." She answered the call. "Hello?"

"Scarlett, how are you doing?" Mike actually sounded a little upbeat.

"Tell me you have good news." Scarlett smiled at Ethan who had come to stand by her side.

"I think it's good. We had permission for wire taps on some phones. One of them was for Simms's mother in case he called home. She still lives in the little town in South Texas where he grew up. I doubt you've ever heard of it." He told her the name.

Scarlett thought a moment. "Wait, isn't it near Corpus Christi? I think we drove through there once. Anna and I took a road trip. We wanted to explore some of Texas. She would only spare me a weekend, but I seem to remember…"

"That's right. You have a good memory. It's a one stoplight town. Not much there." Mike cleared his throat. "Anyway, last night we hit pay dirt. Simms finally called his mother. It was a burner phone so we couldn't pinpoint his exact location, but the conversation was an eye-opener. Seems the man has a son named Tommy Delgado, that his ma didn't know about. That name ring a bell?"

"Delgado?" Scarlett sat in the closest chair, pushing away the empty plate in front of her that reeked of maple syrup. The smell was making her sick to her stomach. "God, Mike, Ron Zenonsky's secretary is Mona Delgado. Could she have anything to do with Simms?"

"You bet your life she could. Research shows us that Ramona Delgado grew up in that same little town. Went to high school with Simms. What do you bet Tommy is their boy?"

"What does this mean? Could Mona have been working with Isaac Crane? We always thought he had to have someone giving him inside information about Anna's program. Then that poor guy who worked near Anna in the lab at Zenon was killed." Scarlett remembered that the computer tech had been knifed. They had assumed Simms, who loved his knife, had killed Henry Littlefield to keep him from talking and that Henry had been the only inside man. Now?

"We plan to bring her in today. I got something else from that phone call, and you're not going to like it." Mike was really serious now.

"What?" Scarlett jumped when Ethan's hand landed on her shoulder.

"We've had a tail on Mrs. Simms for a while now, in case Simms came to see her. You'd be surprised how many hardened criminals have a soft spot for their mamas."

"No kidding." Scarlett couldn't imagine the thug who'd delighted in her screams as he'd cut her having a soft spot for anyone.

"Not long after the phone call, the lady headed for the nearest grocery store. And guess what's waiting for her? A money order from a fella named Roy Lee. Can you believe it? You'd think Leroy would have a little more imagination. We got those records and found out the money was sent from the liquor store down the street from the bar where you've been working, Scarlett. Right there on Sixth Street."

"No!" She almost dropped the phone. Roy Lee. Leroy. So close. All those days she'd been in the bar and could have run into him. She swallowed, afraid she was going to throw up.

"Rangers pulled his mother in for questioning. Didn't take long for her to tell us everything. Leroy is still in Austin. He isn't planning to come see her, but we knew that from the phone call. We're not charging her with anything. Honestly, I feel sorry for her. If my kid was a cold-blooded cop killer, I'd be staring into the barrel of my own gun."

"Mike!" Scarlett looked at Ethan. "Stop talking like that. Just tell me. What's next?"

"We're flooding Sixth Street with cops. Going door to door. I hope when we pick her up that Ramona Delgado will break and save us the trouble of that canvass. If she doesn't, it may take a while to find him, but we *will* find him. As of last night, Simms was still near that liquor store. It's closed on Sundays, state law. But we're tracking down the owner today and hope to get video surveillance soon so we can see what Simms looks like now. That'll help in the hunt."

"I'd like to see what kind of disguise he's using. If you can, send me copies of the pictures you get." She gripped Ethan's hand. "But I'm sure not planning to go to Sixth Street until you catch the bastard."

"Good. Thing is, I'm sure Simms will be moving fast if he finds out we're taking his girlfriend." Mike spoke to someone with him. "They've got the address and are getting ready to hit her apartment now. I'll send you photos when I get them."

"Thanks." Scarlett leaned against Ethan. "I know you'll be too busy to give me constant updates, but please let me know when it's safe to go back to the bar."

"Will do. Tell that boss of yours to stay away too. With any luck, this will all be over soon. Lock yourself in, Scarlett."

"I will. You be careful. Promise?"

"I always am." Mike ended the call.

"Tell me everything." Ethan pulled her back to the couch. "You're white as a sheet. What did Mike say to get you so upset?"

"I should have put the phone on speaker so you could hear him yourself." Scarlett told him just what Mike had said, including the part about policemen covering Sixth Street. "You realize you have to change your plans. You can't meet your mother at the bar today, Ethan."

"You're right about that. I'll call Albert right now. I hope we can head Mama off before she's left her motel." Ethan pulled out his phone. "In fact, I'll call her first."

"Yes, do that." Scarlett walked into the kitchen to give him privacy. She heard him arguing with his mother. Apparently she was impatient to leave town.

"I can't help it, Mama. You want to get caught? Then wait for word from me." Ethan obviously ended the call, then dialed again. "Albert. Change of plans."

Scarlett didn't hear more as she ran water into the bowl she'd used to mix pancake batter. Normal domestic chores should soothe her. But she almost dropped the heavy bowl when she started to dry it because her hands were shaking so much. When would her life settle down? And was she crazy for thinking she could be happy with a man with so much baggage? He would always have this complicated family. But he'd been so patient and understanding with her. She owed him some of the same understanding, didn't she?

Ethan finally put away his phone. "Okay, he'll handle it. Albert's struck up a friendship with my mother and Lisa. They don't have a clue he's working for me. He'll invite them to see a movie or go to lunch. Something to keep them occupied."

"I'm glad." Scarlett began to gather their dirty dishes from the table. "I keep thinking about Mona Delgado. What a snake. I knew she didn't like me. Now I know why. If Leroy is really her boyfriend, she must have hated the fact that he liked cutting on my backside." She shuddered, feeling the humiliation and pain all over again. God, she hated that man. He was an animal.

Ethan gently took the dishes out of her hands and set them in the sink. "She's not the only one maddened by the idea that the bastard carved his initials on you. It makes me want to shoot him in the nuts. Hurt him like he hurt you. Am I really supposed to hide here in your apartment while the cops take him down?" He pulled her in and held her close. Not too tight, just right.

He leaned down and kissed her. But it wasn't a violent kiss. No, it was sweet and hungry and tender. When he picked her up and carried her back to bed, he made such slow, careful love to her, Scarlett felt her heart swell. Ethan Calhoun. How had he known this was just what she'd needed?

Chapter Twenty-Two

There was a chicken in the bedroom, squawking its head off. What the hell?

Leroy rolled over and hit a warm body. Ramona. She'd finally slept over. It was about time. She groped for her phone on the nightstand.

"That's Mama's ringtone. What the hell is she doing calling now?" She answered. "Mama? What's wrong?"

Leroy could hear the crying in the phone from his side of the bed. Time for a retreat. He climbed out of bed and hit the bathroom. By the time he'd taken care of business and brushed his teeth, Ramona was lying back and giving him a stony look.

"You didn't tell me you called your mother last night."

"I told you I was going to. Fillin' her in about Tommy. In case you failed to do it." Leroy climbed back into bed. He knew better than to touch her when she had such a hard look on her face. "So what's got your mama's panties in a twist?"

"It's a bit more serious than that, Leroy." Ramona threw back the covers and began looking for her clothes. Good luck with that. They were scattered around the living room. They'd watched porn last night, one of the few premium channels cheapskate Crane had paid for on cable. Things had progressed from there.

"So tell me. Get back in bed. I won't touch you, if that's what you're worried about. Cover up so I won't be tempted." Leroy hid a grin. Boy, did Ramona hate it when he didn't take her seriously.

"Fuck you, Leroy. They must have wiretapped your ma's phone. Found out about Tommy and paid my mama a visit this morning. Now he knows all about his daddy." Her eyes filled with tears. "Of course that also gave them the connection between us. My mama couldn't hold out. Told them how I worked at Zenon and sent money for the boy. It's more than a simple secretary could afford to send, I'll tell you that." She angrily scrubbed the tears off her cheeks. "You know what this means?"

Leroy sat up straight. "Yeah, those assholes got my ma. If they hurt her…"

"No, they let her go. She called Mama and told her everything as soon as she could. Dorothy Simms is a tough broad, you know that. Had to be to raise a hell-raiser like you."

Leroy knew that to be the truth. "So?"

"So she gave Mama a heads-up before the cops showed. Mama had time to give Tommy the story herself. She sure didn't want him hearing it from some fucking Ranger first."

"Good, that's good. How'd the boy take it?" Leroy hated to see Ramona cry, but he knew this was hitting her hard. Well, hell, he hated it for the boy too. Tommy was a teenager. He'd get on the Internet and find out everything there was to know about his pa. None of it was anything good or to be proud of.

"How do you think? He has a cop killer for a daddy. He ran out of the house, and she's worried sick about him."

"He'll come home when he calms down. Or gets hungry." Leroy knew he hadn't helped when Ramona just looked at him like he was a moron. "He probably didn't want your ma to see him cry, woman. Boys are like that." For a moment Leroy wondered if it would have made a difference, knowing about the boy eighteen years ago. Would he have taken a better path? Worked a nine-to-five and gone to school for a trade?

Who was he kidding? He'd started out bad and gone downhill ever since. There was no use looking back. He needed to figure out what was ahead for them.

"Nothing we can do about it here." She brushed back her hair. "I can't even go back to my apartment now. They'll already have my address, my license plate. Everything."

"I know you, Ramona. You have a plan ready, just in case this happened." Leroy pulled her in. She put up a little resistance but seemed to realize that they only had each other. Time to make the best of it.

"You're right. I knew this day would come. It's a little sooner than I would like, but I know what we need to do next." She toyed with his new piercing. She even sent her hand lower, playing with him. But she wasn't interested in sex. It was a reflex. She was thinking.

"Tell me." Leroy didn't mention sending the money order. He wouldn't be surprised if doing that came back to bite him. "Your mama use a burner phone to call you?"

"Of course. I sent her one a long time ago. You should have done the same, Lee." That got him a pinch.

"You're right. But that's hard to do from jail." He pinched her right back. "Now, talk. What's our next move? We need to get the hell out of here. They might have a way to track my whereabouts from that phone call. Don't know what my own burner phone can tell them, but we can't take that chance."

"Yeah. Gather your shit. We're getting out of here as soon as we have a shower. No telling when we'll get a chance for another one." She climbed out of bed again. "You go first. I'm getting the computer and my clothes together. Plus any food we have left."

"Okay. Pack the beer and liquor. Where are you parked?" He watched her walk around naked. He'd have to jack off in the shower because she sure wasn't going to ease his pain.

"A block away. I'll pick up a license plate from a car in the parking garage. We need to fit as much as possible in the two duffel bags." She looked him over. "Poor Leroy. I see where your mind's at. Forget it." She walked right up to him and poked him in the chest with a sharp fingernail. "You messed up, calling your mother and telling her about Tommy. It'll take me a while to get over that."

"I know. I'm sorry." He grabbed her before she could get away. She smelled like woman, his woman. If he had to go on the run again, he couldn't have a better partner than Ramona. He lifted her chin and looked into her dark eyes. Hair wild, lush mouth defiant, even hip deep in shit, she was beautiful.

"Sure you are." She made a token effort to pull away.

"Really. I am. But you should have heard Ma on the phone. She'll be good to Tommy. She and my grandmother both will spoil him rotten to make up for me being such a disappointment to them. He'll have more family to help him in the future. Look how she already watched out for your mother."

"Yes, she did." Ramona slumped against him. "I'll never get to see my son again, Lee. You realize that?"

"Hell, I never got to see him in the first place." Leroy laid his cheek on her hair. For a moment they just held each other. It was quiet in the apartment. Sunday morning. If they were regular people, they'd be piled in bed with the newspaper and talking about going out for brunch at one of those fancy restaurants down the street. But Leroy had never been a regular guy.

Ramona had claimed to want a normal life, but she had never been satisfied with less than the best. She'd always wanted more. That had made her jump at a life of crime when she'd had the chance. She'd bragged about siphoning money from that tech company she worked for long before Crane had come along with his big score. Ramona's idea of pillow talk. She'd done it all to set up their son for college and buy him whatever he had needed as he grew up. When the boy had run out of his grandma's house, Leroy bet it had been in high-dollar sneakers.

Leroy didn't know what she was thinking right now, but his chest grew damp with her tears and his own eyes were moist. Shit. She was right, there was no time for this. So he let her go and turned to walk into the bathroom. If he lived beyond the next few days, maybe he'd let her give him another child. They'd watch it grow up together this time. Something to look forward to. If they were lucky.

Chapter Twenty-Three

"I've got to go out for a while." Ethan hated to leave Scarlett, but his mother was obviously in one of her moods. Albert had called twice. They were probably going to be kicked out of the motel if someone didn't calm Missy down. "Why don't I pick up a couple of steaks for dinner while I'm out? It's one of the only things I can cook. It's a Texas thing. Daddy taught me how to grill a steak when we were staying at the ranch."

"You have a ranch?" Scarlett slipped her arms around his waist. "What else don't I know about you?"

"Technically, I used to own a fourth of it. We sold it when the price of oil bottomed out after Daddy died." He smiled down at Scarlett. "Never mind. It's not like I have to constantly fight the urge to put on a cowboy hat and sing 'Happy Trails.'"

"Too bad. That would be a real turn-on. My friends back home think all Texas men ride and can two-step to Willie Nelson tunes." She ran a hand down the front of his shirt, the same one he'd worn yesterday. "You going by your place to grab some more clothes? We may be stuck here awhile. If you do, be careful."

"I was thinking about it. I'd love to do target practice on one Leroy Simms." He pulled her in and kissed her. He'd never get tired of her taste, he was sure of that. "And for your information, I can ride a horse, lady. Just wait. I'll take you to a friend's ranch once we get this bar going and can take some time off. Show you more of Texas than some one-stoplight town between here and Corpus." He hummed a tune and two-stepped her around the tiny living room. YoYo almost got tangled in their feet. "See? I have some moves."

"Well, I knew that." She laughed as he spun her out. Then she got serious. "I mean it, be careful. If Simms is still on Sixth Street, he might be desperate enough to take a hostage."

"I'd like to see him try." Ethan patted the gun he'd stuck under his shirt.

"Stop it. Let the cops do their job. No target practice for you, mister. But stop by Amuse Tattoos and tell Carl what's going on. I haven't called Rhett because I don't want to worry him, but everyone at the tattoo parlor ought to be on alert."

"You're right. I'll show them the pictures Mike sent us, in case the cops didn't come by." He kissed her again. "Don't worry about me, either. I'll be fine. Simms doesn't know me. He's bound to be on the run again anyway. Once he saw all those police cars hit the street, he probably hightailed it out of town."

"Those pictures! You realize we probably bumped into him that night when we went to get your car in the parking garage?" Scarlett held on to his arm as she walked him to the door.

"You're right. I'm sure it was him. That's why he kept his hands on his sunglasses." Ethan pulled her close. "Lock up now. We had a near-miss that evening."

"Yes, but he had to have recognized me and just walked on." Scarlett stepped back. "I'm actually optimistic that it's proof he's lost interest in me." She started throwing dead bolts at the door. "Go and come back fast, because steak sounds really good right now. Text me when you're on the way back and I'll start the charcoal in the grill."

"I was surprised to see you had one on the front porch." Once the door was open, Ethan looked around outside. It was automatic now. No sign of anyone lurking around, either bald or with a knife. He shrugged at the role reversal—now he was paranoid and Scarlett seemed to have finally relaxed.

She opened the deluxe grill's lid and frowned. "Damn it, I'll have to scrub the grates. He never does." She picked up the two iron grates and waved them. "Rhett bought this thing when he started dating Casey. You see? It's not just a Texas thing. I think men all over the world like to burn meat to impress women." She laughed and shook her head, in a good mood. "He's still pouting because I wouldn't let him get an enormous butane setup and we have to use charcoal."

"Burn? You insult me, woman. I like my steak medium rare. Prime Texas beef deserves it." Ethan watched her sweet butt sway as she walked into the kitchen to set the grates in the sink. "I'll wait right here until I hear those locks engage, ma'am."

"Yes, sir." She was smiling as she came back and shut the door firmly in his face.

He just stood there. When had Scarlett come to mean so much to him? She'd crept into his heart, and his feelings just kept getting stronger. He waited until he heard all those dead bolts turn and the beep of the alarm being set. He wanted her safe and wouldn't have left her for even a minute if he thought there was any danger that Simms knew where she lived. Thank God she'd had the good sense to move.

* * * *

"Mama, what's got you in an uproar?" Ethan had found her knocking back bourbon in the bar next to the motel where they'd settled on Congress Avenue. Unfortunately it was way too close to his own bar and the dozens of policemen scouring the area for Simms. She screamed at the waitress to hurry up with her refill.

"Seeing Mary Louise in Neiman's brought it all back, baby." She waved at the waitress. "Damn help here is useless."

"Don't you think you've had enough?" The signs were there. Her speech was slurred, and her face was flushed. He shook his head at the waitress who was finally headed their way. "Coffee for both of us."

"Now, listen here..." His mother aimed a fist at him across the table.

Ethan grabbed it. "No, you listen. You're attracting attention. Do you really want to do that?" He looked around. There were few people in here on a Sunday afternoon. But a baseball game played on the TV sets in the corners with groups of men drinking beer in front of them. Thank God the Rangers scored and the men hollered. That sound was loud enough to drown out his mother's surly grumbles as he let her go.

"Of course not. But I've got to get moving, Ethan. Mary Louise will check the Internet. She'll see that I'm supposed to still be in that damn hospital. I'm sure there were news articles in the paper about our escape." She frowned when the waitress brought the coffee and a pitcher creamer. "I really don't want to face this sober."

"Where's Lisa? Not that I want to see her." Ethan watched his mother's hands shake as she added cream and sugar, then tasted her coffee with a grimace.

"She's with Albert. Making a move. She believes he has money. That's all she cares about." Mama's eyes filled with tears. "You think I haven't figured that out? She's using me, Ethan."

"Of course she is!" Ethan grabbed her free hand. "Let me take you somewhere else right now. You never have to see her again." He couldn't believe they'd finally separated the two. This was his chance. If only Albert's men were here.

Mama shook her head and pulled away. "No, I may not like it, but I need her. Lisa is strong. I feel so weak now." She put down the cup, spilling half her coffee. "I'm not the same woman I was before I went into that place. I tell you, they doped me up until I forgot who I was. I've lost all my confidence."

"Mama, I saw how you handled Mary Louise in that shoe department. You were your old self. Smart, on top of your game." Ethan didn't know if it was wise to tell her this. He saw her straighten her shoulders and a gleam come into her eyes. Then she raised her arm.

"We're over here." She smiled. "Lisa and Albert. You haven't met him. You need to thank him for all his help. Pay him back for the times he's taken us to dinner and spotted us cash when we needed it."

Ethan got to his feet when he felt the presence at his back. Now he'd have to test his acting skills. He didn't doubt Albert was good at faking things. He'd been stringing Mama and Lisa along for several weeks now. Yeah, time had been passing, and it was little wonder the women were getting impatient.

"Albert Madison." Albert stuck out his hand as Lisa slid into a chair with a pout. Obviously her plan to part her mark from his money hadn't worked. If that was what she had in mind. Or maybe she'd tried to get him into bed. Albert was giving her space and moved to the opposite side of the table after Ethan introduced himself.

"I hear I owe you for all you've done for my mother and her, uh, friend." Ethan sat back down. "Can I at least order you a drink?"

"Coffee works for me." Albert looked across at Lisa. "What about you, Lisa?"

"You know what I like and it's not coffee." She gestured at the coffee cup in front of her friend, then leaned her elbows on the table. "Missy, what the hell is this? Did he at least bring the passports?"

"No, I didn't." Ethan glanced at Albert, who was supposed to be oblivious to the fake passport thing. "The guy has to go through government channels. You know you have red tape to deal with. I'm paying him an arm and a leg to expedite things, but there's only so much he can do. He told me they'll be in this week." Ethan waved down the waitress and gave the order. "Mama and I were discussing the hospital. Do you feel you were drugged all the time, Lisa?" He was beginning to think his mother had a point. There was supposed to be therapy and hope for a handle on her problem. So she could have a decent future, if not a cure. What the hell kind of hospital was it? If all they were doing was sedating the patients, then Fairhaven was not the best facility for her. He was going to have to talk to his sisters and the lawyer Billy Pagan about a different placement. It had been court-ordered, but Billy could petition the court for a change.

"Of course they did!" Lisa banged her fist on the table. "Do you think we took off just for kicks?" She jumped when Missy grabbed her hand.

"Hush. We're not alone here." Then his mother gave Ethan a hard look. "Why are you discussing our hospital stay with Albert sitting here?" She turned to Albert and narrowed her eyes. "You don't look surprised."

"I'd have to be unconscious, Missy, not to have noticed you have mood swings." Albert smiled and took the coffee the waitress handed him. "Sorry, but you asked. And Lisa let some things slip, didn't you, honey?"

"I don't know. Did I?" Lisa frowned, then sipped her bourbon. "Maybe I've been drinking too much." She shrugged. "We both have. But I'm not drunk now. We've waited long enough, Ethan. This person arranging our new passports isn't making it his priority." She smiled at Albert. "I did tell you Missy and I are determined to start a new life, sugar bear. Our old ones got swept away in that last hurricane that hit Houston."

"Yes, you told me all that. Very hard times. I'm sorry. Maybe it was a sign that you do need to start over." Albert glanced at Ethan. "But then, I'm just a simple man. I'd miss my home and my family. Seems like it would be lonely in a new place where you've never been. What do you think, Ethan? Won't you miss your mother if she just takes off for parts unknown?"

"Yes, of course I would." Ethan kept thinking that the clock was ticking. Scarlett was alone, and he still had to hit his apartment for some clothes. "I'll light a fire under the man taking care of your passports, though, Mama, if it'll make you happy."

"Thanks, Ethan. Yes, it will." Mama was eyeing Lisa's bourbon. "I'll miss you, too." Her eyes filled with tears. "Promise you'll come see me wherever we are. When we get settled?"

"I don't know. I'm starting a new business. You would be the first one to say I should be here to keep an eye on it." Ethan stood. "Which is why I have to go right now. I have something I need to check on at the bar." He walked around to kiss his mother's cheek. He wasn't surprised to see her already flagging down the waitress to switch back to bourbon. Too bad. But at least she'd calmed down and was talking about going to that movie Albert had mentioned. Ethan was almost out the door when he was stopped by a hand on his sleeve.

"I don't know what you're up to, Ethan Calhoun, but I don't trust you." Lisa dug her fingernails into his arm. "If you really love your mother, you'll get those passports to us in the next two days. Otherwise…"

"What? You threatening your gravy train?" Ethan threw her hand off of him. "Listen to me and listen good. You harm one hair on her head and I'll shoot you myself." He lifted his shirt to show her his gun. Yeah, he shouldn't have brought it in here, but he didn't want to be unarmed around this crazy bitch. "Don't think I won't."

"You could try." She sneered at him, then looked him over. "You just got more interesting. But remember, I'm certified crazy. Your mama has her mood swings? Well, I have what they call anger management issues. You don't want to push me, or you will see just what happens when I lose control. I keep my own weapon handy and don't you forget it." She patted her purse slung over her shoulder. She blew him a kiss, then sauntered back to the table, taking a seat next to Albert. Apparently she hadn't given up on the PI, because she suddenly planted a wet kiss on his lips. Albert just leaned back when she was done, then said something that made the two women laugh.

God. Ethan didn't know how Albert had held it together. He would have needed to vomit if Lisa had put her tongue in his mouth. With that thought, he left the bar and got in his car. Sixth Street. He needed to grab some clothes and hurry back to Scarlett. He hadn't forgotten that Simms was still out there.

Chapter Twenty-Four

"You had all this in a storage unit, ready to go? How long you been working on this, Ramona?" Leroy couldn't believe the woman. Parked inside was a silver Honda Civic that looked like a thousand others. She showed him good papers with it registered under a fake name, a driver's license and insurance to match. She had a passport for him under a fake name too. He didn't know when she'd taken the picture for it. It wasn't bad, but a few years old. Didn't matter. He was now David Dansby. He had to love that white bread name. She was Maria Dansby. She'd even come up with a marriage certificate. They were officially a couple. Why? Maybe in her heart she wished Tommy had been legit. He drew the line at the wedding ring she produced. The woman was dreaming.

She had a new laptop in there and a wardrobe to fit their status. He was dressed like he worked at a bank in a dark suit, but he refused to put on the striped tie she tossed at him. She was playing at being a spoiled housewife, wearing what she informed him were designer jeans and carrying a purse she called a Louis. Her blond wig changed her look completely. Hell, she even sported blue contact lenses. He didn't doubt that, if she found a guy who was a real banker with money and the la-di-da tastes she loved, she'd drop her new Dansby husband and take off in a hot minute.

And why not? Bald-headed with a scraggly mustache and goatee, Leroy could only hope his face was unrecognizable. He was planning to let his hair grow into a buzz cut. Like he'd just come out of the service. Oh, yeah, she even had papers to show he'd served a stint in the navy. What a joke. She still teased him about the time he'd gotten seasick taking the ferry from Galveston to Bolivar on a vacation there once.

"Ramona, I got to hand it to you. I had no idea you could manage this kind of cover." Leroy got behind the wheel of the Honda and pulled it out of the storage unit rented to the Dansbys. The car hummed, had a full tank and surprising power. The woman had thought of everything. "But why the fuck did you make me wait so long for these papers?"

"Your passport and your other papers just came in yesterday, so don't give me a hard time about it. I've had years to figure everything else out. While I was squirreling my money away, I knew I'd have to run someday, Lee. How the hell did I know you'd get to go with me? You were in jail, remember? I'm glad, though, that I don't have to make my move alone." She took care of pulling her old car into the unit. They'd unloaded everything they'd need from it, and now she took one last look around.

"You need to wipe it down?" Leroy felt like a third tit. What did he know about these kinds of arrangements? When he'd needed to get away before, he'd stolen the nearest vehicle and taken off. Not a smart move and not usually successful.

"No reason. Once the rental on this unit runs out at the end of the year, they'll finally crack it open. The VIN on the car will tell them it belonged to me once. By then we'll be long gone." She patted the trunk almost fondly, then pulled the garage door down and closed the heavy-duty lock. "Slick as a whistle."

"I'll say." Leroy caught the key, then got behind the wheel of the Honda. For a moment he wished for a high-powered sports car, like that yellow Porsche in the parking garage. But he knew this anonymous car was the right way to go.

"Now what?" He felt a weight slip off of his shoulders. Finally they were away from Sixth Street. She'd rented this unit in northwest Austin not far from the freeway heading out of town. Again, it was a smart choice. There were dozens of such places in the area, and all of them looked alike. He wasn't sure he'd be able to find it again if he had to—Store-A-Lot, Store City, Store 4U. Whatever. He knew better than to write down the name or the unit number, but he tried to remember both. An extra car. Just in case he needed one later, he could come back here.

"I've got Scarlett Hall's new address." Ramona slammed the passenger door and dug in her fancy purse. "She was so careful not to give it away, but I outsmarted her. Played with the computer at work so the payroll clerk had to call and tell her the system for direct deposit was down. We were going to have to mail Scarlett her next paycheck. Trust me, the woman was quick to give out her snail-mail address then."

"You thinking to go after her now, Ramona?" Leroy couldn't believe what he was hearing. "I don't see any cops, so we're in the clear. I say we just head out. We can take the highway here north, then turn toward the west. Bet we could cross the border at El Paso with those papers you got us in less than forty-eight hours. We'd be home free, baby. In Mexico we can catch a boat to the Caymans, get our money, and start our new lives." Leroy slid his hand over her shoulder. "What do you say?"

"I say you're wimping out on me, Lee. I told you that bitch has to die. I'm not leaving town until we take care of her." Ramona fastened her seat belt. "Come on, cop killer. Pick up your balls and drive. She's not expecting us. She lives pretty close to the capitol building downtown." She was punching buttons on her cell phone. "Look. I got the address in my phone and in my GPS. It'll be easy, in and out. I'll even let you play with her for a while before I cut her throat."

"Ramona, baby." Leroy had to admit the idea of getting another shot at Scarlett Hall's plump ass had him hard. But then lots of things made him hard. He could do a stranger in a rest stop if he needed to cut someone. So could Ramona. He told her that.

"A stranger? When I've got the perfect target already, Lee?" She wasn't going to be distracted.

"Not so perfect. Cops have got to be all over her. Protecting her." Leroy thought about just driving. He could see the freeway overpass that they could take out of town just a few blocks away. Yeah, Ramona would bitch about it, but he was the man. He didn't like how she was always trying to tell him what to do.

"Don't be stupid. Cops won't bother with her. She wasn't our target in Crane's operation. Just collateral damage." Ramona glared at him. "I didn't take you for a coward, Lee."

Stupid? Coward? What would she do if he tossed her out of the car right now? After he cut her pretty throat, of course. Leroy gripped the steering wheel. He had those papers she'd bought and knew where the money was. Well, hold on. She'd kept the name of the bank to herself and let him know there were more than a dozen of them on that island. She also had some kind of password to get access to the account that she wasn't sharing with him. He gave her a hard look, and she seemed to realize she'd said too much.

"I'm sorry, baby. It's just that I want this so bad. It's all I can think about. Taking that bitch down. You know the feeling. You told me how it is for you, when you have a score to settle." Ramona turned to him, those startling blue eyes that weren't hers looking him over. "I love you. Don't let this come between us." She even leaned over and gave him a deep kiss.

"Do this. For me? Once it's done, I'll give you that password you've been asking for. As a sign of good faith."

Leroy let her do her thing, kissing him, fondling him, using her sex to get to him. But he was thinking fast. He needed her. Maybe more than she needed him. So maybe he'd go along with this. Because that password was gold. He had to have it to get to the money, and he didn't altogether trust her. Of course she didn't trust him, either. Keeping her little secrets. Like the fact that they had a fucking son.

Damn it, she might just piss him off and make him do something he'd regret before they even got to the Caymans. Yeah, he had a temper. He could cut her throat and then think, aw shit. Better to get the name of the bank and password as soon as possible. He needed an account number too. Hell, the key was probably in her computer. She'd have it all in there. But Ramona being Ramona, she had a password on it too. He just bet it wasn't simple like Tommy4ever or some shit like that. No, she'd bragged that she never used anything predictable for passwords. He'd never guess it in a million years. Right now all he had was a couple hundred bucks in the new wallet she'd given him out of the storage unit. His allowance, she'd said with a laugh. Bitch.

He twitched with the urge to slam her face against the dashboard until she told him everything. But she was just stubborn enough to die before she'd give him the right info. Damn her. He pulled back, disappointed with himself that under her hands he'd started breathing heavy and was as hard as the gearshift.

"Answer me this, woman. Is she really worth it? Think of all that money waiting for us. We could hire a hit man to come get her later. She'll be just as dead."

"Fuck that, Lee. You know how you like to feel and smell the blood when it spills? I got a taste of that when I did Littlefield. I liked it and have been imagining doing Hall in my dreams for months now." Ramona's smile was cold. "Oh, yeah. After the way that bitch Hall ruined my office? You should have seen her. She came in like she was hot shit from Boston. Took my office and turned it upside down. Like I don't know how to do things right. Did you see how I had my stuff ready to go?" She stared out the car window, her bright red nails digging into her fists.

"Yeah. You sure as hell know how to get things done, babe." Lee was beginning to hate the Hall woman too. Not that he really cared about anything but her ass. And she'd had some fine tits as he recalled. Ramona was still talking, wound up.

"Hall ruined more than the office, Lee. She almost blew the Crane deal before we even got started. Made my girlfriend Carla lose her nerve and quit, when I'd spent months grooming her to help me with Crane. Carla knew enough that I had to arrange for her to have a little accident after that. Police still haven't figured out that one." Ramona's cold smile was back.

"Damn, woman." Leroy looked at her with new respect. "What kind of accident?"

"Never mind. Carla's leaving almost messed things up for me. So I'm not forgetting Scarlett Hall, Lee. You need to help me get even with that bitch. Look at all I've done for you." She tossed his new passport and driver's license into his lap. "Could you have gotten these papers for yourself?"

To his shame, Leroy realized he couldn't have. He didn't have a clue how to buy that kind of paper. And he sure as hell didn't have the money for it. Yeah, he had criminal connections, but they were muscle, not brains. You needed someone beat up, blown up, or kidnapped? He could find some guys. But paper? Not a clue. Shit. He needed her, and not just her body to relieve his pain. He needed her mind. He put the papers in the console, then threw the car in gear.

"All right, baby. We'll do this your way. But if it goes sideways, remember this was your idea. We were on the way to Mexico, but you had to complicate things with this play on the woman." He drove the car out of the lot, aware that there were video surveillance cameras. So what? The cops would never think to look here. He drove the speed limit and not a bit over, following Ramona's directions as they headed back toward downtown. Near the capitol building. Shit, that was way too close to Sixth Street for his comfort.

But what choice did he have? He had to keep his woman happy. And what a woman she was. Hell, she'd even packed a couple of shiny new knives in that storage unit, just the kind he liked. They both had good weapons too. She hadn't missed a trick. As he neared the Capitol and saw the dome up ahead, Ramona's hand landed on his leg. Yeah, she was excited. He admitted he was also warming to the idea. He'd get to work over Scarlett Hall again. Maybe risking everything would be worth it.

Chapter Twenty-Five

Scarlett had spent the afternoon cleaning the apartment. No progress report from Mike or Ethan, but she was getting hungry so she threw together some dip to go with a bag of chips and decided to go ahead and fire up the grill. YoYo demanded to go out. Why not walk him around the complex while she waited? She grabbed some small plastic bags to pick up his business and set out.

She waved at a neighbor who drove into the complex. When a silver Honda drove in behind him, she figured it was the neighbor's guest. Ethan had followed her in the same way the night before.

"Good boy!" After YoYo did his duty, Scarlett took care of the deposit and dropped it in the can the complex provided. She picked up the dog and started up the stairs. The Honda had parked, and two people got out. But instead of following the neighbor, who had disappeared into his apartment, they were heading her way.

Scarlett turned and recognized at least one of them instantly. Her grip tightened on YoYo so much he yelped, squirming in her arms. The bald man had to be Leroy Simms. But the blonde with him? It couldn't be... Hell, she didn't care who it was. Scarlett bolted up the stairs. She hadn't set the alarm while she was walking the dog, hadn't even locked the damn door. She fumbled to open it as she heard heavy footsteps pounding up the steps behind her.

Stall them. She reached behind her and grabbed the grill's handle, dragging it across the top of the stairs. She hoped like hell the hot coals would make it impossible for them to move it as she wrenched her door open and dove inside.

"Son of a bitch!" The man screamed.

Before she could turn more than one dead bolt, there was a thud against the door, the frame cracking under pressure. She ran to her bedroom. *Hide.* The panic room was why she'd rented this apartment in the first place. She moved her clothes to one side and found the hidden door, opening it and dropping YoYo inside. Then she slid the clothes back in place to make sure the door would be out of sight if someone managed to get into the apartment. She climbed in after the dog and shut herself into the tiny room. She gathered the dog into her arms and sat with her back against the wall. There was just enough space to keep her knees up against her chin. She bumped the bottle of water she'd set in the room when she'd first moved in. Like she'd drink now. She was paralyzed with fear.

Breathe. She did have air. One side was disguised as an air vent into the bedroom. But the space was so freaking small. She carefully slid the three bolts closed, then leaned back against the wall and held on to YoYo. He was growling low in his throat, desperate to get out of her arms and attack whoever was after her. She kissed the top of his head, then gently wrapped her hand around his mouth. Dear God, he could not bark, not now.

"Shh." Scarlett kept her lips pressed to his fur and prayed. She heard the front door crash against the wall. God, the dead bolt must have given way. Cell phone. Where the hell was her cell phone? For months she'd kept it in her bra. She realized it was in the kitchen, where she'd left it after a call from her mom, her usual Sunday chat. Stupid. She'd thought the danger was over. Obviously it wasn't.

"Where the hell is she?" Mona's voice, she'd know it anywhere. She must have been wearing a blond wig. "Look in the bathroom, behind the shower curtain. I'll look in the bedroom, under the bed."

"Closets too." Leroy's voice. There was the sound of breaking glass. He must have cleared her counter just for the hell of it. Bastard.

"I don't see her." Mona was getting frustrated. Sounds of more things hitting the floor. "Take it easy, Lee. Damn it, someone might hear us. We need to get out of here."

"There's a back balcony off the dining room. Maybe she jumped off of it. You sure you looked everywhere?" Leroy was close.

Scarlett swallowed. That voice. She'd never forget it. She held on to YoYo and prayed he would stay quiet. Shadows moved past the vent. Dear God, he was just feet away. Hangers rattled as her clothes were moved around just outside her hiding place. She held her breath. Then there was the sound of cloth ripping.

"What the hell are you doing, Lee?"

"Testing this knife you bought me. Good and sharp." More ripping. "But I really need to test it on the Hall woman's ass again." He laughed, a deep chuckle that sent chills down Scarlett's spine. If evil had a sound, that was it.

"Seriously?"

"You should see your face. Jealous? Baby, it's all about the feel of the knife going through flesh and then the warm blood on your fingers. You know what I mean? I'm hard just thinking about it."

"She's not here. Let's move." Mona didn't sound happy.

Scarlett couldn't breathe, but YoYo wriggled in her arms and she had to concentrate on keeping him quiet. His throat vibrated under her hand. Growling. Thank God they didn't seem to hear him. They were so close she could hear Leroy breathing, even smell him through the air vent. He'd been drinking beer. She wanted to scream, throw up, get out of there and beat the man to death with whatever came handy. God, but she hated him. And Mona?

"You keep that knife away from me." Mona was so close Scarlett could see her shadow through the vent. "I don't understand how she got away from us. This place is small, and I didn't take her for the type to jump. She'd still be lying on the ground out there if she had. And where's her dog? You saw her outside with it." Mona must have slid back the closet door to look inside again. "We'll have to come back. I'm not giving up. I want that bitch dead."

"Enough. We've been here too long. Come on." Leroy sounded like he'd moved to the living room, his voice fainter. "Burned my hand on that fucking grill. I've a mind to toss that thing in here and set the place on fire."

"And bring the cops here faster? Just leave it for now, Lee. She's probably already calling for help wherever the hell she is. Let's head out of town. We'll finish her later. Just when she thinks she's in the clear." The front door slammed.

Scarlett counted to ten. When she heard nothing else, she eased open the bolts and the small door, being as quiet as possible. She held a squirming YoYo. No way could she put him down with glass on the floor. The bedroom was chaos, her clothes in shreds, but there was no sign of Leroy or Mona.

She had one thought: They couldn't get away. If they did, she'd live in a constant state of paralyzing fear, waiting for them to come back and "finish" her.

She ran to the narrow front window and carefully moved the edge of the curtain aside. The silver Honda was just easing out of the parking lot. No! Once they left the complex, that car would be lost in a sea of similar vehicles. She couldn't even see the license plate number from where she stood.

She ran for her cell phone and car keys. With YoYo in her arms and the phone, she pushed open the broken door as soon as she was sure they wouldn't be able to see her in their rearview mirror. Simms had shoved the grill out of the way, and she hurried down the stairs to her car. She dropped YoYo into the passenger seat, then backed out, staying well away from the Honda. Thank God the speed bumps in the parking lot had slowed them down and they were driving carefully, obviously trying not to draw attention as they left. Luckily a neighbor pulled out from a side lot and drove between them as the gate opened. Forget 911, this situation would be impossible to explain to a stranger. Scarlett hit speed-dial for the first number she could find.

* * * *

Once on Sixth Street, Ethan made quick work of gathering a couple of changes of clothing and stuffing them into a duffel bag. Mike hadn't lied. The street was swarming with cops. He walked into Amuse Tattoos, relieved to see it was business as usual.

"Hey, Carl, Luke. Did the cops come by and show you the photos of the man they're looking for?" Ethan had his phone out, ready to share if they hadn't seen them.

"Sure did." Carl stopped in the middle of an elaborate design of an American flag. "Let's take a break, Al. How about some water?" He patted the customer on his beefy shoulder.

"Yeah, I'd like that. But I don't drink out of plastic bottles. I read a report that those BPAs can cause cancer." Al sat up. He was so covered in tattoos it was a wonder he'd found a vacant spot for a new one.

"No worries. We filter our own water, no bottles. I'll bring you a glass," Carl said as he nodded Ethan toward the back. "Al cage fights but worries about BPAs. Go figure." He pulled down a glass from a shelf and filled it from a pitcher in the refrigerator. "Keep your voice down about the fugitive, Ethan. I don't want to freak out my customers." He took the glass to the man. "Be right back, Al."

"Sure. So what do you know?" Ethan followed Carl to the room where Casey usually worked. Of course she'd taken the weekend off to be with Rhett. Did Scarlett's brother have any idea what was going on? Probably not, or he might have headed back from Houston early.

"A Ranger, Mike Taylor, came by and showed us a couple of pictures. He said he knew Scarlett and had met you. Anyway, Luke recognized Simms immediately. The guy was in here the other night to get his own tattoo."

"You're kidding. That took stones. On the run for murdering a cop and he strolls in here for a new tat?" Ethan couldn't believe it. Leroy Simms had been right next door to where Scarlett worked. God, it made his blood run cold. "What kind of tattoo? You think it'll help the Rangers find Simms?"

"We usually don't share that information, but since he's a fugitive, I guess it can't hurt. He got a heart with the name Ramona over it. Told Luke that she was his woman." Carl had filled a glass of his own and drank it down. "That got the cop excited, I'll tell you."

"Wow. Ramona. That would be Ramona Delgado. Scarlett says she's a secretary at Zenon." Ethan realized that meant nothing to Carl. "Never mind. You have any idea where Simms was living?"

"He gave a fake name, no address, and paid cash. But Luke said he seemed to be on foot. That was all we could tell the Ranger." Carl shook his head. "I can't believe we had him here, Ethan. And let him get away. He had a jailhouse tattoo, Taylor said, but Luke noticed the man had a big Band-Aid on his arm that was probably covering it up. The guy claimed he was healing from a kitchen accident." Carl set his glass in a sink. "Shit. I'm sorry we didn't know who we had."

"He's dangerous, man. Better to let the cops handle it." Ethan was gaining new respect for law enforcement. He should have called them in as soon as his mother had appeared. Now it was too late without bad consequences to himself and maybe Albert.

"You think Luke and I couldn't have taken that bastard down?" Carl sniffed. "I'm armed. Always am in here. See this?" He lifted his loose cotton shirt and showed Ethan his handgun in a holster. "I keep the gun snapped down in the holster so no one can snatch it from me. I learned that lesson the hard way." Carl shook his head.

"You're kidding. What happened?" Ethan knew there was a story there.

"Never mind. The truth is, I take in a lot of cash and people know it. Been robbed a time or two. Or at least they've attempted it. I sure haven't been bothered like that with all the cops cruising the street lately. The real trouble started when your bar was standing vacant and there was no action there. I even had to run off some squatters."

"I appreciate that." Ethan followed Carl back to the front of the shop. "The place still was trashed. You should have seen the bathroom." He turned to Luke. "Scarlett says the women in the ladies' room wrote some nasty things about you. You might want to check yourself, dude."

"Seriously?" Luke shook his head. "I didn't know women did that. Like phone numbers and shit?"

A woman who had seemed to be waiting her turn for a tattoo looked Luke up and down. "Not phone numbers. Warnings." She smiled at Carl. "Word gets around about who is a gentleman and who isn't. Know what I mean?"

"Sure do, Gina." Carl smiled at her. "I'll be through here in ten."

"Can't wait, lover." She settled down with a magazine.

Ethan's phone buzzed. Damn it, what now?

Chapter Twenty-Six

"Scarlett?"

"Ethan! I'm in my car following Leroy Simms and Mona Delgado."

"What?" He sounded shocked. Of course he was.

"They came to the apartment. After me." She took a breath when her voice cracked. "I'm okay. I hid and they didn't find me. But I can't let them get away."

"Stop. Don't do this. What if they see you?" Ethan sounded like he was running. "I'm still near the bar. I see Mike." He was yelling the Ranger's name. "Mike, I've got Scarlett on the phone. She's behind Simms and Delgado, following them in her car. They tried to kidnap her or kill her. Shit, I don't know. I'm giving him the phone, honey."

"Scarlett. What the hell are you doing?" Mike sounded very official and, impossibly, scared. "Back off now."

"I'm not too close. Listen, they're in a gray or silver Honda. I can't read the license plate. I think they put mud on it or something. Anyway, we're headed down Martin Luther King toward the freeway. The one you call Mopac that goes north and south." Scarlett reached down to push YoYo out of her lap. "Oh, no! They've turned. They're going down Guadalupe, that street that runs right in front of the University of Texas. God, Mike, it's swarming with students. Don't send the police after them now. It would be a bloodbath if they decided to pick up hostages and make a stand."

"You think I don't know that? And the first hostage would be you." Mike took a breath. "Girl, you have no business following people who are no doubt armed and dangerous." Mike started issuing orders to people around him. "I've got units headed your way. I've told them no lights or sirens. Both Simms and Delgado are in the car? Did you see weapons?"

"I heard Simms use a knife, ripping up my clothes in the closet. I was in my panic room, right next to where he was slashing at things. Don't know if I told you about that feature in the apartment." Scarlett figured that was something he didn't care about now. "Anyway, I don't know what other weapons they have. But I'm sure they have them. They...they talked about finishing me." *Do not break down.* "Listen, I've got two cars between them and me. I'm okay, Mike. But I'm scared."

"Of course you are. You got a description of the two? How they look now? In case they get away. Which would be fine. Back off and let the cops do their job, Scarlett." Mike said this firmly.

"I can't let them go. I have to keep them in sight, I have to. I saw Mona in a blond wig, jeans and a pink T-shirt. Simms looks bald, dressed like a regular guy in a dark suit with a white shirt. Like he's pretending to be an office worker. He's got a mustache and goatee. But I recognized him, Mike. Right away. Thanks to the pictures you sent us. Bald. Oh, I already said that." She remembered to breathe, then stomped on the brakes when the car ahead of her stopped for a yellow light. Was she going to lose them? She might have except...

"You're not going to believe this, Mike. They're driving through a Whataburger. Like they didn't just try to kidnap me or whatever they had planned. They're ordering food!" Scarlett choked back a sob but didn't let a tear fall. Her hands gripped the wheel. "Mona hates me. I don't know why. What did I ever do to her?" When the light changed, she pulled into a gas station across the street from the restaurant where she could watch them. Crazy! When she saw Mona look around, Scarlett ducked and threw herself across the console. God, if the woman saw her, she wouldn't put it past her to jump out of the car and dodge traffic to come right after her. She really didn't understand it. Why did Mona hate her so much?

"Scarlett, Scarlett! Are you there?" Mike sounded frantic.

"I'm here. I had to get out of sight. I was afraid they saw me. I'm okay." She stayed where she was. There had been a couple of cars ahead of the Honda. How long would it take them to go through the line?

"Listen to me. I'm telling the cops getting close to play this by ear. They know what you're driving and will be careful not to involve you. You're right. We can't risk a shoot-out where there are so many people. I'm on my way. Ethan is with me. He insisted." Mike's voice was rough. "Honey, you can't try to figure out psychopaths. You're a good, decent person with friends and family. Delgado may hate you just for that. Don't let it upset you."

"Tell the cops to be extra careful. I guess classes just let out or something. There are students everywhere." Scarlett peeked over the steering wheel. The Honda was at the window, and she saw Leroy pass money to the server.

"They're paying. So maybe you'll get a chance to take them when we leave this area. If Simms sees the police, no telling what he'll do. Remember how he used that knife before, and he can shoot too. He used a gun when you took out Crane." Scarlett saw that the food had been delivered. "Okay, they're on the move again. I've got to keep following them. If they decide to stop and eat, then you can move in. Don't worry. I plan to stay well back from them."

"You do that. I mean it, Scarlett. You are no match for those two. I'm handing the phone to Ethan. Talk to him while I drive."

"Scarlett, baby, be careful. Maybe you should quit talking and just drive. For God's sake don't let them see you." Ethan sounded scared.

"I won't." She pulled out of the parking lot. A police car went past but ignored them. She figured it was just confirming the identities of the two inside the Honda. "Ethan, don't worry about me. I'm fine."

"Stay that way." He cleared his throat. "We've just gotten started, you know."

"I know." She realized the Honda had turned the corner. "Oh, God. Tell Mike we're going down Thirty-Fifth now. Toward the freeway again." Against her will, Scarlett sobbed.

Ethan shouted that direction to Mike. "What is it, baby? This should be good news. They're moving away from the university. But you sound upset. Have they seen you?"

"No, it's not that. They've slowed down, and I recognize where we are. This neighborhood." Scarlett's hands were damp on the steering wheel, and she had to concentrate as tears filmed her eyes. No, she couldn't give in to the despair that made her want to howl with rage and pain.

"Scarlett?" Ethan was desperately trying to figure out what was wrong with her.

"They're turning in at the parking lot in front of an abandoned grocery store." No, it couldn't be. But it was. The same place where they'd dumped her out of a van onto concrete with her ass bleeding and her body scraped and bruised. "Tell Mike it's the same lot where he found me after Simms cut me before. He'll know the location." Unreal. They were parking. What a fine place to enjoy a burger. Scarlett felt the acid of hate burn in her stomach. God, if only she could run over the bastard, she'd do it, again and again.

"Get out of the car, Leroy Simms." Scarlett wanted to shout it. Aim her car and just gun it. Instead, she drove past and pulled in a block farther down where the car could be hidden behind a bush.

"Scarlett." Mike had taken the phone. "Are you sure?" He rattled off the address.

"Hell yes, I'm sure. I'll never forget it. It's a few blocks from the freeway."

"We're on our way. So are a half dozen squad cars."

"Thanks. I'm hanging up now. I need a minute." She tossed the phone onto the passenger seat and leaned her head against the steering wheel. *Breathe.* Easier said than done. YoYo climbed into her lap and she dug her fingers into his fur.

She'd finally calmed down when her car door was wrenched open. Mona Delgado pointed a gun at her head.

"Hello, Scarlett. Thanks for following us. We even got you a burger."

* * * *

"What the hell do you mean, she needed a minute?" Ethan felt helpless and he didn't like it one damn bit. "I'm calling her back." He grabbed his phone from Mike, who was driving like a madman with one hand. "Her phone's ringing. Why isn't she picking up?" He clicked off when he got her voice mail, then tried again.

"Wish I knew. The squad cars should be there by now." Mike reached for his radio. "Report your status. What do you see? Are you at the site?"

Ethan heard a jumble of the kind of codes cops used and some mumbo jumbo. But one thing was clear. There was no gray Honda in the lot at the abandoned grocery store or any sign of Scarlett's car.

"Look down the street. Scarlett Hall said she pulled behind some bushes about a block down." Mike braked hard when a car pulled out in front of him. He had his siren going, but this character was apparently oblivious because of the loud music blaring from his stereo system. Mike wheeled around him, almost hitting a car coming in the opposite direction. His vocabulary would have impressed Ethan if he hadn't been praying so hard that Scarlett was okay. The Ranger slipped through a space in traffic Ethan wasn't sure was big enough. Ahead of them was a snarl of traffic stopped at a light while a pack of students crossed the street.

"Jesus, Mike!" He didn't know what Mike had just found out, but it had made him throw down his radio and put both hands on the wheel as he gunned the engine.

"Hold on, we're going up on the sidewalk."

Ethan knew his eyes bugged out of his head, but that was nothing compared to the looks on the faces of the students who jumped out of the way. What the hell? But Mike had his horn blaring and siren loud. People got the message that he was a man on a mission and they moved. By the time he got ahead of the crush of cars that had nowhere to go, the way ahead seemed clear.

"What was that about?" Ethan finally let go of the overhead handle.

"They found Scarlett's car, door open and no one inside."

"No!" Ethan leaned forward as if that could get them there faster, and tried to see the street numbers. They passed the Whataburger she'd told them about. There. Thirty-Fifth Street. Mike made the turn with screeching tires.

"You think—" He couldn't say it. Simms and that woman, Delgado. Could they have spotted Scarlett following them and tricked her into stopping? Then, when she'd thought she was safely hidden behind a bush... Ethan gripped the dash. Why the hell had Scarlett taken this on? She must have been so damn terrified, but she had followed them anyway. So freaking brave.

"We're going to get there and make our own assessment of the situation. I hope to God Scarlett took off and she's hiding. Maybe when"—Mike took a breath—"when she sees us, she'll come out."

"You know better than that. They have her, don't they, Mike?" Ethan couldn't think past that. Scarlett in the hands of a knife-wielding psycho. God, no. He spotted a group of flashing lights dead ahead. They were clustered in front of an old grocery store on the left.

Mike wheeled into the parking lot and jerked to a stop. He was out of the car in moments. Ethan clumsily unbuckled his seat belt and tugged at the door handle. Shit. Mike had locked him in. There was no way he could leave the car. He reached over and honked the horn. Mike just shook his head. Great, he was a prisoner in this fucking car. He stayed on the horn this time. He wasn't accepting that.

Mike walked over and jerked open the passenger door. "You can't be in on this. Let the cops handle it. Stay here."

"No. I have to do something. Not sit on my ass." Ethan met Mike's hard stare with one of his own. Mike looked away first.

Mike held the door open with a frown. "Come on then, but you don't touch or say anything. Understand? We're professionals. Let us do our jobs." He held him back when he started to climb out. "I mean it, Ethan. No going cowboy with your gun or I lock you in my trunk."

"Got it." Ethan was on his feet. He knew better than to argue, but it would take more than Mike to hold him back in this search for Scarlett. "Where's her Toyota?"

"Down the block. Come on." Mike strode down the street. Two roadblocks had been set up, and cops were directing traffic to side streets away from the scene.

"What are they doing about Simms and Delgado? Is someone trying to chase them down?" Ethan stopped when he saw Scarlett's car. The door hung open, the key in the ignition. Her cell phone was on the passenger seat. So was some dog fur. She took good care of her car, so that was unusual. When he could speak, he pointed it out to Mike. "You think she took YoYo with her?"

"I've got a unit at her place. There's no sign of a dog there, so I guess she did."

Ethan looked around, whistled, and even called the dog's name. No response. "Then they took both of them. Maybe that's a good sign. They plan to use them as hostages. Not…" He couldn't finish the sentence. Not just kill Scarlett? How could he possibly know what was in the mind of a cop killer or that Delgado woman? They had to be crazy to bother with Scarlett when they had made what had seemed to be a clean getaway from Sixth Street.

Mike shook his head. "Her place was trashed, the door obviously kicked in." Mike leaned against the car's frame. "Did you know she had a panic room? The door to it was standing open."

"No. Seriously? In her apartment?" Ethan realized it was a symptom of just how scared Scarlett had been after the first attack that she'd found a place with such a rare amenity. "It saved her today, though. Except…" He swallowed. "Answer me, damn it. What are you doing now? About tracking them down?"

"Seems the freeway is the likeliest and fastest route they'd take. If they're headed out of town now. I'm surprised they've stayed here this long." Mike shook his head. "There's no point standing around. I've got units going both ways down Mopac. Crime scene techs will dust her car for prints. Let's go. I want to jump on that freeway myself and try to catch up with them."

"Yeah. I'm all for that. Which way?" Ethan couldn't wait to get moving, and Mike had just proved he was a hell of a driver. Thank God the Ranger was on the same page. While he didn't doubt the units already looking would do a good job, no other cop was as invested as Mike in seeing Scarlett safely rescued.

"North. Easy to get lost out that way. Lots of little towns and side roads. Impossible for us to cover them all. If they're heading for Mexico, it's the logical way to go. I say we try our luck that direction. I'm alerting all the local law enforcement agencies in those towns. Silver or gray Honda. Shit, might as well be looking for a needle in a haystack. I can put a helicopter in the air, two. One going each way, but looking for a Honda on a freeway? They'll have the same problem." Mike ran toward his Department of Public Safety unit. Once there, he stopped and looked across at Ethan. "Don't suppose I could talk you into staying here. I can have someone take you home."

"No way in hell." Ethan didn't bother to argue. He just got in the car. He knew better than to show his gun now, when they were surrounded by other cops, but Mike had seen it before, under his shirt. "I have an idea. YoYo has a chip. Scarlett told me that. He's Anna Delaney's dog. Get someone to call her and find out who her vet is, track that chip and we can track the dog. What do you think?"

"I think you have the makings of a detective, Calhoun." Mike got on his phone and started the ball rolling on that. Once he hung up, he glanced at Ethan. "I'm not waiting around for the results of that."

"Then let's go." Ethan slapped the dashboard. "I won't get in your way, and I might be able to help. There are two of them, Mike. I'm a decent shot. Trust me to carry my weight if it comes to a shoot-out."

"That's why you should stay the hell here, Ethan. I warned you, I don't want you in a gunfight." Mike looked grim as he picked up his radio. "But I have a feeling you'd get in that fast car of yours and try to chase them down yourself if I sent you home. I'm not so heartless that I'd have you thrown in a cell for your own safety."

"Thanks." Ethan fastened his seat belt while Mike relayed his plans and request for helicopters to a supervisor over the radio. He didn't mention his passenger. No surprise there. It was probably against regulations to have him riding along. Not that Ethan gave a good damn right now. The car was moving even before they were given the go-ahead. Mike was waved through the roadblock, his car all lights and siren as he drove at high speed toward the nearby freeway.

North. It was as good a guess as any. With any luck they'd get a call that would help them track the dog and Scarlett if the Honda pulled off the freeway anywhere. As for that freeway, the southbound lane was already sluggish with the typical Sunday afternoon traffic. There was a popular lake and parks out south. Mike hit the on-ramp and wove in and out of traffic. Not exactly an empty freeway this direction, either, but at least people moved over when they saw him coming.

Ethan found himself gripping that overhead handle again and praying. *Please, God, let Scarlett be all right.* As long as they were running from the law, surely the hellish duo wouldn't have time to hurt her. They'd be driving with the flow of traffic too, trying to blend in. So Mike just might be able to catch up to them.

Chapter Twenty-Seven

"What did you tell the cops?" Ramona held the growling ball of fluff on her lap. She'd figured out fast that threatening the dog kept Scarlett from trying to bolt out of the car. What a piece of luck.

"Nothing! Give me the dog!" Scarlett reached for him.

"No way. Not until you tell me the truth." Ramona smiled and touched the dog with Leroy's knife. "I'd hate for this cute fella to lose an ear." They were both in the small back seat, Leroy driving.

"You wouldn't—" Scarlett's lips were trembling.

"Sure I would. If I can kill a man, I sure as hell can do a little surgery on a mutt." She laughed at the look on Scarlett's face. The bitch was scared shitless. "Oh, yeah. Everyone gave Leroy credit for Henry Littlefield. I did that one. Sniveling little coward. Begged for his life at the end."

"Monster! Henry was a sweet man. Never hurt anyone." Scarlett's face was red, she was so upset. "How could you kill him?"

"Oh, please. You never gave that twit the time of day. He tried to ask you for a date and you blew him off. I saw it. Now, call me a monster again and I'll prove it with this knife."

Ramona didn't like the bitch's attitude. Had hated her from the moment she'd strutted into Zenon and started changing things with her big ideas from Boston. Those idiots in the office loved her, even that stupid Littlefield. He'd been handy with the Crane op, helping them get info about Anna Delaney's schedule. He'd tried to date Anna first, then Scarlett. When both Boston bitches had given the geek the cold shoulder, Littlefield had been happy to turn on them. But Ramona knew you didn't leave loose ends, and the guy had been one. So he'd had to go. Using the knife had been interesting. And a way to put the blame on Leroy if things went south later.

She just didn't understand it. The same people who talked about the woman they called Mona behind her back and wouldn't give her the time of day sat with Scarlett at lunch and invited her to their baby showers. Had "Mona" ever been included in their little social circles? Hell, no. Her hand tightened on the knife, and she gave Scarlett such a look the woman got smart and scooted closer to the car door.

"I'm getting off this freeway, Ramona. She's bound to have described this car. We can get yours from the storage unit and change out. The exit is coming up." Leroy was watching them in the rearview mirror. "You gotta help me remember which place. Okay?"

"Yeah, good thinking, Lee." She ignored the dog's snarl as she trimmed some fur off its ear and dropped it in Scarlett's lap. Both the dog and the woman were shaking with nerves, and the mutt was shedding like crazy. It made her want to laugh and cut some more. "You described this car to the cops?"

Scarlett shook her head.

"I don't fucking believe you." Ramona held the knife next to the dog's ear again.

"Of course I did! Silver Honda. But look around. There are a lot of them. It won't help them find you. I couldn't even read the license plate." She glared while the dog barked and growled. "Please don't hurt YoYo. YoYo, hush!"

"Stupid name." Leroy snorted. "It's a boy? I had a dog once. Bruiser. Could bite your arm off if you made him mad. Not some useless toy like that little thing."

"I think he's cute. Or he was." Mona trimmed his other ear and the dog yelped. "Damn it, he keeps trying to bite me. Now look what you did, YoYo. I drew blood that time." She held up the blade. "See?"

"Stop it, you bitch!" Scarlett made a grab for the dog again.

"What else did you tell the cops, sister?" Ramona wiped the blood on Scarlett's leg. The woman wore shorts. Showing off some decent legs. Ramona had to give her credit, she actually lunged for the knife. But she was ready for her and slashed her leg, making Scarlett scream.

"What the hell's going on back there?" Leroy stopped the car.

"She made a move. Don't worry, I've got it under control." Ramona tossed some napkins from their lunch bag at Scarlett. Ramona had wolfed down the burger so fast her stomach hurt. The car reeked of the onions Lee loved. "Keep going."

"I can't. I see three storage signs from here. Which one, right or left?"

"Store 4U, on the right." Ramona waved Leroy's bloody knife in front of Scarlett's face. She had her attention now. "What else did you tell the cops?"

Scarlett pressed the napkins on the welling cut. "You had on a blond wig." She straightened her shoulders. "That's it. All I had time for. You don't really think you're going to get away, do you?"

"People always underestimate us, lady. Every time." She grinned as she told Leroy the code to open the gate to the storage facility. "Look here. We're about to change cars. The only question is: Do we kill you now and leave your body to rot here? Or save the fun for later?" She laughed. "Yeah, Lee remembers that ass of yours fondly. He wants to get a good look at it again. Maybe cut a new message."

Scarlett raised her chin and matched her stare for stare. "Seriously? Your boyfriend has the hots for me and you're okay with that?" She reached for the front seat and tapped Leroy on the shoulder. "Hate to disappoint you, Leroy." She said his name like she was spitting out the name of the devil. "But I had your initials erased from my ass."

"The hell you say." Leroy stopped the car across from their storage unit. "How did you do that?"

"Lee, would you forget about this woman's ass? We got bigger issues." Ramona looked behind them. She'd heard sirens off and on since they got on the freeway. Now one was getting louder. It couldn't be. How the hell had this cop gotten close enough to follow them? But coming up fast was a black and white DPS cruiser. They were trapped. She knew there was no back way out of this facility. She'd scoped that out early on.

She tightened her grip on the dog, and the damn thing bit her. "Ow! Shit!" She rolled down the window, ready to toss the fucking furball out.

"Wait! Give me the dog, and maybe I can help with the cops. That is why you brought me along, isn't it? As a bargaining chip?"

"No, damn it. We brought you along to torture and kill you." Ramona sucked on the bleeding bite while Leroy jumped out of the car and unlocked the storage building. What now? Use the second car as a barricade? Run over the cop, who would have backup here any minute?

"Lee! What are you doing?" She threw open her door. To hell with the stupid dog, she left it in the car with Scarlett, along with that ridiculous blond wig that was hot and itching her like crazy. She ran to join Lee.

"I'm backing out so we're aimed at the cops. I saw the lights in the rearview but hoped they would go past us. Guess not." He pulled her to him and gave her a desperate kiss. "Get the woman and the dog, use them as a shield. Hurry, she's trying to get away."

"Fuck!" Ramona ran back and grabbed Scarlett just as she managed to climb out of the car with the dog in her arms. "Move and I cut your throat."

"Then what good am I?" Scarlett jumped when there was a loud crash as the police car rammed the iron gate and came barreling through. It stopped yards away, and both front doors popped open.

Ramona dragged Scarlett behind their open car door while Leroy backed out the other car. He pulled it up beside her, then jumped out and aimed a gun at the cops, shooting a round at one of them.

"Let us go and we'll leave the woman here," Lee shouted. He knew what was at stake and got straight to the point.

"I'll cut her throat if you shoot at us. I swear it." Ramona waved the knife over her head, to prove she had the means. "Sign of good faith, here's her fucking dog." She snatched the dog from Scarlett and dropped it to the ground. When it tried to stay near Scarlett, she kicked it toward the cop car.

"Go, YoYo. Go." Scarlett bent over to push it away with her hands.

Ramona kept her in a strong grip, her knife on the woman's throat. "Lee, don't shoot the mutt. We're bargaining."

"You really think they're going to let us go, baby?" He didn't bother to do more than glance at her, trying to get a bead on whoever reached for the dog.

"They are if they want this bitch." Ramona looked across at her longtime lover. He had a wild light in his eyes she didn't like. He'd given up. Hell, he'd killed a cop. If they took him, he was facing the death penalty and he knew it. They sure weren't going to let him take off down the road in exchange for Scarlett Hall. Now she was screwed too. Why the hell had she bragged to Scarlett about killing Littlefield? Because she'd thought the woman would be dead soon. What a disaster. All those years of careful planning, seeing to details. The money, the sacrifice. For what? Why wasn't the cop saying anything?

The man behind the passenger door called the dog by name, and it finally ran to him. He scooped it up and stuffed it into the squad car. Lee took a shot at him. No sign or sound to say if he hit him or not. More sirens. Of course. The silence had meant the cop was calling for backup and giving out their location.

Ramona could see flashing lights coming down the road toward them, a fucking cop army. She pulled her gun from the back of her jeans and pressed the barrel to Scarlett's head. Yeah, she'd have liked to just use the knife, but time was running out. She'd take down a cop or two if she could after she laid out this bitch.

"Let Scarlett Hall go, Delgado." The cop had the deep voice of authority. "You want a chance at cutting a deal, give her to us now."

"Why should she get to have a life when I'm set to serve time?" Ramona was in a bind. She still had the knife in the hand she'd wrapped around

Scarlett's waist. Now she held the gun in the other. Of course the damn woman was struggling, fighting to get free. She should have tied her when she first got her. But Lee didn't like zip ties, wouldn't have any. And she wasn't good with rope. Besides, they'd been in a hurry. There'd been those sirens in the distance, getting closer.

"Be still, bitch, or I'll cut you right now."

"You could try." Scarlett stomped her foot, clearly trying to make her drop the knife or the gun.

Ramona stabbed Scarlett then, a good one in her waist. Oh, yeah, that got her attention, made her scream. "Feel that? If you keep moving, I swear to God I'm digging in, maybe try for a kidney. Want to test me? I'll be happy to watch you bleed out. Leroy can just look at your dead ass."

"I'm not moving again. Please." Scarlett gasped and held on to Ramona's arm.

"Shut up. I've got an offer on the table. Let me think. It might keep you alive."

"Don't listen to them, baby. You can't believe a word out of their lying mouths." Lee shot at the window in the passenger side of the cop car. Bulletproof glass, but he did some damage. Both men there returned fire.

Scarlett wobbled, like her knees were about to give out.

"Damn it, I said hold still." Ramona finally tossed the knife into the storage unit so she could get a tighter grip on Scarlett. At least the cops weren't shooting at her as long as they were afraid they'd hit Scarlett. But if the hostage went down, they might have a clear shot.

"Let me go. Save yourself. You know Simms wants to die here. You have a chance to get out someday if you don't kill a cop yourself." Scarlett started talking and wouldn't shut up. "That Ranger's name is Mike. You can trust him. He's a good man. If he says you can get a deal, he'll see to it. Don't you have family you want to see again, Mona? Why listen to Simms? Surely you have a mind of your own."

"If I let you go, Lee will shoot me himself. You don't understand. We're in this together." Ramona saw him aiming and firing, having the time of his life. Her lover, the father of her child, and mean as a snake. He was shooting whenever someone moved over there. Yeah, he was crazy. Other cops had pulled in and started returning his fire. She stayed crouched down behind the car where they couldn't hit her. Smoke was thick in the air, and it stunk, like sulfur or something. Lee got off on it, but it was making Ramona queasy. Damn burger.

"We can run into that empty storage unit," Scarlett said as she turned so she was looking at her, the gun barrel now in the center of her forehead.

The woman was gutsy but pale as paper. Ramona's arm was wet with her blood. "Listen to me, Mona. I can yell at Mike, tell him I'm okay and you want to surrender." Scarlett kept her hand over her wound, but blood slid through her fingers and dripped onto the concrete.

"You have no idea what I want." Freedom. A do-over. A cabana on a beach in the Caymans, a cute cabana boy serving her mai tais. To see Tommy graduate from college. Visit his wife and kids someday. Shit. Thinking like that was useless. It made her heart and her gut cramp.

"Come on, Ramona." Scarlett grabbed her gun arm with a surprisingly firm grip. "Yes, I know that's your real name. Let's do this. Separate yourself from Leroy Simms, the cop killer, so you can have a future someday. Life after prison."

"I told you to shut up, I can't think." Ramona didn't want to stare into those blue eyes. Fuck. She still had blue contact lenses in her own eyes. No wonder she felt off. Strange. Leroy spared them a glance and frowned.

"Do something, baby. Take a shot or go ahead and kill the woman. You know we aren't going to get out of this. I love you. No matter what, you did good, baby. Really good. We almost got away with the whole thing." He ducked when more gunfire erupted, then laughed and began shooting at the cops again.

"Aw, Lee. I love you too."

Ramona dragged Scarlett into the empty storage shed. Lee could have been screaming at her that this was all her fault. She was the one who'd insisted they go back for Scarlett Hall. They'd been home free. Yeah, they would be on their way to Mexico by now if it wasn't for her damned obsession with this bitch who smelled like fear and blood.

But Lee wasn't yelling at her. He was going out the way he wanted. Shooting at cops and waiting for his own end with a grin on his face. He had a bottle of tequila in his hand and was drinking between shots. Getting ready for his big finish. Well, this wasn't the way she wanted to go. Hell, no.

Chapter Twenty-Eight

Scarlett staggered as she was pulled into the open unit. Was Mona really thinking of letting her go? Maybe, but she still pressed the gun barrel against Scarlett's forehead. It hurt, but that was nothing compared to the pain of that knife wound in her side. God, but she'd like to grab that gun and turn it on Mona. But she could see Mona's finger twitching on the trigger. What if the gun went off while they struggled? Nice job if Scarlett managed to kill herself.

"Now what?" Scarlett saw spots in front of her eyes and staggered against Mona before she fell to the floor. At least that got the damn gun away from her head. She groped for the knife on the floor nearby. Could she reach it? Mona saw what she was doing and kicked it away.

"You never give up, do you? I can still shoot you. How would you like a bullet in your other leg? That would keep you pinned down."

"No! I swear I'll be still." Scarlett looked down at her blood-soaked T-shirt. Not only was she in excruciating pain, but blood still leaked from her, pooling on the floor.

"You'd better be." Mona kept the gun aimed at her, but she was watching Leroy Simms. He'd ripped off his suit coat when they'd first arrived, and now he'd popped open the trunk of the Honda.

Scarlet realized he wore another knife in a scabbard at his waist. Knife Guy. She'd never forget what he'd done to her with his blade. The pain and humiliation. He liked to degrade women. And Mona was his partner in crime. What did that say about her?

"He ever use a knife on you, Mona?" She had to ask. Maybe if Mona related to her, woman to woman, she'd start showing her some sympathy.

"What? Hell, no. Lee knows I wouldn't put up with that shit." She smiled. "How do you like what I brought for you, babe?"

"This is what I'm talking about." Simms pulled out a scary gun from that trunk.

Scarlett fought dizziness. Dear God. It looked like one of those assault rifles, an AK something. That kind of weapon would be even more dangerous than his pistol.

"Bring me the woman if you're not going to kill her." His words were slurred. The bottle of tequila was empty, and he tossed it away. He grinned and loaded the rifle, then slammed the trunk closed. He stood behind the back passenger door and aimed over it.

"Take this, you fuckers!" He raked the police car with a series of rapid shots that made Scarlett's ears ring. When the car's windshield showed heavy damage, Simms laughed, obviously delighted with the hits. "Look at them cops cower behind their cars." He frowned at Mona. "I said bring her here."

"Don't do it, Mona. You know if he kills me, they'll just rush you both. This is suicide by cop. Obviously Leroy has nothing to lose. You really want to go down with him?" She wondered if Simms could hear her beneath the sound of all the return gunfire. She had no idea how many cops were on the scene now. She'd recognized Mike's voice before. Had that been Ethan calling YoYo? Leroy kept shooting at that first car. Had he missed every time, or were Ethan and Mike lying dead or wounded back there? Oh, God.

"Lee, I can't kill her now, she's our bargaining power." Mona kept her eyes on Simms.

"Fuck that." He ducked behind the other car and was suddenly in the storage unit with them. "They're not going to bargain with me and you know it." He jerked Scarlett up off the ground and stood swaying with her pressed against him. He stared at Mona, one hand biting into Scarlett's arm. He still held the rifle in his other hand. "Don't worry about me, baby. When I'm gone, tell them I made you come with me. Blame me for everything. Big bad Leroy, leading you astray since high school." He leaned toward Mona. "I've always had a thing for you, you know that."

For a moment, Scarlett wondered if he was going to kiss the bitch. With her between them? He was clearly feeling the effects of too much tequila. He must have thought Scarlett had lost so much blood that she was harmless. She took a breath and almost gagged at the stench of booze, onions, and smoke that surrounded Leroy Simms. Even Mona seemed put off and stepped back out of reach.

"Lee, don't give up. Go shoot some more cops." Mona held her gun at her side. She could have shot at some cops, but hadn't yet. Maybe Scarlett had gotten to her with talk of life after prison. Shooting a cop would end that dream. But if she thought Scarlett was going to testify for her later? Claim Mona had been a Good Samaritan in all this? Now, that was a dream.

He ignored Mona's suggestion. "Listen to me, baby. If you get out of this alive, tell the boy I'm sorry I wasn't there for him. You hear me?"

Could Mona possibly care about such a man? Apparently. She was crying. "Please hear me, Lee. Maybe we should surrender. Get a good lawyer. Negotiate for life instead of the needle for you."

"No point in that. It ends here. But not before I take care of this." He pulled out his knife, then tossed the rifle to Mona. She fumbled and almost dropped it in her surprise.

"Do what you want with her, Lee. I don't care. You know I hate her." Mona wiped her wet face with her sleeve. "If you're determined, then finish what you started."

"No!" Scarlett shoved him as hard as she could. He staggered, his hand raised as if to strike her with the knife.

"Still have some fight in you, don't you, woman? I'm happy to play." He grinned and reached for her again.

Scarlett lost her balance and fell back, hitting the concrete so hard she saw stars and had trouble catching her breath. He dropped down on top of her and smiled, his fetid breath in her face. His weight on her body was crushing her and made her desperate to get him off of her. She wasn't going to die today and certainly not by Knife Guy's hand. No way in hell. He raised that damn knife again.

"Scared, chickie?" He laughed. "Aw, she can't breathe. Look, Ramona, the woman is a bloody mess and still fighting."

"Get it over with, Lee. I swear, if you try to look at her butt, I'll shoot you myself." Mona stood over them, the rifle in her hand. Not that Scarlett could focus on anything but Leroy's leering face inches from hers.

"Want to see my butt, Leroy? Roll me over, I'll show you." Scarlett wheezed as she said this, breathing hard but he'd shifted enough to give her air. She would do anything to stall and keep him from killing her. She shoved at him again, but he was a heavy hulk of a man. An immovable object unless he wanted to move.

"Yeah, Ramona. Don't tell me what to do. I may have just moments to live. Don't you want me to die happy? Lean out of the shed and aim another round at those fucking cops. Do it now before they decide to rush us." He rolled until he was on his back, Scarlett now lying on top of him.

Scarlett took a moment to catch her breath and look around furtively for the other knife. It had to be here somewhere. Mona had never picked it up. She'd kicked it and... There! It was lying in the blood that had leaked from her wound.

"You want to know how I erased your initials, Leroy?" It took everything in her, but she pressed a palm to his chest and pushed herself up to a sitting position, straddling him. Even moving that much made her grind her teeth. Her hatred gave her the strength to do it. If she could pretend she was going to pull down her shorts and show him her butt, maybe she could reach the knife. Then she'd threaten him, stick him, do whatever she could to make him let her go.

"Tell me." He watched her with narrowed eyes, not as drunk as he'd seemed a minute ago. He'd ripped open his shirt. Shooting at cops had made him sweat, another stink coming from him.

"Tattoo. You got Ramona's name in a heart on your chest. How... sweet." Scarlett fought dizziness.

"No shit. You tattooed over my initials? Show me." He smiled, pure evil. When he gripped her hips, she gasped and swayed. Pain slammed into her when he touched her knife wound, and she fell forward, her hand sliding on his damp chest. God.

"Changed... my mind." Scarlett's bravery had leaked out with her blood. She couldn't do this. Hurt. "I'd rather die."

"Not yet, sweet thing. Let me see." With a quick move he had her on her face on the pavement, his rough hands ripping her shorts down to expose her butt. "I'll be damned. Look at this, baby. She covered up my initials with a fucking flower garden."

Scarlett lay there, the wind knocked out of her again. Give up? No, she couldn't just lie there and take this. When Leroy stroked her ass, Scarlett couldn't help it, she screamed and bucked. Dear God. No!

"Off. Get off of me!" *Knife! If she could just stretch for it.* She reached back to beat at his head, hit him with one fist while screaming to distract him. A few more inches. Yes. She dropped her hand on top of it and slid the blade toward her, then tucked it next to her side. She almost wept with relief. A weapon. A way to fight back. If she could just find leverage, some way to strike at him. Cut him.

"Stop it, Lee. You don't have time to carve her up. Just kill her and be done with it." Mona had used the rifle, shooting at least two rounds. So she was doing her part to keep the cops occupied.

"Shut up." Leroy must have been studying that tattoo.

"Come on now. You can still let me use her to talk our way out of here." Mona sounded pissed.

"Baby, I told you. I'm a dead man." But he did flip Scarlett over again.

Scarlett fumbled to keep the knife hidden. She could breathe now and might have a chance to fight him off.

"At least let me…" Leroy was on his knees, laughing as he pulled down the front of her shorts.

"If you say fuck her, you're a dead man for sure." Mona stood behind him and poked him in the back with the rifle. "I mean it, Lee."

"Don't tell me what to do. Get back to the door and shoot at the cops." He dragged Scarlett's shorts down even further, looking over his shoulder at Mona, who edged toward the door and shot in the air. "I can have one last fuck if I want it."

Scarlett was exposed, horrified, and she sure couldn't just lie there while he taunted Mona and did whatever he wanted. At least with Mona screaming at him, he hadn't noticed the knife she still held next to her bloody shirt. No, he was busy cutting away her thong and tossing it aside. "With her? Are you nuts?" Mona jumped from the doorway to where Leroy crouched, incensed. She screamed at him but couldn't see Scarlett from where she stood. "You don't have time for this. Cops are shooting at us, Lee." Of course they could all hear that. Bullets pinged off the tin building.

Leroy just laughed again and reached for his zipper, watching Mona as if seeing her reaction was fun for him.

"Don't you dare!" Mona reared back her leg and kicked Leroy in the butt. The move surprised him into losing his balance. He fell forward, right onto the knife in Scarlett's hand.

"Get off her, Lee. Now!" Mona stomped over next to Scarlett's head. "Damn it, I said…" She hit him in the shoulder, surprised when Leroy didn't respond. "Lee?"

Blood spread over Scarlett's chest, hot and wet. One of her hands, the one with the knife, was crushed under Leroy. She tried to push him away, but he was dead weight. His head lay against hers on the concrete, unmoving. Was he breathing? She didn't think so. Had she killed him? She looked up into Mona's horrified face. What would the woman do to her if she had managed to kill him?

"What the fuck happened?" Mona cast aside the rifle and used both hands to roll Simms off of Scarlett. "You had a knife? *My* knife?" Mona dropped to her knees next to Leroy's still body and stared at the knife sticking out of his chest. "My God!"

Scarlett was too shocked to move. She was covered with blood, his and hers, and her chest hurt where the knife handle had slammed into her when it had hit Simms. At least now she could suck in air, and she did, shakily.

"Lee! Baby!" Mona frantically touched his face, then felt for a pulse. "Nooo!" She bent her head and sobbed. But not for long. She soon had herself under control. Standing, she wiped away her tears, then stalked over to pick up the rifle and aim it at Scarlett's face. "You fucking killed him."

Scarlett waited. She was too numb to even say a prayer. She just closed her eyes. She couldn't bear to see the shot come at her. When the silence stretched, except for the gunfire coming from outside, those dozens of metallic pings on the storage shed, she finally looked up.

"Mona?" She wasn't going to apologize or say it was an accident, which it had been. She was glad the bastard was dead. Of course seeing Simms lying there, his eyes wide but already glazed with death, was a reality check she wasn't quite sure how to deal with right now. Taking a human life, no matter how despicable... Well, all she could do was thank God for the miracle that she'd managed to hit him in the heart. He couldn't hurt her now.

Mona wiped more tears from her cheeks. She looked around as if in a daze, finally seeming to come to some kind of decision. She grabbed the handgun in her waistband and put it behind her back, then dragged Scarlett to her feet. "Whatever I say, you back me up. Understand? Pull up your fucking shorts!"

"I, uh, sure. Are you going to let me go?" Scarlett was too weak and stunned to do more than stand trembling after she pulled up her shorts.

"Let's see if you can get me that deal your pal Mike offered." Mona wrestled with the rifle and finally got a good grip on both it and Scarlett. She took a shaky breath, then pushed Scarlett in front of her.

"Hold your fire! I'm surrendering! We're coming out." Mona waved the big gun over her head, first shoving Scarlett out of the storage unit. "Don't shoot! I'm throwing out my weapons." She tossed both guns out of the shed so that they clattered to the pavement in front of the Honda. "If you shoot, you'll hit Scarlett." She shook Scarlett, who was sagging, in front of her, protecting her from the police. "Tell them I'm unarmed."

Scarlett leaned against Mona's supporting hands, the only things keeping her upright as she was shoved forward. She couldn't focus and licked dry lips as she tried to form words. Mona pushed her in the back when she didn't speak.

"Tell them or I'll stick you in that side wound." Mona must have seen her condition and poked her there with a finger anyway.

Scarlett gasped with pain. "Yes! She's unarmed. Don't, don't shoot." She staggered when Mona finally let her go and shoved her toward the police cars.

"Delgado, drop facedown on the ground. Hands out to your sides, palms up. Where's Simms?" Mike's voice.

Scarlett swayed, her hands wet with blood where she held them over her wound. Pain. She could not faint. Had to see... Mona fell to the ground next to her.

"Dead. He's dead," Mona cried out with her face against the concrete.

"He is. I killed him." Had Scarlett said it loud enough? Must have, because suddenly she was in someone's arms. Ethan! Beneath that disgusting gun smell she'd know him anywhere. He picked her up and held her close.

"Scarlett, God, Scarlett!" He kissed her face, her hair. "Mike! She's hurt, covered in blood. Help! Where's the ambulance?" He carried her away from Mona, who screamed that the handcuffs were cutting off the circulation in her hands.

"Ethan. Blood. Not all mine. You okay?" Scarlett said this into his shirt. Raising her head took too much effort.

"I'm fine. Worried about you." He kissed the top of her head again as he walked with her in his arms, every movement a jolting agony. "Who hurt you? Simms? You really took him down?"

"Mona stabbed me." She was pulled away from him. Flat surface. Red lights. Ambulance. She closed her eyes. Safe. Ethan? Cut her shirt. Hurt! At least... Mama always said... Nice bra. Pink. For Ethan. The world fading. Someone said... Blood loss. A prick. Painkiller? Please. Ethan whispering. Love? No sleep. She wanted to say... Too late. The world disappeared.

Chapter Twenty-Nine

Scarlett woke up in a hospital bed. She hurt just about everywhere. The worst was her side, where she remembered getting stitches. She inhaled and smiled despite her pain. The air was perfumed by dozens of roses. Everywhere she looked, there were roses—yellow, pink, red, an exotic orange, and even lavender, in crystal vases. Better than that, though, Ethan sat on one side of her bed and Rhett on the other.

"She's awake!" Rhett said it, but she saw Ethan staring at her like he couldn't get enough.

"Finally." Ethan squeezed her hand. Yes, he was holding on to her left one, carefully like he'd never let go.

"Hey." Scarlett smiled at him. She hoped her heart was in her eyes. She'd never forget how he'd rushed out to pick her up after Mona had dragged her out of the storage unit. She had no idea how he'd managed to talk Mike into letting him be there, but she'd needed him. More than she could have imagined.

"You scared the hell out of us, Ladybug. What were you thinking, chasing those nutcases in your car? And taking the dog with you?" Rhett leaned over and kissed her on the cheek. Then he shook his head. "You look like shit. I'm calling Mom and Dad."

"Don't you dare! I seem to have survived. When they were working on me, I heard the doctor say they won't keep me in here long if I don't show signs of an infection. So what's the point in dragging Mom and Dad here?" Scarlett saw Ethan stand. "Are you going to chew me out too?"

"You'd deserve it. But I'd rather kiss you." He leaned over her, ignoring her brother to give her a leisurely and very claiming kiss. "Promise me you'll never do that again."

"What? Chase bad guys in my car? I hope I never have the need." She reached up and ran her hand over his stubble. So dear. And he looked like he hadn't slept since the day before. "Who's responsible for all the flowers?"

"That's the Texan." Rhett settled back in his chair. "Showing off."

"I don't know one flower from another. Casey said there were a lot of roses in your tattoo, so I figured they were a safe bet. You'll have to tell me which color is your favorite. For the future." Ethan brushed her hair back from her face. "I wouldn't be as blunt as your brother, but you don't look great. How are you feeling?"

"I hurt like hell where Mona stabbed me in the side. Otherwise, weak and achy." She pulled Ethan's hand to her lips and kissed the back of it. "I do love roses. I think I like the yellow the best. Isn't there a song about the Yellow Rose of Texas?"

"Sure is. I'll do us all a favor and not sing it. Though, as a good Texas boy, I know it by heart." He glanced at Rhett. "Could you leave us alone for a few minutes?"

"If that's what Scarlett wants." Rhett stood when she nodded. "Okay, but, sis, give me a shout if you need me back in here. I *am* calling our parents. I'll downplay this, or Mom would be on the next plane."

"You know I love her, but she's absolutely smothering when you're sick or hurt." Scarlett would never forget when she'd had the flu in college. She still couldn't face a bowl of chicken soup.

"I know. She moved in when I broke my foot skydiving and I thought I'd never pry her out of there." He stood in the doorway, frowning. "We'd be looking at something a hell of a lot more serious if that bitch had hit a vital organ. And all bets are off if you do end up with an infection."

Scarlett blew him a kiss. "Thanks, big brother. If she freaks out, promise Mom I'll come home for, um, Mother's Day. Next month. That should make her happy."

"Yep. That'll do it." He glanced at Ethan. "Hope your boss is all right with that."

"Whatever she needs. Boston. Hell, I'll go with you, Scarlett, if you want me. The bar opening can wait." He wasn't letting go of her hand.

Scarlett watched Rhett smirk as he left the room. She knew what her brother was thinking. If Ethan went home with her, that would signal a real relationship to her parents. They'd be all over the Texan. Was she ready for that? Was Ethan ready for that?

"You're awfully quiet. Did my threatening to go to Boston with you do that? I didn't mean to pressure you when you're still weak from blood loss. But I told you we're just getting started and I meant it." Ethan leaned against the bed and studied her face.

"Do I really look that bad?" She wished for a mirror, then decided it was probably a good thing she didn't have one. She ran a hand through her hair and realized someone must have combed it, but it needed a wash. And her forehead hurt.

"You're just so pale. Damn it." His fingertips slid across her forehead. "You even have a bruise here. Round. Did Delgado put a gun to your head?"

"Yes, to keep me in line."

"God, the hell they put you through." He swallowed. "There was a pool of blood in that storage unit. Scarlett, it's a miracle you didn't bleed out."

"Some of that blood belonged to Leroy Simms. I killed him, Ethan." Scarlett stared up at the ceiling. Should she be sad? Sorry? All she felt was a deep relief. "I mean, he fell on the knife. He and Mona…" She looked away.

"You don't have to explain anything. I'm glad he's dead. I know you are too."

"Yes! Does that make me a horrible person?" If it hadn't pulled her stitches, she would have laughed out loud with relief. Oh, she was horrible. A man was dead. No, a monster was dead. She wanted a pain pill and oblivion so she didn't have to think about any of it.

"Look at me, damn it." He squeezed her fingers, not hard, just enough to get her attention. "Scarlett, you are not horrible. You were fighting for your life. That bastard tormented you. Don't you dare feel guilty about what happened."

"Guilty? No, not that. Well, maybe a little for not…" Scarlett pulled his face to hers and kissed him. "My brain is fried. Obviously I have no idea how I feel about what went down. But you were there for me. I remember that much. How you ran out to pick me up at the end."

"Yes, I did." He pulled her into his arms, treating her like delicate porcelain because of her injuries. "You scared me. I thought I'd lost you for a while there. If you did kill him, I say well done."

Scarlett held on to him, his warmth wonderfully soothing. When she finally let him help her lay back on the pillows, she tried to explain how she felt. "It's just that I've been afraid for so long, I'm finding it hard to believe it's really over. Is Mona locked up where she can't escape? And are they sure Simms is really dead?" She looked him in the eyes.

"I promise you, he's dead. Mike made damn sure of that. Mona, Ramona, whatever the hell she goes by, is in a very secure place. After Simms escaped, believe me, they're taking no chances with her."

"Good." Scarlett shuddered. "I never want to go through anything like that again."

"Damn it, I'd like to go to that jail and wipe the floor with Delgado. I was raised to never hit a woman. Never have. Yet. But the idea that she…" Ethan looked away, staring at a vase of pink roses. "I knew Simms had a thing for you, but the woman. Why was she so dead set on hurting you, Scarlett?" He met her gaze again, held her hand. Strong and there for her.

Scarlett shared some of the things Mona had told her. The resentment at work that she'd never even noticed. Of course her coworkers had avoided Mona. She'd flaunted the fact that she was Ron Zenonsky's secretary and privy to company secrets. She acted like she was better than the rest of the office staff and then wondered why no one wanted a happy hour with her.

"Call it jealousy or the irrational behavior of a woman who wasn't wired right, I don't know or care. But she focused all her hatred on me. Ethan, I just hope I never have to see her again." Scarlett had never meant anything more. "What will happen to her now? They need to throw the book at her."

"Mike says so far the charges are kidnapping, assault with a deadly weapon, of course. Look what she did to you. Then there's resisting arrest and aiding and abetting a fugitive." He frowned. "That last one makes me shudder. It could be what they pin on me if I get caught helping my mother. Mike's become a friend. I'm beginning to think I should tell him everything and see what happens."

"Tell me what?" Mike stood in the doorway. "Something you need to get off your chest, Calhoun?"

"Mike!" Scarlett held out her hand. "Never mind that! I have something important to tell you. About Mona Delgado. When she had me in that car, she confessed to a murder."

"What?" That got Mike's attention. He hurried to her bedside. "What murder?" He tossed his cowboy hat on the foot of the bed and pulled out his notebook. "Glad to see you awake, by the way." He leaned down and kissed her on the cheek, a rare thing for the Ranger. Then he settled into the chair abandoned by Rhett. "Your brother said to tell you he'll be back in a while with Casey."

"Good. I need some things from my apartment. She can pick them up for me. Maybe I'll call her." Scarlett looked around for her phone. When had she had it last? "Ethan?"

"Scarlett, tell me about the murder first. This is a priority." Mike frowned at her.

"What do you need? I'll leave you here to tell Mike about Delgado and run and get your things for you." Ethan was on his feet, obviously anxious to take off. He probably wanted to hear about the murder but was even more worried about Mike's interest in his own secret.

"Oh, would you? That would be great. Let me make a list." Scarlett looked around for paper and pen.

Ethan took her hand. "Let me guess. If you're like my sisters you want a hairbrush, makeup, nightgown, and robe. Slippers and a change of clothes for when they let you leave here. Is that it?" He avoided looking at Mike. Or maybe that was her imagination. He smiled down at her, giving her his full attention.

"That's perfect. I seem to be missing my purse and phone. They were in my car. Mike?"

"We didn't keep them. Look around for them, Ethan." Mike was fidgeting, obviously ready for the murder details.

"I'll check in the apartment, maybe Rhett got them." Ethan leaned over for a kiss. "You going to be okay for a while? I can call Rhett if you want me to stay." He finally glanced at Mike.

"No, go. I'll be okay." Scarlett squeezed his hand and gestured for him to come closer. She whispered in his ear. "Take your time, you know why." Then she kissed him again and watched him straighten with a smile. "Check on YoYo while you're there, if you don't mind."

"Sure. The little guy and I are buds now. I sure was glad he came to me when Delgado let him go. He's our hero. His chip helped us track you when Simms turned off the freeway. Can you believe it?" Ethan tucked the covers more securely around her while Mike explained how they'd figured that out. "You take it easy. Mike, she's weak and in pain. Don't stay too long."

"Yes, I am." Scarlett did hate to see Ethan go, but knew it was better for him to get away from Mike for now. "Did you know YoYo took a chunk out of Mona?" She turned to Mike when he laughed. "Hey, he's little, but he has a protective instinct, just like all men."

"I'll have to give him an extra treat for that. But if he bit Delgado, he may need to go to the vet for a checkup. That woman is bound to be toxic." Ethan knocked fists with Mike on his way to the door.

"Ethan, wait! Do you have a key?" She couldn't remember if she'd given him one.

"Rhett gave me a copy." He waved at her from the door, obviously anxious to get out of the room. "Be back in a flash. Love you." And with that bombshell, he was gone.

"He's a stand-up guy. He was determined to stick with me when we were trying to find you. Not surprised he used the 'L' word." Mike shook his head. "You look a little surprised."

"I guess I am. We haven't said it yet. Though I thought I heard it after the rescue."

"Rescue? Honey, you saved yourself." Mike patted her arm. "Don't know how you managed to take down Simms, but the whole force is talking about it. You're our hero."

"No. It was an accident. Mona was jealous of the attention Simms gave me. When he got on top of me, well..." Scarlett covered her face, shocked when sobs burst out of her. Oh, God, she did not want to relive those moments. But she couldn't forget Simms reaching for his zipper. He'd been so big, so heavy, and there was nothing she could do to stop him. She stammered out the story, finally telling someone all that had happened. Mike didn't say a word. Didn't even write it down. He just kept his warm, strong hand on her arm, reassuring. There.

When she got to the part where Mona kicked Leroy, Mike grunted, the only sign that she'd surprised him.

"So you see, it was an accident. I think Mona loved him. She said she did anyway. Simms claimed to love her too. He was even willing to take the blame for everything." Scarlett took the handful of tissues Mike passed to her and blew her nose. "When Mona realized Leroy had fallen on the knife and was dead..." She took a breath. "Well, I thought for a minute that she was going to shoot me on the spot." Scarlett wiped her face and looked at those beautiful roses. Alive. She was alive and had a man who loved her. This inner trembling had to stop. She looked at Mike, who sat patiently, never judging. "But then she gathered herself. Mona is a hard woman and always seemed to have a plan. Anyway, she ordered me to cooperate right before she dragged me out of there. You saw what happened next."

"Yeah. Sure surprised the hell out of us. We expected to see Simms pop up and start shooting when you two came out." Mike sighed. "Now, what's this murder you threw out there to distract me from whatever is going on with your boyfriend?"

"Nothing gets by you, does it?" Scarlett shook her head. She sure wasn't telling Mike a thing about Ethan's problem. "Mona claimed she killed Henry Littlefield. She bragged that she used a knife on him. Had him begging for his life at the end."

"Wow. We thought Leroy Simms killed him." Mike wrote that down. "Did she give you any more details?"

"Just that she got off on the blood. Used a knife on me to prove it. She said she knew law enforcement gave Leroy credit for it, but that she'd done the deed. She and Simms had matching knives." Scarlett really didn't want to talk about this anymore. Thank God a nurse appeared at the door.

"It's time to take Ms. Hall's vitals and for her medication. If you'll step out, sir." She smiled at Mike. She might have been flirting. He certainly was handsome in his Ranger uniform.

"Can we talk later or tomorrow? I *am* tired." Scarlett sighed and made a show of yawning. Not that it was a stretch. Whether it was weakness from blood loss or just the drain of reliving everything she'd been through, she wanted nothing more than oblivion right now. She hoped one of her medications would provide that.

"Sure. But I'll need a complete statement. A blow-by-blow of everything that happened with Delgado and Simms from beginning to end." Mike put on his cowboy hat and smiled at the nurse. "Take good care of her now. She's a brave lady."

"Yes, sir." The nurse carried in a container of supplies. "We take good care of all our patients. I hope you never get wounded in the line of duty and we have to fix you up."

"Me too." He glanced back at Scarlett. "I'll call you later." He walked out the door.

"My, I do like a man in uniform." The nurse took Scarlett's arm so she could check her blood pressure. "He married?"

"Afraid so." Scarlett leaned back and closed her eyes while the nurse chattered and checked the dressing on her wound. What if she hadn't followed Simms and Delgado? Would they be in Mexico by now, planning how they'd come back to finish her? Maybe she'd been foolish following them. It had certainly been dangerous. But she'd done it for peace of mind. Fine. Simms was dead. Delgado locked up tight. So where was the peace?

At least her pain meds kicked in and Scarlett was just drifting off to sleep when a distant buzzing woke her. Phone. She groped in the nightstand drawer. Aha! Her missing cell phone.

Still a little out of it, she answered.

"Ms. Hall?"

"Yes?"

"This is Nathan McFee. I'm representing Ramona Delgado."

"Representing?" Scarlett wasn't sure she was fully awake.

"Her attorney, Ms. Hall. She asked me to call you."

"Why?" Scarlett almost dropped the phone. What kind of joke was this?

"She'd like to speak to you."

"You can't be serious." Scarlett laughed, the movement hurting her side. "You can tell Ms. Delgado to go straight to hell."

"Wait! Don't hang up." The lawyer seemed anxious. If he was smart, he was probably afraid of Mona. Surely she couldn't hurt anyone from jail. Public defender? Or was she somehow paying him big bucks? Didn't matter.

"I'm lying in a hospital bed because of your client, Mr. McFee. She has nothing to say that I want to hear. Tell her I'll see her in court when I testify against her." Scarlett ended the call and dropped the phone on the bed beside her. What the hell could Mona want? Scarlett knew what *she* wanted, never to see or hear from that bitch again.

Breathe. Mona is locked up and can't get out. Then why was her heart pounding and her stomach queasy?

Scarlett put a hand on her side. Did the wound feel hot? Was she getting worse? She pressed the call button for the nurse, then picked up the phone again. Ethan. Rhett. She didn't want to be alone.

Wait a damn minute. Since when did she need someone to hold her hand? She sure hadn't had anyone helping her in that storage shed. She took a breath. Shaky. Another one. Better. And the pain meds were kicking in. All right. Yes, she loved her brother. And Ethan. But she didn't need either one of them right now. She was safe, recovering, and Mike had called her a hero.

Well, that was a stretch. She'd survived anyway. She lay back on her pillow and closed her eyes. No more nightmares. No more cowering in panic rooms. From now on she was looking ahead to a future without fear. She smiled as she drifted off to sleep.

* * * *

Ethan had just put the last thing he thought Scarlett would want into a tote when his phone rang. He really didn't need this now.

"Mama, what's up?"

"This isn't your mother, Ethan. It's Lisa. I'm using her phone."

"Why is that? Yours run out of minutes? Don't you feel even a little guilty for using my mother, Lisa?" Damn it, he had to get this settled and soon. But right now, Scarlett was his priority.

"Missy used *me* to get out of that hellhole. Trust me on that. Now, listen. We drove by that bar of yours a while ago. Guess what we saw? A street full of cops. What the hell have you done, Ethan? Turned in your own mama?" Lisa's voice rose on that last word. "You will sorely regret that, mister."

"Turn on the news. Sixth Street is where that killer, Leroy Simms, has been hiding out. If you saw cops, it's because they were searching for him.

Now that he's dead and his partner in crime has been caught, I'm sure the heat there will die down. Wait and see if it doesn't." Ethan's phone beeped with an incoming call from Scarlett. "Look, I'm getting another call I need to take."

"Don't you dare hang up on me!" Lisa screamed. "I don't trust you. I don't believe a word out of your lying mouth."

Ethan realized Scarlett's call had gone to voice mail. Shit. "Lisa, calm down. I've done everything you've asked of me. Put my mother on the phone."

"She is unavailable." Lisa sniffed. "Both of us are fed up with your stalling. Bring us cash, a lot of it, and we'll buy our own fake papers. Somewhere else. Maybe Albert will help us."

"I wouldn't count on that. He seems like a nice guy. Honest. What's he going to say when you tell him you're changing identities so you can leave the country?" Ethan knew this was all going to shit. He had to arrange a meeting. Lisa had no answer for that, so he plowed ahead.

"Tomorrow. Meet me in the bar tomorrow. I'll have what you need. I promise you. Mama had better be there. You sure I can't talk to her?"

"She's passed out. Too much bourbon. You saw how she was drinking. Drowning her sorrows. When you told her you'd be too busy to visit her in her new country, she went down into what we call the black hole of misery." Lisa laughed. "Yeah, Mama's got real issues. So drinking is one of the few pleasures she has left, Ethan. Me too. If I can't get Albert in the sack soon, I'm moving on from him to someone else. You're right. He's a nice guy. Maybe too nice for me." She fumbled with the phone, and Ethan heard her pour a drink.

"Let me tell you something. Those drugs they gave us in the hospital dulled our appetites for everything except food. That should be a crime, don't you think? Now that I'm away from that shit, I'm finally feeling it again. Urges. You know what I mean?" She howled, then laughed.

"I don't need to hear this, Lisa." He sure didn't want to think about it in connection to his mother. "Just agree to meet me in the bar tomorrow at three. I'll either have the money or the papers. That work for you?"

"Fine. But all those cops better be gone when we get there or we're picking another place." She hung up.

Ethan dialed Scarlett. "Ethan?" She sounded half asleep.

"What is it? Everything all right?" He heard her take a breath.

"I must have rolled over on my phone. I'm sorry. But Mike is gone if you want to come back." Big yawn. "Any idea how long that will be?"

"I'm on my way." He smiled at how dopey she sounded. "Go back to sleep, baby. Let yourself heal. I think I've got everything you need here."

"You're everything I need." She sighed, obviously half asleep. "I love you."

"Well, I guess you heard me. I love you too. But we shouldn't be saying it like this over the phone. I want to say it right next time. Looking into your eyes. See you in a little while." Ethan ended the call and stuck his phone in his pocket. Love. Yeah, he'd meant it, and he hated that he'd said it so offhandedly in the hospital. Love you. Without the I. He'd heard his sisters when they were teenagers gripe about that. It was a cop-out. Say the three words, Ethan, they'd told him years ago. And not just after sex, but all the time.

He'd never said those three words. Not to his hookups, that was for sure. No, he'd never said them until he'd held Scarlett while she was almost unconscious from blood loss. He had to do it right next time. But he couldn't quit smiling. Because she'd said it back. Without hesitation.

So despite the looming Mama and Lisa confrontation, he was happy as he said good-bye to YoYo, locked Scarlett's apartment door, and headed to his car. He had a future to look forward to now. Surely Scarlett would be okay that he wasn't on board with the secret bar thing anymore. With her out of danger, they could plan a different kind of place. Fuel would be a club they could both be proud of. If he wasn't serving time for aiding and abetting. Because leaning against his Porsche was a tall, dark Texas Ranger with a grim look that meant business.

Well, hell.

Chapter Thirty

Scarlett still was a little weak but glad to be home. YoYo was thrilled to see her, jumping at her feet until she settled on the couch. She noticed everything was in order, with no sign of her nightmare except for new wood framing the front door.

"Thanks for bringing me home." She pushed YoYo back when he tried to sit in her lap, wincing when he trod on her stitches. "Down." Of course he ignored her, but he did settle beside her.

"I'm surprised Ethan isn't here." Rhett brought in the vase of yellow roses. The rest had been donated to other patients at the hospital.

"He had a special delivery at the bar. I told him to go ahead and take care of it since you'd volunteered to bring me home." Scarlett knew Ethan was finally handling a confrontation with his mother. She was dying to be there with him, but he'd insisted he had it worked out. No details. Which was driving her crazy. Yes, it was his family. Not her business. But if they were in a relationship... She realized Rhett had probably said something and she'd missed it.

"What?"

"I said, you're still managing, even from your sickbed. It's his bar, let him handle it." Rhett set the roses on the kitchen table. "You okay?"

"Getting there." She stroked YoYo's fur and noticed the cut on one ear. That bitch Mona. It was healing, but she'd trimmed the fur unevenly. A trip to the groomer was necessary—and soon.

"Anna called. She and King are coming back from Boston in a couple of days. I'll miss this little fellow when she picks him up." She hugged YoYo. "Mona used him to keep me in line. What a heartless bitch."

"Yeah. No doubt about that. Look what she did to you, Ladybug." Rhett moved over and settled next to her on the couch. "Maybe you can get your own rescue dog after YoYo's gone. Ethan told me this little guy even bit Delgado trying to protect you."

"I didn't know the pup had it in him." Scarlett blinked back tears. She refused to start crying at the drop of a hat. No way.

"I still can't believe you went after them." Rhett squeezed her hand. "I would have done the same thing. But Scar, my God, you had to be scared shitless."

"I was. But they'd threatened to come back later and finish me. With that hanging over my head, I knew I'd never have a moment's peace if they got away." She let go of his hand and stood. "I think I'll go to bed now. Don't you have a date with Casey? All I want now is to sleep in my own bed for hours. I'll see Ethan when he gets done at the bar."

"You sure you don't need me for anything else?" He followed her to her bedroom door.

"Who fixed the door and cleaned everything? I know Simms wrecked my bathroom and slashed my clothes." Scarlett held on to the door frame.

"Your boyfriend sent his contractor over here. Got the door fixed right away. Casey assessed the damage in the bathroom and replaced the broken stuff. We put the clothes that could be salvaged back in the closet and tossed the rest. You'll need to go shopping. Your closet is looking a little bare." Rhett kissed her cheek. "Relax. Simms is dead, and Delgado is in a maximum-security cell block. She can't get out. The DA is trying to work it so you won't even have to go to court. There are enough charges to put her away for decades."

"Good. Right now I can't imagine testifying. But I will if I have to do it." Scarlett walked over and looked in her closet. Yes, she needed to shop. When Anna got back, they could have some fun. As soon as she got her strength back.

"Hey, did you know there was a reward for information leading to Leroy Simms's capture? Mike says I should get it." Scarlett grabbed the closet door when a wave of dizziness hit her. She ended up sitting on the side of the bed.

"Hell, yes, you deserve it. I'll look into it for you, if you want me to." Rhett moved into the room. "You sure you're okay?"

"Tired. Which is stupid. All I did was ride in the car over here and climb the stairs." She smiled at her brother. "The reward. Yeah, that would be great. He trashed my wardrobe. It would be justice if he paid for it." Oh, crap, dizzy again. She flopped back on the bed.

"Take it easy. Maybe I should stay." Rhett stared down at her. "I'll get you some juice."

"No, don't bother. I'm going to just fall asleep right here." She toed off her shoes and let them fall to the floor. "Where's my phone?"

"I'll put it by the bed." He went back into the living room and returned to set it on her nightstand.

"Thanks." Scarlett hadn't told anyone about the calls from Delgado's lawyer. She'd finally blocked his number. If he showed up banging on her door, she'd call Mike. No way was she talking to Mona Delgado. But she did want her phone nearby. "I'm set now."

"I'll take off, then. If you're sure Ethan is coming back, I'll stay over at Casey's tonight. Give you and your guy some alone time." Rhett was watching her from the doorway. "You sure you want to be alone? You still look pale and wobbly."

"The doctor said it was natural to feel weak. I have pain pills if I need them in the bag you brought in from the hospital. You might put them in the bathroom for me. Don't need them yet. So go, take off. Tell Casey thanks for her help. Please. And thanks for bringing me home." Scarlett closed her eyes. "See you tomorrow."

"Okay." Rhett messed around, putting her pain pills and a glass of water by the bed before he finally left. Best brother ever.

As soon as she heard his key in the lock, Scarlett bent over with a groan and put on her shoes again. The pain pills beckoned, but she didn't dare. She knew it was probably not a good idea, but she was desperate to go to the bar. Ethan had told her enough that she knew Mike was going to be there to help Ethan with his mother and her situation. Her guy had been way too vague on details, and it was driving her crazy.

She loved him. Ethan said he loved her. So this was something she should be able to help with. He'd clearly been worried about this for weeks. He might even face criminal charges for not turning in his mother when she first showed up in Austin. If nothing else, Scarlett could offer moral support. Talk to Mike for him and plead Ethan's case. She stood and looked for her car keys and purse. By the time she found them on the kitchen bar, she was dizzy again. No, this wouldn't do. She found some juice in the fridge and drank a glass. That helped.

Rhett had walked YoYo before he left, so she locked the dog inside the apartment, then wobbled down the stairs. Ridiculous to be so weak. They'd replaced the blood she'd lost and she'd only been in the hospital for two days. No reason to feel this way. Like an invalid. But she held on to the railing and carefully walked down the stairs and to her car, the effort taking a lot out of her. Damn it.

Getting in her car was surprisingly difficult. She dreaded it. She knew Mike had arranged to have it brought back to her apartment complex after it had been "processed." Why hadn't Scarlett locked herself in that day? Stupid beater. When she turned off the key, the doors automatically unlocked, and she hadn't given them a thought. She'd been so freaked out...

Her heart was pounding, and it wasn't easy putting the key in the ignition, but she finally got it done. Mona was in jail. Simms was dead. No one was going to get the drop on her this time. But she locked herself in anyway before she backed out of her parking slot and got on the road. Sweat popped out on her forehead. The effort to leave the apartment and get in the car had taken more out of her than she could have imagined. She turned on the air conditioner and aimed the vent at her face when she saw spots dancing in front of her eyes. Damn it, she didn't have far to go. She had to pull herself together and do this.

Luck was with her and traffic was light. The cold air helped her focus and, by the time she pulled into her assigned parking space in the garage, she was feeling better. Ethan's Porsche was in its usual spot. He was already at the bar. Had his mother arrived? Maybe Scarlett had missed the whole thing.

The walk across Sixth Street took longer than she remembered. It was hot for April, and she was sweating again by the time she got to the back door in the alley. Which was ajar. That wasn't good. When she heard raised voices, she stopped and listened.

* * * *

Ethan had told Mike everything. It hadn't been easy. The Ranger had a stone face that made Ethan feel like a criminal. Well, hell, maybe he was. But after spilling his guts to the guy, he felt better. Somehow he knew the big man would help him put things right. Maybe that was naïve of him. But here they were now in his bar, and he had his mother and Lisa in front of him. He'd told Albert to stay away. He hoped his investigator did just that. If Albert lost his PI license over this, that would be just one more thing he'd be guilty of.

Mike and three of his fellow officers were hidden in the bathrooms. They would help with the takedown. Shit, he hoped no one got hurt doing this.

"So where are the passports, Ethan?" Lisa was all business.

His mother had gone straight to the bar. "Leave him alone, Lisa. He said he had them. Look around. He's made good progress here fixing up the bar. I'm proud of you, son. When can we meet that new manager of yours? And how about the investor? Do I know him?"

"Mama, please lay off the booze." Ethan laid a file folder on the bar. He didn't like the way Lisa was eyeing him. She had that purse of hers clutched in her arms. He knew she had a gun in there.

"It's happy hour. Why shouldn't I have something to drink to celebrate? You have our new identities? The works?" Missy Calhoun laughed. "We'll be on the road and out of your hair soon. I'd think you would be ready to hoist a few yourself."

"And never see my mother again?" Ethan walked over to her. "Mama, that's the last thing I want."

"What are you saying, Ethan." Lisa stared at him. "You'd better not be backing out of our deal."

"Did you really think I'd help you leave the country?" Ethan kept an eye on Lisa and that purse.

"Now, Ethan, you know I can't be happy here." Missy put herself between Ethan and Lisa. "Let me talk to him. I'm sure he'll come through when he sees how much it means to me."

"There's been enough talking. Weeks of his empty promises." Lisa paced in front of the bar. "I'm sick of waiting, Missy. I've had it with you and your family. Now, listen to me, Calhoun. You can keep your precious mama, but, damn it, I need money so I can get the hell out of town. Missy, you're on your own. But you owe me for breaking you out of that hospital."

"Wait, what?" Missy grabbed Lisa's arm. "We're supposed to be in this together. You promised. I can't do this on my own, Lisa."

"Shut up. I'm sick of you. Get away from me." She shoved Missy and pulled out her gun. "Ethan, money. Now. Don't you have a safe in this place?"

"Calm down, Lisa. Mama, are you all right?" Ethan moved toward his mother, who was crying.

"She promised we'd do this together." Missy shook her head.

"I'm not giving you a dime, Lisa."

"I had a feeling you were stringing us along." Lisa's eyes darted around the room. "I asked you a question. You got a safe? Money in it?"

Ethan pushed his mother aside. "I use a bank, Lisa. Like most people do. Use that gun, and you're just going to make things worse for yourself."

"He's right." Mike, along with his men, came from both sides of the bar, two from each bathroom. "Put down the gun, Lisa. You're surrounded. I won't tell you twice." He had his own gun pointed at her.

"You called the cops? Ethan Calhoun, you'll pay for this!" Lisa aimed at him, her face a mask of hatred.

"Lisa, no! Ethan, look out!" Missy cried out, throwing herself at him just as a shot rang out.

"Mama!" Ethan caught her before she fell to the floor. Blood bloomed on her shoulder.

Mike tackled Lisa to the floor, and her gun went flying.

"Bastard! Let me go!" Lisa struggled as Mike cuffed her hands behind her back. He handed her over to two other Rangers when she kept screaming.

"Ambulance is on its way." Mike was suddenly by his side, a bar towel in his hands. "How does she look?"

"How the hell should I know?" Ethan pressed the towel to his mother's wound. "It's not her heart, I don't think."

"Ethan." Mama opened her eyes. "I'm sorry. That bitch made me..." She closed her eyes.

"Mama, hang in there. Paramedics are on the way." Ethan kissed her pale cheek. He looked up and saw Scarlett standing behind Mike. "Scarlett. What are you doing here?"

"Never mind that. Are you all right?" Scarlett's eyes were big in her pale face. "Ethan?"

"Liar! I didn't make her do anything!" Lisa struggled between two grim Rangers. "This was all Missy's idea. She paid for the gun. Got the money from her son. Yeah, that one right there." She nodded toward Ethan. "The rich guy. Let's see you put *him* in handcuffs." She turned to one of the men and spit at him. "Watch where you put that hand, asshole." She kicked, then gasped when she was jerked off her feet.

"Read her her rights, Stephens, then get her out of here." Mike looked thunderous. "We'll take statements later. From everyone involved."

They heard Lisa scream again from the alley. "You can't put me in jail. I'm sick. Certified crazy. There's paperwork to prove it. Take me to a hospital. I need my medicine. Let me go, you fucking moron!"

Scarlett laid her hand on Ethan's back. If she was shocked at Lisa's outburst, she didn't show it. "Your mother's breathing, Ethan. That's a good sign." She looked up, then stepped back. "The ambulance is here. That was quick."

"St. David's is right down the street." Mike pulled Scarlett aside so the paramedics could take over. They gently moved Ethan out of the way.

Ethan felt helpless as they staunched the bleeding and began hooking his mother up to IVs before lifting her onto a gurney. She was whisked away in the ambulance, but he wasn't allowed to ride along.

"She's a fugitive, Ethan, now in custody. I'll follow the ambulance. You can follow, too, but she'll be handcuffed to the bed once she's stable. Sorry about that." Mike hurried from the bar. "You're lucky I'm not reading you your rights. Understand?"

"Yeah, sure." Ethan felt helpless as he watched the Ranger stride away after the paramedics.

"Are you all right?" Scarlett held on to his arm, and Ethan realized he was covered in blood, his mother's blood.

"Sure. Just a little shook up. That was intense." He took a breath and held on to her hand. "I've got to go. Follow the ambulance." Ethan wasn't sure what he could do, but he had to see what shape his mother was in. All that drinking and Mama wasn't exactly in prime condition to begin with. "Did they take Lisa away?"

"The shooter's in custody." One of the Rangers said quietly. "Mr. Calhoun, Officer Rogers will get your statement at the hospital, but there will be some explanations necessary. Maybe charges coming." He frowned as he looked around. "I'm his supervisor. I don't know what your association with Taylor is, but he's already stuck on desk duty because of his decision to let you ride with him to the takedown of Simms the other day. The only thing helping his case for taking you with him is that you were apparently the one who thought about using the chip in the dog to track the fugitives' car. Good idea." He paused. "But this latest snafu can't be overlooked. Shots fired and a fugitive wounded. Taylor's going to have a lot to answer for." He gave Ethan a hard look. "Do him a favor and don't say a word to anybody. Got that?"

Ethan nodded. He understood. Damn it. He'd helped women who'd broken the law. Just because one of them was his mother was no excuse.

"Is it okay for us to go the hospital?" Scarlett hadn't been given a gag order.

"Yeah. Get out of here. But if you disappear, then I'll put an APB on your ass, Ethan Calhoun." The Ranger hit speed dial and started talking on his phone.

"Yes, sir." Ethan walked away as quickly as he could, Scarlett by his side. When she stumbled, he stopped and really looked at her. She was barely able to stand, he could see that now. After the hellish few days she'd just lived through, she should be home, in bed. "You don't have to go. This is my mess. I'll clean it up."

"Not without me, you won't. I love you. Come on." She took a breath, then managed a surprisingly firm grip on his arm and pulled him out toward the door. "You want to drive, or shall I?"

"I'm driving." He stopped and kissed her. "Thanks. I love you too. I sure can use the moral support. I've got to call my sisters."

"And your lawyer. You're in trouble." She ran a hand over his cheek. She did that a lot, and he loved it. "*We're* in trouble. So let's check on your mama and then you can give me a list of who to call. I've got you, Ethan. Don't you forget it. We'll both clean up this mess together."

Chapter Thirty-One

"I really like your sisters. And your brother-in-law." Scarlett let her head fall back on the couch.

"But you thought they'd never leave." Ethan grinned as he settled next to her. "You look exhausted."

"I am. But in a good way. I'm healing. No signs of infection, thank God. Your mother's situation is getting settled, and you aren't in jail." She kissed Ethan's cheek. "I count all of those as wins."

"Billy is amazing, isn't he?" Ethan picked up her hand. "The fact that Lisa held a gun on me helped. Clearly I was coerced. Then she shot Mama. Billy's got it looking like I feared for Mama's life. How could I not do what I could to help her with the situation? Even Albert stepped up as a witness to say I tried to figure out how to return them to Fairhaven as soon as I could."

Scarlett shuddered. "That Lisa. She's one scary woman. When I heard her screaming at you in the bar, she reminded me of Mona Delgado, a stone-cold killer."

"Exactly. That's why Lisa is being reevaluated now. I don't think she's going back to a hospital this time. Assault with a deadly weapon with a pack of Rangers as witnesses? She didn't go into her crazy act until she realized she was caught."

Scarlett snuggled against him. "I feel bad about the grief Mike is getting. I hope helping both of us doesn't ruin his career."

"Billy will make sure he comes out all right. Remember, Mike managed to track down Simms and Delgado, then get a hostage released, almost unharmed. Delgado is behind bars and going away for a long, long time. Mike gets the credit for that." Ethan moved away and looked at her, his face serious. "He took a lot of flak for letting me ride along that day, though. It was totally against the rules."

"Guess you threw some kind of fit and wouldn't get out of his car. What could he do short of tossing you bodily on the parking lot?" She smiled and touched his cheek. So dear to her. "It's behind us now. I'm ready to move on."

"Time to get back to work on the bar." Ethan stared down at his feet.

"What's the matter?" She knew the bar was his dream, but he didn't sound excited about it. "I'm eager to get back to it."

He took both her hands. "I have a confession to make. About the bar."

"What?" Had he changed his mind? Given up the bar idea? Everyone in his family was involved in Calhoun Petroleum. His sister Megan had told her how valuable Ethan had been when he'd worked there. They all wanted him back in Houston. Was he thinking about it? Houston was his home. She'd only been there once, for a weekend. All she remembered were flatlands, tall skyscapers, and packed freeways. Would Ethan want to go back? Would he ask her to go with him?

"I ordered a sign. Without consulting you, manager." He reached for his laptop. He'd brought it in and left it on the coffee table.

"Oh. For a moment..." Scarlett began to breathe again. "Never mind. Show me."

"It's big. Stainless steel. There's a guy in Waco who does this amazing work cutting out letters in heavy sheet metal. I saw some of his stuff, and it just spoke to me. Reminded me of the trucks in the oil fields for some reason. I grew up riding with Daddy in his pickup and seeing the oil tankers with the Calhoun logo on them. All of us kids did at one time or another." Ethan pulled up a website and then there it was.

"Fuel. Bold and it is big. I like the font." Scarlett read the dimensions. "You won't be able to hide that."

"I know. I can see it backlit over the front door." He set the laptop back on the table and took her in his arms again. "I don't want to hide it."

"But if it's a secret bar..." She knew. Of course. The secret bar thing had been her idea. Before her last encounter with Simms, they'd visited those secret bars and Ethan hadn't exactly been thrilled, had he? She turned to face him.

"Okay, here it is. I hate the whole secret bar concept. Those bars we saw? Creepy. Too dark, too hidden. I want my bar to be open, in the spotlight. I mean, the interior can be dark and sexy. That's okay." He gestured. "But I want people to drive by and see that big sign. They'll stop and join the lines waiting to get in because we'll be so popular. I'm hoping everyone will be talking about how cool it is. There will be a waiting list for reservations and big write-ups on the Internet about the music and the food." He jumped up. "Don't hate me, but Fuel needs to be out there, not hidden behind some door with a secret buzzer or whatever you had in mind."

Scarlett leaned back and studied him. Tall, handsome, and flushed with the excitement of imagining his place full of people eating and drinking, maybe dancing to good music. God, how she loved him. She shook her head.

"You know why I wanted the bar to be a secret, don't you?"

"You thought it was cool. A neat concept." He sat again. "For some people, it's the right thing."

"I was hiding, Ethan. Because I didn't feel safe. Even when Simms was in jail, I always felt like someone was watching me." Scarlett sighed. "Paranoia, Ethan. I was so traumatized by the attack in January, I couldn't eat, sleep... Hell, I had panic attacks. You saw me in the middle of one when we first met."

"Yeah, when Casey's tattoo needle hit you. But you pulled yourself together pretty fast." He took her hand. "You're one of the strongest women I know, Scarlett Hall. Never doubt it."

She leaned in, kissing him with all the love in her heart. When she finally came up for air, she had her thoughts together.

"Okay, here it is. I may still have nightmares. And look over my shoulder when we're out somewhere." She gripped his hand. "That's why I decided to start seeing someone about this, Ethan. Albert gave me the name of a good therapist. I should have done that months ago."

"Good." He shut up when he saw she had more to say.

"Even though Simms is dead and Delgado is locked up, I need time to come down off the ledge." She stood and pulled Ethan up beside her.

"I get it. Whatever you need." He wrapped his arms around her, gently. "What about the bar?"

She grabbed his lean cheeks in her hands so he was looking into her eyes. "I can't wait to make Fuel the hottest club in town. We'll see those lines go out the door and down the block. Together."

"You sure you're not disappointed?" He took her hands and leaned in. His kiss was easy, as if he still thought he had to be careful of her healing wound. He drew back and studied her.

"The only way you can disappoint me, Ethan Calhoun, is if you keep treating me like I'm too fragile to take to bed." She grinned and tugged him toward her bedroom. "Now, come on, Texan, I'm ready to celebrate that our troubles are over. I can't think of a better way to do it than in your arms."

Lovin' this Lone Star Suspense?

Don't miss
TEXAS LIGHTNING
Available now

And keep an eye out for
More books in the series
Coming soon from
Lyrical Press

Printed in the United States
by Baker & Taylor Publisher Services